Live Out Loud

Live Out Loud

MARIE MEYER

New York   Boston

Copyright © 2017 by Marie Meyer
Excerpt of *Long Road Home* copyright © 2017 by Marie Meyer
Cover design by Brian Lemus
Cover copyright © 2017 by Hachette Book Group, Inc.
Hachette Book Group supports the right to free expression and the value of copyright. The purpose of copyright is to encourage writers and artists to produce the creative works that enrich our culture.

The scanning, uploading, and distribution of this book without permission is a theft of the author's intellectual property. If you would like permission to use material from the book (other than for review purposes), please contact permissions@hbgusa.com. Thank you for your support of the author's rights.

Forever Yours
Hachette Book Group
1290 Avenue of the Americas
New York, NY 10104
forever-romance.com
twitter.com/foreverromance

First ebook and print on demand edition: April 2017

Forever Yours is an imprint of Grand Central Publishing. The Forever Yours name and logo are trademarks of Hachette Book Group, Inc.

The publisher is not responsible for websites (or their content) that are not owned by the publisher.

The Hachette Speakers Bureau provides a wide range of authors for speaking events. To find out more, go to www.hachettespeakersbureau.com or call (866) 376-6591.

ISBN 978-1-4555-4274-1 (ebook edition)
ISBN 978-1-4555-4277-2 (print on demand edition)

For Nenna.
You've been so patient.

Live Out Loud

CHAPTER ONE

HARPER

The door signaler flashes. I look up from the hospital's extensive patient counseling materials and glance at my clock. *Had I really been studying for three hours straight?* With my pharmacy clinical rotation at St. Louis Children's Hospital starting next week, I plan to be more than prepared; I want to be at the top of my game. I'd have to be. If that means spending hours reading and rereading the hospital pharmacy's patient counseling literature, then so be it. I'll gladly give up my Friday night.

Tossing the binder to the floor, Bobby—my little white-haired West Highland terrier lifts his head, not pleased that I interrupted his twentieth nap of the day. He is the laziest dog I've ever met, and I love him for it.

I stand and stretch, climbing my hands up an invisible ladder, my back realigning.

LED lights flash again. Someone's at my door.

Reaching for the knob, I pull it open. My roommate, Chloe stands on the other side, a beatific smile on her face and her hands on her hips. Wearing a tiny denim skirt, cowboy boots, and a hot pink shirt that hangs off one shoulder, it's no mystery she has big plans for the evening. She's braided her hair to the side so the dramatic transition from the black tresses at the top of her head transform into a trail of blond perfection near the end. How she gets away with such an extraordinary dichotomy, I'll never know; I couldn't pull off an ombré look if I tried.

The way she's dressed and the look on her face, she's up to something…and I'm certain she means for me to be involved as well. *"What?"* I sign, palms up.

Bobby uncurls himself from his bed and trots to the door, greeting Chloe. Crouching on her heels, she scratches Bobby on the head as he sneaks in a few licks on any patch of skin he can reach. Glancing up at me, Chloe stands back up, leaving a tail-wagging Bobby dancing at my heels.

Chloe raises her arms, and in a flurry of motion, her hands form words in impeccable American Sign Language. *"Don't say no, okay? Promise me you won't say no. There's this hot band playing at Mississippi Lights tonight. They're my new favorite, and I really want to see them. Will you come? Please?"* She juts her lower lip out and bats her eyelashes. *"Oh, and I heard T-R-E-Y is supposed to be there tonight,"* she adds, sticking her tongue out. *"If he sees me having a good time, maybe it will make him realize what an idiot he was for breaking up with me."*

I love Chloe. She's my best friend. We've been roommates for the last three years, but to be honest, she falls in love with a new band every other week. Her enthusiasm over this new group doesn't have me psyched to give up on the intriguing world of hospital protocol and patient care. And the fact that she wants to make her douchebag ex-boyfriend jealous doesn't light a fire inside me either. I've always known Chloe is too good for his cheating ass; I only wish she could have beaten Trey to the punch and dumped him first.

I cock my head, irritated. Why is she such a softie for him? *"Chloe, we've been over this, you can do so much better than T-R-E-Y."*

"Yeah, yeah." She rolls her eyes. *"I just want him to see that I don't need him. That I'm getting along just fine—better even—without him."*

Yes. Yes she is. I just wish she believed that.

"Mississippi Lights?" I ask. There are worse places to see a band. At least the venue is small and they crank the volume. If I stand near the side of the stage, right in front of the speakers, well, I still wouldn't be able to hear the band, but at least I could feel the music's pulse.

Chloe's eyes widen, waiting for me to cave. She is the master of the sad Puss in Boots face. When she brings out the eyes, she could persuade the Pope to commit homicide. Hand against her chest, she makes a slow clockwise circle. *"Pleeeease?"* Her lower lip pops out again.

"I guess." I drop my hands to my sides and let out a long breath.

An enormous smile breaks through the pleading look she just heaped on me. Bouncing on the balls of her feet, she throws her arms around my neck and squeezes. When she pulls away, she's beaming. *"Thank you, thank you, thank you,"* she repeats, tapping her chin with the tips of her fingers.

I nod. *"I'll be ready in a few."*

"Great!" Turning around, she bounds down the small hallway and disappears into her room.

I shut the door and turn around, sighing. *"What did I get myself into, Bobby?"* He may not know sign language, but my little guy gets me. He cocks his head, his ears perked up in understanding. As much as I didn't want to go out tonight, I know Chloe needs the distraction, and knowing Trey will be there, it's best that I go, just to keep Chloe as far away from him as possible.

Walking back to the bed, I bend over and pick up the hospital's book and toss it onto my desk before heading to the closet. Flipping hangers from one side to the other, a blue, mid-thigh bodycon dress catches my eye. I yank it off the hanger and lay it on the bed. As I wiggle out of my yoga pants and T-shirt, I reach for the dress and bring it over my head, mourning the loss of my comfy clothes.

After touching up my makeup and taming my red curls, I'm presentable and club-ready…well, at least I *look* club-ready, my mind-set anything but.

The door signaler flashes again—Chloe's subtle way of telling me to hurry up. I grab my keys and purse from my desk, give Bobby a goodbye pat on the head, and open the door.

"Ready," I sign, before she has a chance to chastise me for taking too long.

Her smile grows and her eyebrows pull up as she takes in my outfit. *"Holy shit, girl! Why didn't you tell me you're looking for a man?"*

"Is it too much?" I gesture to my ample assets and cringe.

There is no hiding in this dress. If my parents knew I had a dress like this, I'd get a lecture on modesty and be sent back to my room to change. I bought this dress because I knew my parents would disapprove if they ever saw it, not to draw male attention.

Chloe shakes her head. *"No freaking way! You look hot! I'd give my right arm to have boobs like yours."*

I roll my eyes and squeeze past her, walking down the stairs. Once we're in the living room, I turn and face Chloe, *"And I'm not looking for a man,"* I tell her. I do not have time for a man.

"I hate to break it to you, sweetie, but that dress is going to be like a lighthouse in a dark sea."

"Well, it's a good thing I have you by my side." I smile. *"You and those sexy boots, and your legs that go on for miles will distract all the guys before they even lay eyes on me. I pale in comparison."*

"You're delusional." Chloe rolls her eyes this time and picks up her keys. *"I've been dying to see Mine Shaft!"* With a little shimmy of her hips, she opens the door and I follow behind.

I walk to the passenger side of Chloe's purple Jeep Wrangler and wait for her to unlock the door when I notice she's waving her hand, trying to get my attention.

I adjust the thin strap on my purse and sign, *"Yeah?"*

With a sincere look that melts my heart, she says, *"Thanks for going out with me tonight. I know you're worried about starting your clinical rotation next week, and I know you didn't want any distractions, so this means a lot to me."*

I walk around the backside of her Jeep and stand beside her. I won't vocalize how much she means to me, as I gave up trying to verbalize a long time ago, but I squeeze her in an all-consuming hug. I hope she knows that I would do anything for her.

Four years ago, I was a deaf girl in a sea of hearing pharmacy students. So many people told me I'd never make it, and I'll be the first to admit, nothing about school has been easy. But, Chloe was the first person who believed I would make a great pharmacist, and she told me so on a daily basis our first year, after I'd had three different interpreters quit before the end of the semester. She also learned to sign for me…something my own parents struggled to do. If putting down some boring hospital procedural textbook in order to support my best friend and help her find her confidence again, then I was glad to do it.

I pull back and look into Chloe's eyes, letting her shoulders go. *"You know I'd do anything for you, Chloe."*

"Yeah, I know. Now scoot." She directs me back to the passenger side with a hip-check and a smile. *"I want to be close to the stage. Have you seen these guys?"*

I shake my head as I climb onto the passenger seat.

"Well, I have." Chloe drops her hand to the ignition, and I feel the Jeep rumble to life. Before she pulls out onto the street, she adds, *"And let me tell you, we have some serious eye candy to consume this evening."*

I squint my eyes and give her a questioning look. *"What are you waiting for then? My sweet tooth is hurting!"*

CHAPTER TWO

HARPER

The last remnants of Indian summer linger as a warm breeze tosses my curls into my face. I swipe them back as Chloe and I come to a halt at the end of a long line. The line in front of Mississippi Lights.

Chloe faces me and pouts, irritated. *"What are all these people doing here?"* Her hands fly.

I shrug. *"You said the band was hot."*

The line inches forward and Chloe shuffles ahead of me. *"Yes, but…"* She throws her hands up, not finishing what she was about to say.

"But what?" I ask.

"But they're my hot, new band!"

I grin and shake my head. *"I hate to break it to you, Chloe, you have to share them."*

"I liked Mine Shaft before all of these"—she gestures to the gathered crowd—*"poseurs."*

It's a good thing our conversation transpires in ASL, I don't think this crowd would take kindly to being called poseurs.

I point over Chloe's shoulder and she turns around—it's our turn to go inside. We hand the bouncer our IDs, along with the cover charge, and he waves us through the door.

Taking in the number of people packed into the small club, it's safe to assume everyone had Chloe's idea to arrive early.

I grab her hand, so we aren't separated in the massive crowd, and we weave through the dance floor toward the bar.

Leaning against the wooden bar top, I read the bartender's lips. "What can I get you?" he asks.

Opening the note application on my phone, I type, Cosmo, please, and turn my phone around. He leans closer, squints at the text, and nods. He directs his attention to Chloe, takes her order, and gets to work.

With our drinks in hand, Chloe and I make our way back across the dance floor. Chloe knows I like to be near the front, close to the speakers.

I take a sip of my drink, and keep my eyes glued to the stage. A guy with sandy blond hair is busy adjusting the height of the cymbals on the drum set.

Turning to face Chloe, with my free hand, I quickly sign, *"Is he one of the Mine Shaft guys?"* I point in the direction of the drums.

Chloe's dark eyes widen and a know-it-all grin blossoms on her face as she bobs her head up and down. *"See? What I'd tell you. H-O-T!"* she spells. *"Wait until you see the rest of them."* She nudges my shoulder with hers and puts her beer bottle to her lips, taking a generous pull. As she swallows, she adds, *"In my opinion, the lead singer is the hottest. G-R-F-F-I-N. Oh my*

God." Her eyes roll back in her head and she fans herself. "*I wonder if I can get him to come on* Sweet Nothings?" She wags her eyebrows.

Sweet Nothings is Chloe's—and sometimes, her sister Megan's—massively popular YouTube baking show. Having just surpassed fifty thousand subscribers and gaining a slew of new advertisers, she's making a killing. I wonder why she's still in school, and when I ask, she just shrugs and signs, "*I've made it this far, why quit now?*"

I shake my head and smile. I bet she'd love for any one of the guys in Mine Shaft to join her on an episode of *Sweet Nothings*, that's the Chloe I know and love.

Glancing back up at the stage, I watch the drummer tinker with the different instruments in his drum set. I stare, fascinated by each calculated adjustment he makes.

I'm sure all the careful fine-tuning is what separates good bands from great ones, ensuring the music will sound its best. For me, if there's a decent bass line or a heavy drumbeat, I can usually find the rhythm of a song through the vibrations of the sound waves. I love watching the people who make the music, especially when they're in caught up in a song. It's like being privy to a secret, or sharing a deeply intimate moment.

The drummer finishes his adjustments and looks over his shoulder. Seconds later, three more guys join him on stage. The fine hairs on my arms rise, excitement tingles in my veins. There's nothing like a live concert.

The band members take their places on stage. The lead singer, Griffin, I presume, steps toward the microphone and begins moving his hand over the strings of his bass guitar. He's as gorgeous as Chloe mentioned. For a guy to even register on her radar, they have to be taller than her five eleven. By the looks of it, Griffin Daniels is well over that mark.

I watch Griffin's lips move, trying to decipher a few words to the song, but I'm not close enough. Then, I feel it. I'm engulfed by waves of sound. I sway my body in time to the rhythm. I take note of the vibrations under the soles of my feet, rising up through my legs. Closing my eyes, I "listen" the only way I know how.

The skin on my cheeks prickles as each crest of sound washes over me. My heart finds the beat, and I know I'm in the same place as the guys on stage. A place where you can't tell where your own body ends and the music begins, they're one in the same.

When the intensity of the pulse fades away, the song comes to an end. I open my eyes and notice the guitarist for the first time. Yes, Mine Shaft lives up to the eye-candy status Chloe had billed them as, but damn, the guitarist is in a league all by himself.

I still my body and watch him, mesmerized. Every now and then, he shifts his weight, licks his lips, and presses his mouth close to the mic. I can't read his lips, but that doesn't mean I can't pull my eyes away either. The way they move…the way *he* moves. His body, the way his fingers roam over the strings of his guitar…he's enchanting.

My gaze drifts from his mouth, upward, following the five-o'clock shadow of his square jawline…and then his eyes. Intense, focused, he stares at something far away, lost in the music.

Watching him, I wonder what he sees…what images the song conjures in his mind. He blinks, shifts his body, and locks his eyes directly on mine.

Holy crap! I suck in a breath and hold it, almost tearing my eyes away from his in embarrassment—he caught me gawking. But I can't. I can't look away.

No longer in profile, I have the perfect view of his whole gorgeous face. And he's staring right at me.

Stunned, I hold his gaze for one beat…two…three…long enough for the heat blazing in my core to work its way to my cheeks. It's impossible. There's no way he can see me, not with the stage lights beaming down on him. But, I'll be damned if it doesn't look…*feel* like he's looking straight into my deepest, darkest thoughts.

His stare is so consuming, if I don't look away, I may burn up.

As I pull my eyes away I catch the corner of his mouth turn up in a subtle half smile.

Now I know I'm imagining things! Turning to Chloe, I tap her on the shoulder. When she looks at me, I ask, *"Who's the guitarist?"*

Her fingers work over the letters of his name. *"T-H-O-R-I-N K-L-I-N-E."*

I set my eyes back on his whiskered, brooding face. His eyes are closed now, giving me the chance to resume my ogling without getting caught in his seductive stare. I don't know what passed between us in those few seconds, but whatever it was, it left a current of electricity running through my veins. My insides are still buzzing like a live wire, which is completely ridiculous because I know he couldn't have seen me. There's no way.

I trail my gaze downward, across his broad shoulders, over his well-defined biceps, wishing I could get a close-up look at the intricate sleeve tattoos winding down his arms. I settle on the sinuous movement of his hips—a counter rhythm to his right hand stroking the strings of his guitar. I bet those fingers can work all kinds of magic. I shiver at the thought.

Despite my lusty thoughts, something else about him catches my eye: the play of emotions across his face. Usually, I can tell when one song ends and another begins, because the vibration of the music changes. I know if a song is fast or slow by the tempo of the beat, and if the song is popular—getting lots of radio exposure—I can usually guess the title. Each song has its own pulse; its own identity. But tonight, I don't have to rely solely on what I feel. Thorin Kline, whether he knows it or not, tells a story when he plays his guitar. I may not be able to hear the words to this melancholy song, but thanks to him, I understand it just the same.

And then, there's a shift in the tempo, and he's smiling and happy.

* * *

Griffin, the lead singer, lifts his hands in the air and says something into the microphone. Chloe, standing beside me, jumps up and down in response.

With a little nudge from my hip, I get her attention. *"What did he say?"*

"We're the best crowd they've ever played for," she signs quickly, turning her attention back to the stage.

I glance around the club, watching all the cheering bodies, when my eyes fall on Trey, Chloe's ex. I've never truly hated anyone, but Trey Carver is in the lead to earn that distinction.

Dammit! I hope Chloe hasn't seen him. I've got to get her out of here before she does. Trey is Chloe's personal brand of meth. I don't know what it is about the guy, when they were together, he treated her like shit and she always took him back.

I knock my hip into her side again. When her dark eyes focus on mine, I tell her the most convincing lie I can think of. *"I'm not feeling well. I really want to get home."*

"Really?" She raises an eyebrow, confused. *"The band's finished, but we could get another drink, mingle a little."*

No mingling. Mingling is bad. That is exactly what I'm trying to avoid. I shake my head and repeat myself. *"No. I want to go."*

With a dramatic sinking of her shoulders, she signs, *"All right. Let's go."*

I know she's disappointed, but what I'm doing is for her own good.

As we turn to leave, I sweep my eyes across the stage one more time, hoping to catch a final glimpse of Thorin Kline. This time, my shoulders deflate like a popped balloon. The stage is bare. Thorin's gone.

I pivot on the heel of my shoe and nod to Chloe to go to the right side. The last time I saw Trey, he was behind us, but toward the back. Standing on my tiptoes, I scan the crowded room but don't see him.

Chloe moves right and we press through the crowd. We're almost to the exit when a heavy hand presses down on my shoulder.

CHAPTER THREE

THOR

Shit, sweetheart, where's the fire? "Hey, Red, hold up," I say, trying to get her attention. I don't want to startle her, but it's no use, she can't hear me over the noise of the club. If I don't stop her now, she'll leave and I won't get her number. I drop my hand onto her shoulder and she goes rigid under my touch.

Smooth, Kline. Way to scare the poor girl.

Very slowly, she turns around, almost as if she's expecting to see the Grim Reaper standing behind her. When our gazes meet, her shoulders relax and she lets out a deep breath. Up close, she's even more beautiful. And Jesus...her eyes. When I caught her gaze for a few seconds on stage, I knew there was something special about her eyes; I just couldn't see them clearly. Up close, they're extraordinary. I've never seen eyes like hers before...the color of emerald sea glass. A long forgotten memory surfaces, one of my earliest...walking along the beach as a kid...with my dad...before everything went to hell.

I shake off the phantom thought and focus on the girl.

"Sorry. Didn't mean to scare you. It's just…I…" I stumble over my words like I'm a thirteen-year-old boy. What the hell's my problem? *She's not the first chick you've ever talked to. Spit the damn words out, Thor.* "I saw you while I was up on stage, and I was hoping to get your number, I'd really like to take you out sometime."

There. I said it. Not hard.

She smiles widely and nods. Lifting her hands between us, I notice her fingers move. Graceful and deliberate hand motions. *Is she using sign language?*

"She can read your lips."

I glance to my right. A tall girl with long, half black, half blond hair flanks her side. Pretty, but pales in comparison to her friend.

"Read my lips?" I shake my head, not understanding. I point to the redheaded beauty and direct my question to her friend. "She's deaf?"

There's a tap on my shoulder and my eyes snap back to Red's. Moving her hands again, she signs something, and I'm clueless. Her lips move, but she doesn't speak. And apparently, I'm shit at lipreading. But at least her expression is playful. That's a plus, right?

She lowers her arms and smiles. Damn, I love how the right side of her lips pulls up higher than the left.

Since Griffin and I started Mine Shaft, I've never had to chase down a girl. For some reason, chicks dig guys in a band. They've always pursued me. But, the one time I see a girl so gorgeous, and take the time to run after her, she can't even hear me.

I look at her friend. "What did she just say?"

Red's friend folds her arms over her chest, wearing the same beatific smile she did when I stopped them. "She answered your question. Yes, she's deaf. She also asked if you still want her number."

I stare at the girl. With wild red curls framing her face and a mischievous smirk, she waits for my answer. *Hell yeah, I do.* I want the opportunity to get to know this woman. There's something about her...I don't understand what...but I know want to find out. And damn, I want a chance to run my hands over the curves of her body.

I look her square in the eye, "So, what about it, Red? You gonna give me your number?"

She cocks her head, glances at her friend, makes some complicated movements with her hands, and holds her phone out to me.

This whole situation is so damn weird. Red's friend laughs and says, "She isn't going to give you her number, but she'll take yours."

I scrutinize Red's face. Is she serious? "You want my number?"

She nods, again.

My lips pull up at the corners. *Huh.* This is a first. No girl has ever denied me her number and asked for mine instead. "Sure thing, Red."

I look into her eyes and deliberately fold my hand around hers, lifting the phone from her fingers. I've been dying to touch her ivory skin, and now that I have, I want more. Even beneath my callused fingers, her skin is silky and warm. I can only imagine what she would look like with that dress on my floor, and I sure as hell want the chance to find out.

She nods, green eyes flashing.

I wink at her and look down at the phone in my hands. Behind the apps a little white dog peeks out the side of a purse. "Cute mutt."

The friend chuckles. Smirking at both ladies, I tip my head in the direction of her screen and tap on the phone app. Adding my name and number to her contacts list, I go a step further and add myself to her "favorites" list, and put myself on top. Then, dammit, images of her on top of me in bed pop into my head. *Shit! Calm yourself, Kline.*

I click the button on the side of her phone and the screen goes dark. Holding it out to her, she reaches for it, this time, wrapping her hand around mine, just like I'd done. That small gesture, the heat of her touch, and the infinitesimal connection of our bodies has mine aching for something deeper.

Dropping her phone into her purse, she glances up at me. Pressing the tips of her fingers against her chin, she lowers her hand, pulling it away from her face.

"She says, 'Thank you.'"

I mimic the gesture. "Thank you," I say in return, keeping my eyes glued to her brilliant green ones.

The girls smile, then turn to walk away. With their heads bent low, I can see the conspiratorial glances, hear the friend's hushed giggles, and see Red's fingers move.

"Hey!" I call after them. "What did she say?"

Over her shoulder, Red's friend says, "Harper will let you know."

Harper. She had me so flustered, I'd forgotten to ask her name. I am such a douche.

Harper and her friend make it to the back of the club and slip out the door. The second they're out of sight, I turn and make my way back to the stage. Pauly, Griffin, and Adam have the mess well contained.

I blow out a long breath, lift the last cabinet, and start down the hall to the back exit. Images of Harper play on a continuous loop in my head: her lips…her eyes…her freckled, ivory skin…the way she moved her skillful, elegant fingers. They're so long and slender. I bet she's good with her hands.

Kicking open the propped back door with my boot, I see Griffin in the back of the van arranging the equipment. "Hey, man. Got one more." I walk over and pass the amp to him.

"Where've you been?" he asks.

"Just talking to someone."

"Yeah? The Hammer arranging a post-concert hookup?" Griffin hops down from the van and lands a punch to my shoulder.

"Nah. Not tonight." I think of Harper. Why hadn't I insisted on getting her number? Damn, she's got me all fucked up. "I promised my mom I'd stop by tonight."

"She doing okay?" Griffin throws the van doors shut, the echo of slamming metal reverberating down the small alley behind the club.

For the first time in twenty years, I can answer with a confident, "Yeah. She's good."

"That's great, man. If anyone deserves some peace, it's your mom."

Damn straight she does. "Thanks."

Griffin locks the van. "I'm going to give Pauly the keys, then I'm heading back to the apartment. I need some fucking sleep. That drive from Rhode Island was a bitch."

"How's Jill?" I ask, knowing it's killing him to have his best friend halfway across the country. They've been inseparable since they were kids.

Scuffing his foot in the loose gravel of the cracked pavement, he shrugs and casts his eyes downward. A beat later, he pulls in a large breath of air, settles his attention back on me, and says, "She's going to kick serious ass at that school."

I have no doubts. Jillian is going to be a famous designer one day. "Damn, right," I agree.

"I'll catch you later, man," I say, walking toward the side of the building.

"See ya." Griffin steps toward the door, pulls it open, and disappears inside.

I glance at my watch and pull a pack of cigarettes from my jacket pocket. Slapping the pack against my palm, I take one out and slip it between my lips. With a quick flick of my wrist, the lighter catches. I shield the flame and bring it to the end of the cigarette, inhaling those first glorious puffs of nicotine. The tension in my shoulders ebbs.

It's a soundless night. As I make my way around the building, toward my car, all I hear is the crunch of gravel beneath my boots and the faint crackle of burning tobacco when I take a long pull on my cigarette. Once again, thoughts of Harper come flooding back. She can't hear. To her, the world is truly soundless.

Am I a complete idiot? Can I really go on a date with a woman who can't hear? How the hell are we supposed to communicate?

So many questions have me scared shitless. This is uncharted territory. When it comes to one-night stands, I'm the king. I don't do relationships. I'm the Hammer for fuck's sake. My reputation precedes me.

But with Harper, there's an inexplicable desire for more than just one night, the glimmer of hope that she might text me, and I'll get the chance to know her, and for some reason, that silences all of my fears.

CHAPTER FOUR

THOR

I kill the Charger's engine and pull the latch on the door. Stepping out of the car, I glance around the quiet parking lot. A couple of the large security lights are burned out and the lot's darker than it should be. Mom's new townhouse isn't in the best neighborhood, but at least she's out of *his* house, and that makes her a million times safer by comparison.

Walking along the cracked sidewalk, I scan the address numbers nailed into the brick, to the right of each front door, and stop at 12B—Mom's new place. I'm so fucking proud of her, this move was a long time coming. She should have left my drunken asshole of a father years ago—why she stayed so long, I'll never understand. He beat the shit out of her...out of the both of us, for years. But, nine months ago was the last straw—when he put her in the hospital with a handful of broken ribs and a concussion. The police tried to track him down, but he skipped town. I begged her to file a restraining order and leave him. She agreed it was time to move out and start fresh, but didn't want to get the courts involved, content that he was truly gone this time.

I press the doorbell and hear its faint chime inside, followed by Mom's footsteps. I glance at my watch and notice it's just after one in the morning. Why did she insist that I come over this late? What's going on?

"Who is it?" Mom calls from the other side.

"It's me, Mom."

She turns the deadbolt and I can hear her sliding the chain off the latch. With a yank, she opens the door and smiles. "Thor," she says with a sigh. "Thanks for coming."

"Sure thing. What's up?"

She opens the door wider and I step inside, locking the deadbolt.

Mom stands in front of me, smiling from ear to ear like she's won the lottery or something. "Ma? You okay?"

She stretches her arms out wide. "Come here. I just need a hug."

I step into her arms and swallow her tiny, five-feet-four-inch frame with all of my six feet two inches. My height comes from *his* side of the family…the Kline traits dominating any of Mom's Gilbert genes.

Mom rubs her hands up and down my back, squeezing me as tightly as she can. "So glad you're here. Love you," she mumbles against my chest.

I tighten my biceps, squeezing her closer. "Love you, too. But what's so important that you needed me to come over in the middle of the night?" I break our hug to give her a sidelong glance. I know she has an ulterior motive, but hell if I know what it is.

"Can't a mom just want her only son to stop by?" She gives my arm a squeeze.

"I know you, you're up to something." Walking over to her couch, I plop down and toe-off my boots; my feet are killing me.

"You're right. I do need you to do something. I need some pictures hung."

Pictures? I pull my eyebrows together. "I don't think your neighbors would appreciate me driving nails into the walls in middle of the night. I could have come tomorrow and taken care of the pictures, Ma. What's really going on?"

With a heavy sigh, she falls into the oversized armchair. She's quiet for a moment, avoiding my eyes. When she does finally turn her gaze back on me, her eyes are shiny with fresh, unshed tears. "You got me."

I sit up. "What is it?" Anger boils in my veins, and as much as I hate to acknowledge it, so does fear. For so long, it was fear of what he could do to the both of us, now it's fear of what he can do to her. I can take care of myself. "Is he back? Did he come here? Did he hurt you?" We haven't heard from him in nine months, but that doesn't mean he won't come back. He's like a horrible disease you can't get rid of.

Mom shakes her head and tries to wave away my panic. "No, it isn't that. He hasn't been here."

Blowing out a heavy breath, I lean back on the couch, rubbing a hand over my close-cropped hair. If that man comes anywhere near her again, I will tear him a new asshole. Over my dead body will he ever hurt her again.

"You want some coffee?" she asks, standing, not waiting for my answer before heading down the narrow hallway toward the kitchen.

I heave myself off the couch, exhaustion washing over me. I'm so fucking tired, I could drink an entire pot of coffee and still fall asleep. "I guess," I mumble, following her down the hall.

In the kitchen, Mom's at the counter pouring water into the coffeemaker, her back to me. Pulling out one of the chairs, I flip it backward and straddle it, watching her. "It's not the pictures. I can tell something's up. Talk to me."

She busies herself, measuring scoops of coffee grounds into a filter, ignoring my question. Flipping the lid closed, she presses the power button and the machine wheezes to life. I need to get her a new coffeemaker, one of those one-cup pod contraptions.

Mom turns around and joins me at the table. Sadness is etched on her face, extinguishing the light in her eyes and pulling her smile down. I reach across the table and clutch her tiny hand in mine. "Talk to me."

Her eyes catch mine and she gives a closed mouth smile. "It's stupid."

"If it's bothering you this much, it's not stupid."

She sighs heavily, shoulders slumping. "It's so quiet here," she says. "I'm not used to the quiet."

I wish I understood what she meant. I treasure the quiet…crave it, actually. When I was younger, Dad's noise sucked the life out of Mom and me, and now, with Mine Shaft booking bigger gigs, there's a constant buzz in my ears, like I've stood to close to the speakers at a concert. It's rare that I can escape to my quiet place. "Isn't it nice to be able to hear your own thoughts for once?" *And not get the shit beat out of you for having an opinion?* That's what I really want to say to her, but I'm not here to make her feel bad.

Pursing her lips, she shakes her head. "That's just it. I went from living with my parents, right into a place with your dad. I've never been on my own, and to be honest, I'm scared. At least when I know you're going to visit, I've got something to look forward to."

"Being by yourself has got to be better than living with *him*." I bite my lip, tasting blood, trying my damnedest to dial back the vitriol I want to spew. I hate that he still has an effect on her. Even when he isn't around, he's cinched around her neck like a goddamn noose.

"It is. I should have left him a long time ago." She stands, her chair scraping against the worn linoleum. Turning around, she walks to the cabinet and pulls down two mugs and fills them. Two cups of coffee in hand, she returns to the table, the hint of a smile on her face. "Being alone is hard, too. But, I'll adjust." Sliding a cup across the table to me, she sips hers. "I've survived worse than loneliness and an apartment that makes weird noises in the middle of the night," she laughs humorlessly.

"Ma"—I put my hand on hers, forcing her to look at me—"you are the strongest woman I know. And I'll always be here for you."

It breaks my heart to see her like this, what that man has

done to her. There are no words.

She pulls her hand from beneath mine and sits back, nursing her coffee and grinning widely. "Enough about me and my shit. How was the concert tonight?"

"Good." I nod. "Standing room only."

"Look at my boy getting all famous!" she squeals while she shrugs her shoulders in rapid succession.

"I wouldn't go that far. Hell, we can't get a record label to give us the time of day."

"But, your fans do, and that's what counts, right?"

I take a swallow of my watered down coffee, recalling the screaming crowd that had packed into Mississippi Lights tonight. Our biggest gig yet. But it's Harper's round face and wild red curls that my brain zeros in on. Could she feel my eyes on her tonight? It seemed like she could. When our eyes locked for those brief seconds, everything around us fell away. It was just the two of us...fucking amazing. And her body. *Damn.* The sultry sway of her hips as she danced to the music was intoxicating. Won't get that image out of my head for a long time, not that I'd want to.

Mom smacks my arm. "Thor?"

My eyes snap to hers and I'm pulled away from the Harper movie reel in my head. "Yeah." I clear my throat. "Sorry. What'd you say?"

Mom's eyes widen, stretching her lips upward into a sly grin. "What were you thinking about?" She points her index finger at me, circling it around. "I know you, Thorin, only a girl can put that look on your face. Do you have a new girlfriend?"

"Jesus. No, I don't." I bristle at the word "girlfriend." Wrinkling my nose, I throw back a swallow of coffee.

"Oh! It is a girl! You *always* get like this." Her hands beat a wild, circular path in front of my face.

I can't hide anything from her. "Like what?"

"Like this." Her hands move faster, making wider circles, as if that clarifies her meaning. "All defensive and brooding. Girls eat that shit up, don't they?"

I look up at ceiling and roll my eyes. Inhale. Exhale. Repeat. Lowering my chin, I meet Mom's enthusiastic stare and cave. "Yes. I met a girl."

"Ahhhh!" She claps. "I knew it! It's the brooding, gets 'em every time."

I blow out a huge breath, my cheeks puffing. Telling her about Harper was a mistake. She is going to take this news and run with it. Tomorrow, Harper and I will be married. By Sunday, we'll have a couple kids. "Relax, Ma. I didn't propose. Hell, I don't even have her number. Time to lay off the soap operas and Hallmark movies."

Mom falls back in her chair like I've taken a pin to her balloon. "You can't ask the lady out if you don't have her number, Thor."

I nod. "Thanks for that pro tip, but the ball's in her court, she's got my number."

She bites her lip, working over this nugget of information. "Oh. Well, do you want her to call? What's she like?"

Fuck yes, I want her to call, she's sexy as hell. Curves that warrant a caution sign. A sassy, lopsided grin that dares a man to come closer. And let's not forget about those deft fingers…I definitely want to find out what those can do. "Yeah, I really hope she calls. She's beautiful. Curly, red hair. Petite. Pink cheeks. Ivory skin. Freckles." I rattle off the mother-friendly list of Harper's physical attributes.

"Sounds like she made quite an impression." Mom wags her eyebrows.

You have no idea. I put the cup to my lips and finish off the cold, poor excuse for coffee.

"Then don't ruin things with her. You aren't getting any younger."

I give her a dirty look, offended. "I'm only twenty-four."

"Exactly. Don't waste your youth and good looks, they won't last forever. And you were already five years old by the time I was your age."

I roll my eyes. I need a fucking cigarette. If there's one person in the world that should want me to stay away from anything serious, it's my mother. She should be first in line to shoot down any potential romances, not the one making a damn love connection. Jesus, and the thought of kids? That makes me want to vomit. No fucking way. I will not be responsible for screwing up a tiny human's life.

Relationships aren't my thing. Never have been. From the time girls hit my radar, I knew I wasn't looking for more than just a short-lived good time. With my old man as a role model, I wanted no part of anything that resembled a relationship. One-night stands are easier…safer…no one gets hurt.

But dammit, Harper pops into my head. After a ninety-second conversation with her, I'm itching for a second date before

I've even been on a first one. What is it about her that's got me wanting more, tossing aside my strict one-night stand policy? Yeah, she's different from the girls I usually hook up with, and it's not because she's deaf, there's something else. I felt it when I couldn't tear my eyes away from hers while I was on stage. I don't know what it is, but I'm willing to go on a thousand dates if it means I get to figure it out.

CHAPTER FIVE

Harper

I watch the last kid leave, then turn around and survey the mess left behind. The room looks likes a fairy war zone. Glitter everywhere. At the time, making cosmic silly putty sounded like a good idea, in practice, not so much. This is why pharmacy school is a better career choice for me than teaching. The kids have way too much fun and now I'm left with the chaos my crazy idea generated. After working at the YMCA's Deaf Youth Outreach Program for the last three years, one would think I learned my lesson about messy projects. Nope. The bigger the mess, the more fun the kids and I have. With a sigh, I resign myself to the fact that I'm going to be here all night, up to my eyeballs in glitter, and that's okay.

Walking over to craft area I collect the dripping glue bottles and toss them in a basket. I set a trashcan at one end of the table and swipe my hand across its length. A dozen empty glitter containers, paper, and ruined markers plop into the can. I pull my hand away and wiggle my fingers covered with wet glue, multicolored sparkles, and some other unidentifiable gooey substances. Kindergarteners aren't known for their hygiene skills. *Smart, Harper.*

Clapping my hands over the trash, some of the glitter comes off, but I'm still a mess. I'll be leaving a trail of pixie dust in my wake for weeks. I turn around and head to the bathroom to wash my hands just in time to see Chloe barreling through the Y's door.

Chloe skips over to me, bouncing like Tigger with a beatific smile on her face. Her black-blond braid is wild, pieces coming loose all around her face and sticking out in every direction. I'm not used to seeing her so disheveled. *"I've got huge news!"*

"What?" Half-dried clumps of glitter glue fall from my sticky fingers.

"Months ago, I sent in an application and a video to the Food Network for a chance to appear on their show, Cupcake Wars. *They called. They want me on the show!"* Chloe bounces on the balls of her feet, excitement pouring from her.

I wipe my hands down the sides of my pants getting off as much gunk as possible. *"O-M-G! Chloe, that's amazing! You've wanted to be on that show forever!"*

"I know, right? They're doing some sort of Internet baker episode, so I'll be going to war with another YouTube baker."

"I'm so proud of you, Chloe!" I stretch out my arms and pull her into a hug. I don't care that I'm covered in a layer of kindergarten muck; this is the kind of news that requires hugging. After a tight squeeze, I pull away and ask, *"What are the details? Where do they film? When do you leave? When will you be on TV?"*

Chloe shakes her head, a permanent smile on her face. *"I don't know the details yet, but Megan said she'd go with me, be my assistant. Unless of course, you want that job?"* She waggles her eyebrows.

Still smiling, I shake my head. *"I happily give Megan the title of 'Assistant to the Cupcake Queen.' It's the perfect gig for your sister."*

Consumed by excitement, my eyes well up and I pull her back into my arms, holding on longer than a normal hug should last. It isn't until Chloe starts to squirm in my arms that I let go. She holds me at arm's length and gives me a once-over. *"What happened to you?"*

"A fairy threw up on me." I shrug.

She wrinkles her nose and sticks out her tongue while picking glitter out of my hair. *"Got an extra rag, I'll help you clean up."*

"You don't have to do that. You should be out celebrating."

Chloe waves me off and pushes by, swiping the roll paper towels off the end of the table. Tucking it under her arms she mouths, along with signing, *"I cannot subsist on a smattering of ten-minute conversations in a week. I miss my friend. Our clinical rotations are killing our social lives. At least this way, we'll have a chance to catch up."* Taking the paper towels from under her arm, she rips off one long piece and walks to the sink, running it under the faucet.

Chloe's right. This last week has been one exhausting rollercoaster ride. Chloe and I are on opposite clinical paths. While she spends her first semester learning the ropes of filling prescriptions in a commercial drugstore setting, I'm learning the hospital side of pharmacology—which I love. To know that I have the opportunity to help manage a patient's pain, especially a child's, it's the greatest feeling.

At the end of the semester, Chloe and I will switch. It's actually kind of nice that we didn't have the same track, this way, we know what's coming down the line—and for me, it's always helpful to have some insight into the future, so I can prepare.

Whipping back around, Chloe cups her hands beneath the wet towel and runs, plopping the soggy towels on the table. Together, we wipe down the mess. *"Thanks for staying to help."*

"It's nothing." She gives me a thumbs up and huge smile. *"Not like I have anywhere I need to be. Although"*—she stops signing, her brow furrowed—*"it wouldn't be a bad idea to start practicing for* Cupcake Wars. *Hope you like cupcakes, that's all I'm baking for a while."* She winks at me, pivots on her heel, and shoots the dirty paper towel into a trashcan like Lisa Leslie.

Whirling back around, she eyes me, pointing.

"What? Something the matter?" I underhand toss my wet rag into the trash, raising an eyebrow at her incredulous stare.

"I might not have anywhere to be tonight, but why aren't you getting ready for a date?" She gives me the stink-eye. *"Does the name T-H-O-R-I-N K-L-I-N-E ring a bell?"*

Shit. I thought she'd forgotten about that; it's been over a week. I cringe. Yes, Thorin Kline is hot. Yes, he's a musician (and damn Chloe for knowing my weakness for musicians). But, I have zero time for the opposite sex right now. *"Yes, I re-*

member him. I'm choosing not to engage. Now is not a good time to get involved with someone."

"Fuck that!" She shoves a chair under the table and stalks toward me. *"It's just a date, Harper, not a friggin' marriage proposal. Text the guy, go out with him. My eighty-year-old grandma has more of a social life than you."*

I yank the chair from under the table and flop onto it. She's so right. I have no life.

Chloe drags another chair over and sets it backward, right in front of me. She straddles it, resting her elbows on the back, chin propped comfortably in her folded hands. She blinks, waiting.

That's the thing about Chloe, she knows me too well. She knows I hate long periods of silence. She'll wait me out. My need to fill empty space with words has gotten me in trouble so many times, I've lost count.

Not this time, though. I can sit here quietly. If I get tired of sitting, I'll just finish cleaning up. Text Thorin Kline? That's the one thing I will NOT do.

One minute.

Two minutes.

Chloe licks her lips, checks her watch, blinks, and resumes her stare of opposition.

Three minutes.

GAH! Dammit! I want to scream. I stand up, sending the preschool chair falling behind me. *"Why is it so important to you that I text him?"* I sign furiously, angered by her sit-in protest against my love life.

Chloe stands, her face in line with mine. She scoops up my

hands, gives them a couple of squeezes, then lets go. *"You're like a sister to me. I want you to be happy. Let loose once in a while. It's okay to have fun. All you do is study."* She flinches, shaking her shoulders in repulsion.

"If I went out with him, you know better than anyone how the date will go. My track record with guys isn't stellar. I'm tired of the same old shit. Pity dates suck. He didn't know I was deaf before he asked for my number, and once he found out, he didn't want to be the prick who walked away. If I don't text, I save him and me a lot of awkward staring."

"Okay. Whatever you say." She pulls her bottom lip into her mouth and walks away. I watch, stunned. Chloe never gives up an argument. And she *never* turns her back to me in the middle of a conversation. *What the hell?* I wasn't done making my point.

At the closet, Chloe drags out a vacuum cleaner. I tap her shoulder, forcing her to turn around. When she looks at me, I lay into her. *"Why did you walk away? I wasn't finished yet."*

"It looked like you were. Obviously, your mind is made up. What else is there to say?" With a shrug, she bends over and unwraps the cord from the machine.

This time, I wait. I know she'll look at me eventually. With the cord unwrapped, Chloe squats, pushes the plug into the outlet, and stands. Her eyes on me, she flips the switch and the light on the handle glows red. I can feel the vibrations of the beater spinning on the floor. A great thing about being deaf, conversations can continue even in the noisiest places. *"Give me one good reason why I should text him. Why I should give him a chance? Why you think he's somehow better than all the other idiots I've wasted my time on."*

Chloe moves the sweeper back and forth, eyeing me. I can see the wheels turning in her head. The vibrations under my feet stop. The red light, off. Pushing the handle upright, she walks around the vacuum and comes to stand in front of me. *"Because he spoke to YOU!"* She points at me.

I pinch my eyes together. *"What does that mean?"* That was not the answer I'd been expecting. *He's hot*, or *Have you seen his ass?* Those would have been the typical Chloe answers.

"Even after he found out you were deaf, he spoke to you. You're always saying that hearing people have a terrible habit of not speaking directly to you in a conversation. He did. Without having to be told. Doesn't seem like a prick to me, or pity. Just a guy hoping the pretty girl will text him."

I roll my eyes. When she puts it like that…

"Honestly, right now, you're the one who's being all condescending and judgey. You get upset when people assume you're an invalid just because you're deaf, and here, you're labeling him a douchebag before he even gets a chance to prove you otherwise. Yeah, you've had some shitty dates in the past, who hasn't? Want to compare lists? Don't be that person. He spoke to you, Harper, not me." Shaking her head, Chloe grabs my hands and pulls me in for a hug, squeezing tight. A clinical, antiseptic smell clings to her clothes and hair. I can tell she's spent the whole day at the pharmacy.

She's right. And dammit, I hate it when she's right.

Stepping back, I look her in the eye. *"Okay, I'll text him."* I sigh my concession.

Chloe shakes her head. *"Don't text him because I guilted you into it. Only text him if you want to."*

I do want to. I have all along. The excuses just clouded my vision. *"You're right. I'm not being fair. He deserves a chance."*

"Damn right he does!" Chloe smacks my shoulder. *"Have you seen his ass?"*

And there it is! That's the Chloe I know.

CHAPTER SIX

HARPER

"Chloe, why am I doing this?" I shake out my hands and arms, my stomach in knots. Forget butterflies, they've been forced to evacuate the quaking, twisting mess of my insides. *"This is stupid. A waste of time."* I haven't been on a freaking date in ages and for good reason—the language barrier is a crusher. I get it, communication differences are a huge deal and more often than not, they're the deal breaker.

Chloe shakes her head and glares at me in her much perfected "I love you, but you're ridiculous" way. *"It's okay to have some fun every now and then. Even you can take a day off from saving the world. And what other reason do you need to go out with him?"* she asks. *"He's hot."* Her eyes widen, trying to burn her reasoning into me like a laser beam. *"And he's in a band."*

"Not all hot-guy musicians are date worthy." I cock my head and return her glare. *"And I'm not saving the world."* I roll my eyes.

"When you aren't studying, so you can become the world's

greatest pharmacist, you spend all your free time with kinder-
garteners at the YMCA. Admirable, but you can afford to be a
little selfish once in a while. As much fun as the pill and tablet
counter, finger paints, and glitter are, you are in serious need
of some excitement." She wags her eyebrows. *"And you'll never*
know if T-H-O-R-I-N-E K-L-I-N-E, Mr. Hot Band Guy, is
date-worthy unless you go on an actual date with him." Chloe
steps closer and puts her hand on my shoulder, her eyes focused on the window behind me. Snapping her attention back
to me, she pulls her hand away and quickly signs, *"He's here."*
The corners of her mouth pull into a playful grin and the knots
in my stomach tighten to the point that I feel like my whole
body is going to fold in on itself.

Hi, Thorin. Didn't realize you were going on a date with a
pretzel, huh? I cringe at the thought.

All I know about Thorin Kline is that he's twenty-four, an
only child, a native St. Louisan, and he taught himself how to
play the guitar and piano because his parents couldn't afford
lessons. According to his band's website, I have nothing in
common with this guy. I'm two years older than him, not from
St. Louis, and unfortunately, my knack for playing Name that
Tune doesn't count for actual musical talent. I don't know how
this date is going to be anything more than an awkward, silent,
stare-fest. I hope he has nice eyes; otherwise, it's going to be a
long night.

Bobby dances at the door, ready to greet a new friend, because, let's face it, all company comes to see Bobby, at least
that's what he thinks. I don't have the heart to tell him otherwise. Chloe pats my shoulder, bringing me out of my growing

nervous breakdown. *"He's walking up to the door. Stop worrying. Enjoy yourself,"* she signs, emphasizing each word, then pulls me in for a hug.

"Get the door, Harper." She winks with a grin, picks up Bobby, and scampers off toward her bedroom.

Filling my lungs with a huge gulp of air, I blow it out and give the knob a twist, pulling open the door. Thorin Kline stands on my porch looking like a cross between bad-boy rock star and the boy next door. My jaw drops. What the hell happened to my memory? He wasn't this ruggedly sexy a week ago. I try to swallow. I've got nothing but a dry mouth and a staring problem that I have no intention of correcting.

My eyes travel down his body and back up again, unapologetically. Can't help it. The other night, at the club, I was so preoccupied with getting Chloe out before she saw Trey and dumbfounded that the guitarist from the band wanted my number, I didn't have time to appreciate how gorgeous Thorin Kline was. Not to mention it was kind of dark in the club, so there was that.

It's not dark now. I lock eyes with Thorin, and he holds my gaze. His eyes are a crystalline sky blue, like the anhydrous form of cobalt chloride, the same substance used to make invisible ink. And his eyes aren't giving away any of his secrets. But his body speaks volumes. Uber sexy, cocky, brooding rock star, Thorin Kline, is nervous! And it's so friggin' adorable!

Over the years, I've become an expert on reading people—their facial expressions, body language, a tell-all stare. In the span of just a few minutes, I can learn so much about a person. Thorin shifts his weight between his feet while his left thumb and forefinger worry over the tail of his red button-down shirt. He lifts his right hand to his cheek, rubbing his palm against the dark stubble. "Hey," he says, a flirty, cautious smile on his lips. Damn, he's hot.

I wave and smile back, relaxing a little, knowing that I'm not the only one who's anxious about this date. Pulling the door open wider, I wave him inside. Taking my cue, he pushes his hands into his jeans pockets and crosses the threshold. Holding up my index finger, I gesture for him to wait a minute, then turn around and grab my purse and phone off the coffee table.

Spinning back around, I face him. He's looking around, admiring my place. I cast a glance over my shoulder, hoping Chloe's not eavesdropping—I wouldn't put it past her, when it comes to a guy and me, she's incorrigible. I don't see her, which means Thorin won't see her either, thank God. This whole scenario is awkward enough, I don't need her prying eyes as well.

There's a light tap on my shoulder and I whip my head back to the front. Thorin's looking right at me, his eyes still revealing nothing. I smile, an attempt to ease the tension that's creeping back into my chest, and hold my phone up between us. I type out a quick message. We can use our phones to talk. I hit send and look back up.

Thorin pulls his phone out of his back pocket and glances at the screen, nodding his head. Unlocking his phone, his thumbs peck at the keyboard, then he looks up, regarding me.

My phone vibrates in my hand. Cool. BTW, you look stunning. Cute piercing. Ready to go?

I brush my fingers over the side of my nose, touching the dainty hoop. My nose ring was my first rebellious act when I left for college…well, second really, if you count moving out of my parents' house to go away to school. My parents disapproved of the move, but I felt liberated having done it. I needed to get out on my own, to prove to Mom and Dad that I didn't need them to shelter me from the world. I love my parents and I know they love me, but the sidewalk of our relationship has always been paved with eggshells. They danced around me, never quite comfortable with having a deaf child, and I tiptoed around them, trying to prove to them in subtle ways I was just as normal as all of their friends' hearing kids.

"Thank you," I sign, mouthing the words. I don't know why that small compliment means so much to me, but it does. So often, people are consumed with trying to figure out how to act around the "deaf girl" they fail to see me.

Thorin dips his chin and grabs my hand, winking. With a gentle tug, he's pulling me out the door and to his car—an old, sexy as hell, black Charger. Thorin Kline is the total package: a talented musician, a killer body, and he drives a fast car. I say a silent prayer to the dating gods, *Please let him be a nice guy, too, because I'm liking everything he's got going on.*

Thorin opens the door for me, and I climb inside, basking in the glorious scent of the aged leather bucket seats. There's nothing like the smell of an old muscle car—gasoline and exhaust mingled with the faint scent of stale cigarette smoke.

A shadow darkens the driver's side, and I look over just in time to see Thorin slipping behind the wheel. He turns the ignition and the engine stutters a few times before it kicks to life, purring like a well-loved kitten. It's a glorious machine, in pristine condition.

I have my grandfather to thank for my love of fast cars. Running my hand over the wood paneling on the door, images of when I was a little girl flash through my mind. I spent countless weekends with my grandparents, usually hanging out with Papa in his garage while he tinkered on one of his babies. He loved classic cars, his collection spanning the infancy of the automobile to the late seventies, where the cars were noisy and labeled the owner a badass.

I'm still clutching my phone, so I type a quick message and send it to Thorin before he backs out of the driveway. This car is amazing! '69 Charger?

He looks at his phone lying in his lap and picks it up. Deep lines at the sides of his mouth frame a relaxed smile, the nervous vibes he was giving off a moment ago, gone. Biting his lower lip, he responds. Both of his thumbs slip over the screen, punching out a quick staccato beat.

His message flashes on my screen. Thanks. It's a '71. You like cars?

I nod enthusiastically and sign my answer, while mouthing the words. *"I love them!"* Caught up in the moment, I forget that he doesn't sign, but a look of understanding passes over his face and he replies.

"Nice. Me, too," he says. My eyes focus on his mouth. Pressed together, his upper lip has a slight dip in the middle, at the top, and his bottom lip comes to a subtle point at the bottom, making a perfectly shaped heart. It's a lovely mouth—a kissable mouth, for sure. And I get to stare at that mouth all night. Lucky me!

He licks his lips and continues speaking. "I…you said you liked…? Ever been to the…Bar?"

I watch his mouth move, puckering and then thinning out, his tongue caressing the tops and bottoms of his teeth, forming beautiful words, words my brain doesn't register because it's a hormonal ball of mush. All I can think about is how it would feel to have his lips puckered against mine. And don't even get me started on his tongue. My imagination runs wild with all the places I'd like it to caress.

I'm good at lipreading, and even still, I don't understand every spoken word. Lipreading isn't an exact science and it's certainly isn't like actual reading. It's more like taking a fill-in-the-blank test without a word bank. I never fully understand what's being said. Lots of guesswork on my part. Of all nights for my brain to take a vacation and leave my libido in charge, I just missed half of what he said.

Pull it together, Harper! If I want to get through this date without looking like an idiot, I need to concentrate on his words, not his lips…or his tongue.

Shaking my head, I lower my eyebrows and sign, *"Sorry, What?"* It usually takes me a while to get used to a person's unique speaking cadence. But misunderstanding Thorin, that's on my raging hormones, not his speaking; he's doing just fine.

He nods and licks his lips before repeating his question. I pay attention this time, hard focus. *Keep your mind on the words, Harper.* "When you texted me, I remember you said you liked seafood. Ever been to the Broadway Oyster Bar?"

Making a fist in my right hand, I shake it, signing, *"Yes."* I'm pleasantly surprised at how well Thorin is reading my lips, so I continue signing and mouthing short answers. *"Love that restaurant."*

"Great." He smiles, shifting into reverse and backing down the driveway.

Looking out the window, my stomach twists into knots again. Pretzel Harper is back. Now that he's driving, it's more difficult to converse, which makes things all the more awkward. When I'm nervous, I get chatty. And right now, there's no way for me to be chatty with him.

Drumming my fingers on my purse, a small thread tickles the underside of my palm. I catch it between my thumb and forefinger, rolling it back and forth. Anything to give my twitchy fingers an outlet to move. I steal a glance his way and wonder if he's feeling as jumpy as me.

On cue, he turns his head in my direction and catches my eye, giving me a relaxed, easy smile. Nope. Not jumpy at all. He's the picture of calm coolness—the rock star I saw on stage a couple weeks ago.

Every now and then it hits me, I'm on a date with a friggin' rock star. *How is this real life?*

Thor winks and puts his eyes back on the road, and the knots in my stomach pull tighter. How is he so at ease when I'm a nervous wreck?

Reaching for the knob on the dashboard, Thorin slides through different channels. As he climbs higher on the FM frequency, he settles on the local alternative station and turns up the volume. He puts his hand back on the wheel and his fingers start tapping out the beat of the song on the steering wheel. I bite back a smile, an idea blooming in my head.

If I concentrate hard enough on the thump of the beat and the unique vibrations of the song, I can usually guess what song is playing. I can't hear the music or the lyrics, but each song has it's own rhythmic signature that I can feel. It's really not that hard to guess, radio stations play the same songs over and over again, if anyone pays close enough attention to the beat and the way it feels, they could do the same thing.

Shifting my focus, I study the way the pulse reverberates through the metal of the car, into the seat and up through my body, the way the mirrors thump in time with the beat, but I'm not getting anything. The music isn't loud enough. I hope he doesn't mind, but I lean in and twist the volume control higher.

Thorin's eyes leave the road, looking at me in astonishment. "Can you hear that?" he asks.

I shake my head and answer, *"No, but I can feel the beat and guess which song is playing."*

Thorin watches me with interest, but he doesn't respond. He has no clue what I just said. Okay, different approach. I pick up my phone, even though I know I shouldn't text him. I'll make it short: I can feel the beat.

In his lap, the screen brightens and he glances down at the message. Nodding his head, he smiles and reaches for the knob, cranking it as high as it goes. Now my seat is thumping.

I shake my head, cringing. With the radio that loud, it has to unbearable for him, yet he doesn't seem to mind. Leaning forward, I place my hands on the dashboard, palms down, and concentrate on the vibrations, while I watch the side mirror shake. *Thump, thump. THUMP. Thump, thump. THUMP. Thump. THUMP, thump, thump. THUMP...*

The pattern cycles in beats of four, varying slightly in the transition zones, where the heavy thumps even out. I nod. I know this song, it's on the radio *all* the time. Picking up my phone, I type: "Radioactive" by Imagine Dragons. Pressing send, I watch Thorin's phone light up.

He sees my message and looks at me just long enough to say, "Wow" before putting his eyes back on the road.

Even in profile, I can see he's still grinning. *Gah!* What does that mean? Is he impressed by my parlor trick? Does he think I'm an idiot? Should I name another song? Is he wondering what the hell he's doing on a date with me? My mind conjures up a dozen thoughts—some horrible, others, not so bad.

In the middle of thinking terrible thought number four, Thorin glances back in my direction. "How about this one?" he says, tapping the radio dial.

Sure enough, the song had changed. The beat pulses steady, little variation, very different from "Radioactive." This isn't a bass-driven song, making it harder to guess. Biting my lower lip, I touch the dashboard and close my eyes, counting the beats. I don't want to get this wrong. Two songs come to mind, "Safe and Sound" by Capital Cities, and "Kids" by MGMT. Both have similar rhythms. My gut instinct is to go with "Safe and Sound" because it's a newer song. I own my answer and send Thorin the text, hoping I'm right.

With a quick glance at his lap, he reads the message and looks up at me. "That's fucking amazing, Red!"

Whew! I got it right! I relax, leaning into the seat, relieved. I'm surprised at how much I want to impress him. That almost never happens when I'm on a date. Most of the time, I'm counting down the minutes until I get to go home, because the guy I'm out with is so freaking uncomfortable around me, it's a miserable time for the both of us. Not Thorin, though. He doesn't seem put off by our communication differences in the least, treating me like he would any other person. And don't even get me started on the nickname. He called me Red the night we meet, at the club. I didn't think anything of it then, but now, it makes my whole body tingle, like that first sip of a freshly poured soda, fizz tickling my nose.

We continue the game, Thorin's smile growing with each correct answer I give, even playfully teasing me when I get one of the songs wrong. The awkwardness dissolves into normal, like we've known each other for years. I glance at my phone, noting the time. We've been together for thirty-three minutes and it's already shaping up to be the best date I've had in years.

CHAPTER SEVEN

THOR

I slow the car and turn into the tiny parking lot, my gut sinking. There aren't many parking options at the oyster bar, it's the lot or the street. And being downtown on the same night as a Cardinals home game, there's no way in hell I'm parking on the street. Some drunk fucker plowing his car into the side of my baby is the last thing I need. I'll risk a door ding in the parking lot.

Killing the engine, I hop out and stride over to Harper's side. I offer my hand and she slides her palm against mine, standing. My eyes roam over her body, drinking her in like a bottle of the finest tequila. Despite being short, she has long, shapely legs. Her tight black jeans accentuate each curve, especially her ass. *Damn.* I shake off the image of running my palm over her backside and blow out a breath, slipping my hand into my pocket—a nonchalant attempt at adjusting my pants around my hard-on. *Concentrate on safer territory, Thor.*

My eyes zero in on her chest, not safer territory on most occasions, but tonight, Harper is wearing a leopard-print scarf, effectively hiding any skin. *God bless you, Harper.* The scarf is cute and will help keep my head in the "get to know you" game instead of the "let's fuck" game, where I'm so used to spending my time. Getting to know someone is a foreign concept to me.

Harper flips her long hair over her shoulder, exposing the ivory skin of her neck, and I wonder what it will feel like on my lips. *Shit.* My attempt at pure thoughts didn't last long. I'm going to have to settle for getting to know her and wanting to take her to bed, because in all honesty, I want to do both.

Hand in hand, we walk down the sidewalk. Dixieland jazz blasts from inside the restaurant, pouring out onto street, and I hope we can get a seat away from the stage, my ears are still ringing from having the radio up so loud in the car, not that I have any regrets. I would have turned it up louder if it had been possible, anything to keep her smiling.

I glance at Harper and squeeze her hand. She turns her head in my direction and gives me an easy, crooked smile. God I love her smile, it speaks louder than any words.

* * *

I shove my empty plate away, and fall against the back of my chair, stuffed. I need a cigarette, but I'll wait. No way am I leaving Harper sitting alone while I go outside for a smoke; that would be a jackass move.

Harper picks up the pen sitting beside her plate and writes on the napkin, having given up texting in place of writing. She mentioned earlier that she prefers writing to texting; it's more

personal. I agree. Texting is cold, no intimacy. There's something sexy about Harper's loopy, half-cursive, half-printed
words on the white napkin.

Would you like my last oyster? I'm full. She lays the pen
down and slides the napkin toward me, pointing to her plate.

I snatch the pen and napkin from her and scribble my comment beneath her question, **No thank you.** I flip the napkin
around so she can read my answer.

She makes her hand flat, touching the tips of her fingers to
her head and pulling it away while lowering her index, middle,
and ring fingers. *"Why? Don't like them?"* I read her lips.

"I'm allergic to shellfish," I say, wondering what her voice
sounds like. She hasn't spoken all evening. I want to ask her
why she doesn't speak, but for some reason, that question
seems too personal for a first date.

Harper's eyes go wide, a look of horror on her face. She pulls
her plate closer to her body—any closer and her scarf will be
swimming in cocktail sauce. I laugh and touch her arm, "It's
fine. I can be around oysters, just can't eat them."

Exaggerating her relief, she wipes imaginary sweat from her
forehead and exhales, her shoulders deflating. Grinning, she
pushes her plate to the side and picks up the pen, writing, **Are
you allergic to anything else? Please say you're not allergic
to peanuts!**

I opt for writing my answer this time. Gives me the opportunity to touch her. With the pen in her hand, I deliberately
brush my fingers over hers, lingering longer than necessary,
sliding my fingertips over her slender knuckles. Clutching the
pen, I swivel the napkin around and lean over, pressing the tip

to the paper. This close, I can feel her breath on my hand. My eyes flick upward, landing on her parted lips. Her tongue slips between them, licking, and it takes every ounce of my self-control not to lean in a little farther and pull her tongue against my mouth.

Harper looks at me, raising her eyebrows, waiting for my answer. I shake off my lusty urges and focus on the paper. **Only shellfish. And why shouldn't I be allergic to peanuts?** I raise an eyebrow, smirking.

She motions for the pen and I drop it into her waiting palm. **Oh, good! Reese's Peanut Butter Cups are my favorite food! It would be tragic if I didn't get to share them with you. What's your favorite?**

I lift my head and stare into her sea glass–green eyes. Her words cut deep, touching a place no one has ever been—a place I keep sealed off. In all these years, no woman has ever told me her favorite food. Favorite positions, yes. But not food. That would be too domestic, too personal. Although, I never cared enough to ask. When it comes to my past liaisons, there was never much talking, period. It's easier to fuck, then to let someone get to know me. Just as the old adage says, "Like father, like son." The risk of becoming my father is too great. With a one-night stand, no one gets hurt. There are no expectations other than a good time. So, what am I doing letting Harper get close to me? I pick up my beer and drain it. Harper is a cool chick, why would I lead her into a relationship knowing how it will inevitably end—my parents aren't stellar relationship role models, and I'm a fucking moron for getting involved with this woman.

Tossing back the last swallow of her cranberry martini, Harper sets the glass on the table and taps her index finger on the napkin, next to her question, just as our waiter appears at the table.

"Can I get you two anything else?" he asks, shifting his gaze from Harper to me, and back again.

Harper shakes her head and smiles.

"No dessert?" I offer, trying my damnedest to get my head focused on positive thoughts.

She shakes her head again and signs, *"Too much. I'm full."* I'm glad she mouths the words, or I'd be lost. Although, I like watching her sign, her movements are so fluid; it's mesmerizing.

"All right then, I'll get your check." The waiter shuffles the menus he's holding and turns to leave.

Harper smiles and picks up with our conversation, splaying the fingers of her right hand outward, a slight bend in her middle finger, tapping it on her chin. She points to the napkin. Lowering my gaze, I reread what she'd written last: **What's your favorite?** I set the ballpoint to the paper and scribble down the first thing that pops into my head, **Chicken and dumplings. When I was a kid, I used to ask my mom for chicken and dumplings every year on my birthday.** I turned seven the last time she'd made them. I hate talking about this shit. I've got to change the subject.

Harper pulls the pen from my grip and slides the napkin toward her. **What's your family like? Any brothers or sisters?** Laying the pen on the napkin, she pushes them back to me.

Fucked up. I think it, I don't write it. For the first time tonight, I notice how loud the restaurant has gotten. Wall-to-wall people. Everyone vying for airtime, trying to make their words louder than the band rocking on stage. If Harper and I had been talking, we would be shouting. It amazes me how quiet our conversation has been, like we're the only two people in the room. But with that one question, the world comes crashing back in—reality, louder than feedback on a live mic, and just as painful.

What is there to say about my parents? Everything started off normal, then one day my dad gambled away his life savings, started drinking, and used my mom and me as punching bags? She doesn't want to hear that shit. **No siblings. My parents are separated. Mom's great. Dad's an ass. What about yours?** Short and simple. I toss the question back to her, hoping she has it better in the parent department.

"Sorry," she signs, just as her phone flashes. Picking it up, she glances at the screen and rolls her eyes. It's subtle, but I catch the hint of annoyance. I wonder who pissed her off. Setting the phone facedown, she turns her attention back to me, along with a smile.

All evening, I've studied her smiles: big ones, small ones, and those in between. I may not be able to hear her voice, or speak her language, but I know when she squints her eyes, and fine lines appear at the outer corners, accompanied by a full-on, toothy grin, she's bubbling over with excitement, or happiness. Or when she's embarrassed, her smile is faint and she rolls her eyes before averting them, looking downward as she tucks her head into her left shoulder, trying to hide. I'm a quick study when it comes to Harper King. And, when she

signs *"Sorry,"* her features soften and fall. All telltale lines of
joy disappear from her face, and I know she really is sorry. Not
a passive "sorry," the kind you'd give an acquaintance, but a
heartfelt, meaningful sentiment saved for someone you care
about. But, in between all of her smiles, there's the look I saw
when she read her text message.

Pen still in hand, I yank the napkin back and add another
sentence. **Everything all right? It's cool if you need to text
someone back.**

She takes the pen from my grasp, her fingers sending sparks
of electricity through my body when she touches me. I watch
as her hand gracefully forms each letter, curling it into the
next. When she's finished, she turns the napkin around and
pushes it toward me.

**I don't have any brothers or sisters, either. My parents
and I have a complicated relationship. They live back east,
in New Hampshire. I live here. Less drama. My mom's texting, but she can wait.**

After reading her words, I look up. She presses her lips together and shrugs. Like me, she just scratched the surface, not
giving away too much, but just enough. It seems we've found
kindred spirits in each other when it comes to our families. I
make a fist and repeat her motion, signing, *"Sorry."*

Harper's thin-lipped smile grows, the creases at the corner
of her eyes fan out, and she nods in approval, pointing to my
hand before giving me a thumbs-up.

"Can I ask you a personal question?" I get the words out
faster when I speak, steering our conversation away from all
the family talk. I do not want to talk about my fucking dad.

Harper pulls her eyebrows up and nods, giving me the go-ahead.

"Have you always been deaf?" I hope she doesn't think I'm a dick for asking.

Bending her head over the napkin, she writes fast. **I was almost three when I lost my hearing. Meningitis. I was really sick. My parents said I almost died. I was so little when it happened, I don't remember being able to hear. Just vague memories of being so sick. I was in a lot of pain.**

Shit. How am I supposed to respond to that? I take up the pen, buying myself an extra second to come up with a response that doesn't make me sound like the world's biggest prick. **I'm sorry.** I scrawl, for lack of a better reply.

Harper waves away my comment, and the expression on her face doesn't scream "offended." **No reason to be sorry. Being deaf is all I know. It's my normal. Can't miss something that I don't remember having, right?** She shrugs.

She is right. There really is no such thing as normal—only the sum of an individual's perspective and experience. I rub my cheek, scratching the stubble on my chin, soaking in my philosophical revelation. I should be writing this shit down, there's a song in there somewhere.

Harper holds up her index finger and quickly jots something else down. **Now it's my turn to ask something personal**—she lifts her head, wagging her eyebrows—**where did the name "Thorin" come from? It's so different.**

Her hand is wrapped around the pen and I pluck it free, like it was stuck in an inkwell. **My grandpa—Mom's dad—was a huge Tolkien fan. He passed away before I was born, but**

my mom honored his love of Middle-earth and named me after Thorin Oakenshield, the king of the dwarves. It could have been worse. You could be on a date with Bilbo or Frodo. I look at her, cringing. **Everyone calls me Thor, though.**

Harper laughs silently, shoulders shaking. Brushing her index finger twice on the tip of her nose, I read, *"Funny!"* on her lips. With her right hand, she tucks her thumb between her index and middle fingers, deftly moving them into four different positions, while mouthing my name.

I've been entranced by her signing all night, but damn if that wasn't the sexiest. My name on her lips…and in her hands. My dick twitches as dirty thoughts invade my head…other parts of me are eager to meet her mouth and hands.

"Mind if we get out of here?" I say, "There's some place I'd like to show you." I know it's late, but I want more time with her, alone. It's a bad, fucking idea to go down this path, I don't even come close enough to being good enough for her, but selfishly, I can't let go.

Harper nods and picks up the pen again. **I'd like that. What's the place?** She turns the napkin.

Somewhere I go when I need quiet, I write. Smiling, I rub a nervous hand over my chin. Town and Country Pools: it's abandoned, secluded, and been my hideout for years. The one place I can go to disappear from the world for a while.

Once I settle the bill, Harper lays the napkin from her lap, on the table, and shoulders her purse. I come around the table and slip my arm around her waist. We make our way through the heavy crowd.

As I put my palm to the door, ready to push it open, I remember the napkin with our conversation. Tapping Harper on the shoulder, I hold up one finger and say, "Forgot something. Be right back." Before I know if she understood, I turn and jog back to our table, dodging servers and customers, hoping the table hasn't been bussed.

It's still a mess, the napkin with our conversation lying next to Harper's plate. Picking it up, I fold it into a small square and slide it into my pocket. I can't explain it, but the thought of our first real conversation ending up in a landfill doesn't sit right with me.

I pat my pocket and make my way back to Harper, ready to share with her the one place I've never shared with anyone.

CHAPTER EIGHT

Thor

The full moon casts a whitewashed glare over the cracked pool deck just beyond the chain-link fence. It's noisy tonight, the chirps and croaks of horny frogs and crickets vie for the title of Loudest Mating Call.

I peel back a small section of fencing where the aluminum has rusted out. Holding it open, I wave Harper through. She cringes, shaking her head. "It's okay," I say and immediately regret it. "Shit," I curse under my breath. I'm a fucking idiot. During dinner Harper mentioned that it's downright impossible to lip-read in the dark, and here I am making her do just that.

Letting the torn fence fall back into place, I stand up straight and pull my phone out of my back pocket. I type quickly and turn my phone around to show her the note. It's okay. I come here all the time. There's never anyone around.

Harper reads the message and tugs my phone from my hands to reply. Are you sure?

I nod, grinning light and easy. A need deep inside screams for me to ease her tension; I don't want her to be anxious or worried when she's with me.

Reaching for the torn fence, I pull it back and coax her closer. Harper slides her feet a couple inches in my direction, close enough for me to slip my hand on her lower back just as she bends down to fit through the hole.

Her body is warm against my palm and I'm not even touching skin…but damn do I want to. She drove me fucking crazy all through dinner—in the best possible way. Just watching the way her fingers moved when she signed…the way her mouth shaped words…the patch of skin on her neck, right beneath her earlobe…the dusting of freckles covering her visible skin. My thoughts moved from R rated to NC-17, fingers itching to find out if she has freckles anywhere else.

Easy, Thor, I warn myself. For now, I'll be content with having my hand on her back. Freckle exploration will have to wait until later…hopefully.

Once Harper is through, I follow behind, careful not to get caught on the ragged ends of the fence. Done that a time or two—gashes and ripped clothes, not cool. Standing up straight, I take in my private sanctuary. Fallen leaves skitter over the ground, their dried edges scratching over the concrete before the wind tosses them into the neglected depths of the empty swimming pool.

So many people talk about their muse as an ethereal being, whispering beautiful words or lines of music into their ear. Not me. This decrepit, abandoned swimming pool has been the source of my creative outlet for years. I love this place, and will be sad as fuck when it's finally leveled for the new subdivision that's slated to be built on the property.

Harper turns around and looks at me, trying to hide her trepidation behind a thin-lipped smile. My chest seizes, making it hard to breathe. I can't take my eyes off her, not that I want to. Bleached moonlight shines on her wild, coppery hair. One defiant curl has managed to break free from the confines of her left ear, tapping an irregular beat against her chin every time it catches the breeze. God, she's beautiful. The urge to shove my fingers into all those curls, pull her face to mine, and taste that smile is overwhelming. I want to kiss away all her fear and anxiety, prove to her that she's safe with me.

Instead, I reach for her hand, slipping my fingers between hers, reminding myself to take it slow. I want…no, I *need* more time with this woman. There has to be a second date. I can't fuck anything up.

With a gentle tug on Harper's arm, I tip my head to the right and lead her through the maze of the weed-infested pool deck. It's been a couple weeks since I've been here, and with all the rain we've had, the weeds sprouting through the cracks are thriving.

We skirt around a waist-high thornbush and round the corner toward the deeper pool—my favorite hiding place in the world. I've never come here with anyone…never even told anyone this place exists. Now Harper's in on my secret.

I let go of her hand and hold up a finger saying, "Wait here, okay?" I hope the moonlight is bright enough for her to read my lips.

She nods, understanding, and I let out of sigh of relief. I

don't want her to think I'm being rude or inconsiderate...I need that second date. A small chuckle escapes my lips. I can't recall ever wanting to impress a chick as much as I want to impress Harper. Who the fuck am I?

I turn around, reaching for the pool's rickety ladder and swing my leg over, stepping onto the first rung. Three rungs down, I wave Harper over, gesturing for her to follow my lead.

With wide eyes and biting her bottom lip, she grabs the handles, and very timidly, lowers her body onto the ladder. I wish I knew what she was thinking. Was it a bad idea to bring her here? Fuck, I hope this isn't the worst date of her life.

Sighing, I place my hands at her waist and guide her downward. Our bodies are pressed close, my front to her back. I try my best not to think about how perfectly she fits against me and how gorgeous she smells—the faint scent of the outdoors clings to her hair along with something soft and flowery. I pull in another deep breath, my eyes slipping closed for a second, committing her scent to memory.

With both of us situated on the ladder, I take another slow step, holding on to Harper with my right hand and the ladder in my left. The rusty metal wobbles and groans under our combined weight and Harper starts shaking. "I've got you." I lean in closer, wrapping my arm all the way around her. She pulls in a sharp breath and doesn't let it out. Shit. Did I scare her? I don't let go, keeping a strong hold on to her, until she exhales. *You're safe with me, Harper.* I hope she knows that...*feels* that. I will the thoughts from my head into hers as we take the next two rungs.

My boot hits the last rung. Slowly, I pull my arm from

around Harper, and jump the last two feet. Harper glances over her shoulder, a look of terror on her face. I reach up, rubbing a comforting circle on her back before putting my hands at her sides. At my touch, her face softens and she exhales. "Almost there," I say. I doubt she can see my lips, but she relaxes anyway.

One foot after the other, she lowers herself downward. When her feet tap down on the last rung, I tighten my grip on her waist and pull her backward, snaking my arms around her. Trusting me, she lets go of the ladder and falls gracefully, her body sliding against mine on the way down. Lust rips through me like a bolt of lightning, zapping every nerve ending in my body. I want her in all the ways I know I shouldn't.

Harper's feet touch the ground and she turns in my arms, resting her hands on my chest, looking up at my face. She pulls in a breath, and I swear, the world comes to a fucking halt.

Staring, unblinking, her lips part, and all I can think about is how much I want to taste her pretty little mouth. I refuse to surrender my hold, she feels too good in my arms. Perfect. The way my guitar feels when I strap it on, like a part of me had been missing, and then suddenly, it isn't.

Harper exhales, her warm breath fanning out over my face, still smelling like her cranberry martini from dinner. I know she'd taste just as sweet as the fruity drink, and that sends all the blood in my body rushing southward. I lean in, dying to feel her lips on mine…and with the slightest pressure on my chest, Harper gives a shy push and steps out of my grip.

Fuck. Doesn't she want me to kiss her? Maybe she isn't as into me as I'm into her.

I ball my hand in a fist and move it in clockwise circles on my chest. *"Sorry."* This is becoming a handy sign to know, I have a feeling I'm going to be using it a lot.

Like she did when I signed at dinner, her face lights up, mouth splitting into a crooked megawatt-smile. The urge to kiss her hasn't gone away, it's worse now, and I fucking love that I put *that* smile on her face.

Reaching for me, Harper touches my fist, stilling my circular motion with her palm. Ever so slightly, she moves her index finger along the top of my thumb, sliding it to the side of my hand so that my thumb rests at the side of my fist, not the front. When she's happy with the placement of my fingers, she nods, pleased.

Pulling my hand away, I study her handiwork, committing the small adjustment to memory for next time.

Harper tugs her phone out of her back pocket and leans in close to the screen, typing quickly. When she finishes, she turns it around for me to see. You have nothing to be sorry about.

Plucking the phone from her fingers, I type my response below hers. Didn't mean to be forward. Wasn't cool of me.

Handing the phone back, Harper scans the message, a bluish light shines over her features as her eyes dart over my words. Biting her lip, she types, I had shellfish for dinner, remember? I wouldn't want our first kiss to send you into anaphylactic shock.

Relief washes over me. So she does want to kiss me. Thank. Fucking. God. I grab the phone from her hands. I'm willing to take my chances. ;-) I hand it back to her, winking.

Eyes squinted, she considers my comment, smirking.

Good, playful Harper's back. Scooping her hand in mine, I give her arm a tug, leading her to my favorite spot in the whole world, under the diving board.

I look up, admiring the plank above my head. Countless nights I've spent under this board, endless hours. Some of the best music I've ever written was born in this very spot.

Lowering my gaze, I look at Harper and silently welcome her to my sanctuary. I keep the words locked in my head, knowing it's too dark for her to read my lips, but I'm determined to let my actions speak for me, to communicate to her just how important this place is to me.

Since I was sixteen, this place has been my safe haven—the place I've come to meditate, commune, and hide away until all the shit in my life settles. To an outsider, this place has all the makings of a nightmare, hell on earth—broken concrete, weeds, rusted and decaying chaise lounges, puddles of stagnate water, and two eerie, deserted pools. People always judge books by their covers, but sometimes, the rough exterior is just a stumbling point to get to the good stuff inside. Same goes for this place. To the naked eye, it's a mess, but the comfort it's always brought me makes it fucking gorgeous.

I don't know if there's a God, hell, with all the shit Mom and I've endured over the years, I'd be more inclined to say there isn't. But, when I'm here, engulfed by darkness, hidden from the fucked-up world, it's easier to believe there could be. And now, sharing my place with Harper, maybe the idea of a God isn't that far-fetched—the fact that she's here with me, there has to be a God, right?

It's a stroke of luck that the space under the diving board isn't covered in sludge, giving Harper and I a dry place to sit. With my boot, I kick away a few twigs and park my ass on the ground, looking up at Harper. Patting the light blue concrete beside me, I invite Harper to sit. She casts a dubious glance around and plops onto the pool floor beside me.

Now we're talking!

A chilly gust rushes over us, whistling and howling, turning the empty pool into a large wind instrument. Angling her body toward me, Harper tucks her left shoulder behind me and buries her head against my chest. Strands of her hair blow up in my face and I have no desire to swipe them away, enjoying the gentle lashing against my cheek.

Once the wind dies down, I tap Harper on the shoulder, getting her attention. She lifts her head from my chest and locks her eyes on to mine, her long lashes brushing against her skin when she blinks.

And fuck me. She does it again. Her eyes are so expressive, it's like she sees beyond my tough exterior, straight to all the fucked-up parts I try so hard to hide. The girl has superpowers.

Swallowing, I ignore her scrutiny, and lean forward, holding up my index finger. I shrug off my button-down shirt. The thin, cotton tee I've got on isn't much against the chilly wind, but making sure she's warm is higher on my priority list than my own comfort.

I laugh inwardly. Mother Nature is on my side tonight, making all my usual moves way to easy to execute. Holding my shirt out, I stretch my left arm behind her and drape the button-down over her shoulders.

Looking comfortable and happy with my shirt wrapped around her, she smiles—the right corner of her mouth quirking up a few millimeters higher than the left side. She has such a fantastic smile. I make a mental list of everything I've learned that makes Harper King smile, and I hope to keep adding to it.

She glances down, and with a feather-light touch, hesitant, she traces one of the images on my sleeve tattoo. The largest clock face. I twist my arm, bringing it closer to her, giving her permission to touch as much as she wants. I'm proud of my ink. And I'm loving the way her fingers are brushing over my skin.

Since my senior year of high school, I've had an obsession with tattoos. When I'm angry, the bite of the machine can quell my rage faster than anything. But I'm picky. I don't get just anything inked. There has to be a significant reason why I'm adding the art to my body, and it's usually something I don't want to forget. My own version of a ribbon tied around my finger. When I was little, my grandma used to do that, tie a ribbon around her finger, so she wouldn't forget.

Lifting her phone, I watch Harper's fingers sweep over the screen as she punches out a message. Your tattoos are impressive. Can I ask what they mean?

She passes me the phone.

Shit. I want to tell her everything. I don't want any secrets between us, but for me to tell her what the clocks on my arms mean, that would mean I'd have to tell her about my dad—that each time he beat me, I recorded the time the beating ended in a notebook. The clock face she traced, the biggest one, has the time I fought back. The last time he hit me.

That story is too fucking sad for a first date. If I want a second one, I've got to keep my response vague. I like clocks. Each one reminds me of growing up. Becoming a man.

After reading, Harper glances up at me, her long lashes fluttering against her eyelids. I wish I knew what was going through her head. I suck at reading people.

Lifting the phone from my hand, she looks down and starts typing. They're beautiful.

I laugh as I drag my thumbs across the onscreen keyboard. I was going more for badass, but if you think they're beautiful, I can live with that. I hand the phone over and wink.

Harper smiles. Didn't mean to wound your manly pride. ;-) Nothing wrong with being beautiful and badass. Kind of like this place. Won't we get caught for trespassing?

She holds up the phone and I take it from her hands, adding my response. Harper leans in close, reading as I type. Nah. I've been coming here for almost eight years. Never been caught. The owners sold the property. It's supposed to be subdivided, but the developers—an incoming text appears at the top of the screen, so I can't finish my thought—Mom: Why are you ignoring me, Harper? Please respond ASAP.

"Shit. Umm…" Not quite sure what to do, I tap on the text before it disappears and hand the phone back to Harper.

Reading the message, she throws her head back, her face contorting into an angry scowl. Signing something, no clue what, she double clicks the home button and flips back to our conversation on the note screen. Sorry about that. My mom. Again.

Sure you don't need to get back to her? Seems important. I type and give her the phone.

She takes her frustration out on the keyboard, smashing her fingers against the glass. A chat about the weather would come attached with an ASAP. She can wait. Finish your story, please? Harper glances at me, eyes pleading. She'd mentioned her relationship with her parents was complicated; I'm picking up on that vibe.

"You sure?" I say, hoping she can read my lips.

She nods. *If you say so, Red.* If there's anyone on the planet that understands parent issues, it's me. I scroll up, find my original comment, and scan over it, mumbling, "It's supposed to be subdivided, but the developers..." Okay, got it. Memory jogged.

The developers haven't gotten around to subdividing. Not sure what the holdup is, but I'd be fine if the project never went through. Don't want to lose this place. It's quiet. I can think here. I make a move to pass the phone back to her, but think of something else, so I pull it back. I already know "sorry," will you teach me some other signs?

Teasing, I hand the phone to her, but yank it back each time she tries to grab it. On the fourth fake-out, she makes contact, latching on with her right hand as she pokes me in the side with her left. "Ow! Damn, Red, you play dirty!" I laugh, doubling over to avoid any more of her assault.

Harper's shoulders bounce in silent laughter as she works her fingers over the screen. It hits me hard how much I want to hear her laugh. She's got the best smile on the planet, I bet her laugh is just as perfect. Who am I kidding? There's nothing about this girl that isn't perfect. She hands the phone over. Gotcha! Somebody's ticklish! *filing that away for later* ;-) I'll teach you all the signs you want to know, if you teach me to play the guitar.

I take the phone from her hands. Deal. Show me how to sign your name. I've wondered how to do that all night.

Showing me, she holds her right hand between us. I watch as she extends her index and middle fingers outward, tucking the rest beneath her thumb. Bringing her fingers up to her face, she wiggles them on her upper cheek.

I raise my right hand next to hers and copy the shape. Nodding, Harper repeats the motion, tickling the skin just below her eye. Clumsily, I do the same, not even close to matching her fluid, refined movement.

After a few tries, I lower my hands. Harper picks up the phone. That's my name sign. It's the sign for freckles, but the fingers make the letter "H," for Harper.

I lay my hand out flat, palm up, waiting for her to pass the phone. What's the sign for Thor?, I type. It was a turn-on watching her spell my name, can't wait to see how hot it is when she signs it. I pass the phone back to her.

A gust of wind blows over us, kicking up a swirl of dead leaves. The long tree branches hanging over the pool creak in protest. Midway through typing, Harper curls her body closer to my side and I welcome the opportunity to hold her tighter, squeezing. She smells nice and she fits so perfectly against my side. This is fucking paradise.

Glancing up at me, she shivers, but doesn't look uncomfortable, quite the opposite actually. When she's finished typing, she hands the phone back. Names don't automatically have signs. Name signs can only be given to someone by a deaf person. My dad always called me Freckles as a kid, so my second-grade teacher gave me the name sign to match.

I rub a hand over my face, then type out my answer while Harper watches. Can't wait for you to give me one, then. Shooting a wink in her direction, she fires back with a smug grin and a noncommittal shrug.

Her eyes roam over my face and it's crazy, but I can *feel* it. Heat trails over my skin, down my cheeks at the same time a shiver rolls up my spine. How does she do that?

I'm sure a minute passes, if not more. With each breath, my pulse kicks up, heavy and raging. The urge to grab the side of her face and pull her mouth to mine is almost unbearable.

Drenched in moonlight, her pale, freckled skin is set in contrast against her wild red hair. She could be some sort of forest nymph or spirit—to beautiful to be a part of this world, for sure. "Teach me more?" I whisper, her eyes fixed on my mouth.

Lifting her hands, she presses the tips of her fingers to her thumbs and touches them together, slowly bringing her right to her pursed lips as she turns her body into mine. No clue what she signed, but her body language is screaming, *Kiss me.* Fuck, I want to.

My eyes are locked on hers, blood pounding in my ears. Reaching for me, the tips of her fingers brush up my face, scratching against the stubble on my jaw, until her whole palm rests against my cheek. She licks her lips and that's it, I can't take it anymore. I need to fucking kiss her.

Bowing my head to meet hers, I shove my hand into her hair. Knotted spirals catch between my fingers until I'm cradling her head in my palm. With delicate pressure, I pull her closer, watching her eyelids fall shut. Our hot breaths mingle in the centimeters dividing us. I inhale, she exhales. We breathe each other in.

My heartbeat thunders in my ears and with one yank, lightning strikes.

Hot and searing, her mouth is on mine. She melts against me, pressing her fingertips into my cheek, begging me closer. Her lips are strong and soft all at the same time. I can't get enough, and I fucking want it all. Opening my mouth on hers, I run my tongue along the seam of her lips, tracing each curve and dip, until she parts them. I push into her, tasting, wanting, my body craving the sustenance a kiss only hints at.

With my arm still behind her back, I pull her forward, guiding her onto my lap. My shirt falls off her shoulders as she straddles me, and now I have all the leverage I need. Burying my other hand in her hair, I draw her closer, deepening the kiss, my tongue thrusting against hers.

Harper presses her palms on each side of my face, changing the angle, her body rocking each time our tongues meet. I'm so fucking hard. My dick begs for her to keep grinding, at the same time mourning the fact that it's not inside her.

A soft groan rumbles in my throat as I lower my hands down her back. The fabric of her shirt is smooth beneath my callused fingers. Following the path of her spine, I move lower, over her bra strap, and the dip in the small of her back, until I curve my hands around her ass, thrusting her against me. I thrust again, my dick right at her opening, separated by the fabric between us. *"Fuuuuuck."*

Grinding against my hard-on, Harper sucks in a sharp

breath and bites my lower lip, her tongue plunging into my mouth one last time before she pulls away, panting.

I stare into her eyes, my dick throbbing. "Shit," I sigh, smoothing the curls off Harper's face. That was fucking close. The last time a girl made me come in pants I was fourteen, and my self-control was shit. Seems I've met my match in Harper King, when it comes to her, she's the one in the driver's seat.

Harper shifts on my lap, and I suck in a breath, "Whoa." I try to calm myself, but my dick is still rock hard, cramped as fuck in my tight jeans, and craving release.

Glancing down at my crotch, Harper's eyes go wide with realization. She signs furiously, her body rocking with the motion of her arms. This is not helping. My hands at her waist, I lift her tiny body off my lap, and do my best to readjust without being too vulgar.

Harper says something in sign language, but I only catch the word "sorry" here and there. I clasp my hands around hers and shift my body (very uncomfortably) around, so we're face-to-face. The moon's still bright and I hope it's enough light for her to see my face. "You"—I press my index finger onto her collarbone, shaking my head—"have nothing to be sorry about."

She bites her lip. Looking unsure, her eyes dancing from mine to my lap. Pinching her chin between my thumb and forefinger, I draw her face back up, forcing her to look at me. *Please, Harper, understand this.* I don't want her to think all I want to do is fuck (well, I do, but God, it's so much more than that). "I not going to lie, taking you back to my place and getting you naked is high on my list right now." Not that she doesn't already know; there's no hiding the bulge in my pants. "But, not just that. I want to get to know you. Everything about you." There's a first time for everything.

Harper scrambles, twisting and shifting her body, patting the ground, coming up with a phone. Hurriedly, she unlocks the screen and types, then hands the phone to me. OMG! I am so sorry! I didn't mean...

I swipe the phone from her hands. Don't apologize! I'm glad you were into it as much as I was. It was amazing. Already looking forward to the next time.

The flustered, concerned expression on her face morphs into a sultry grin as she types her response. On the bright side, I didn't send you into anaphylaxis! Kissing me didn't kill you! ;-)

Oh, Red, give yourself more credit. You were most certainly killing me.

CHAPTER NINE

HARPER

Lying in bed, I stare at the ceiling, the events of last night on a continuous loop in my head. I touch my lips—still a little sore—and a smile creeps to my mouth. I don't know what came over me; I've never reacted like that on a first date. I don't know this Harper, but damn, if she gets to have more make-out sessions with Thorin Kline, I welcome her with open arms.

Squeezing my abs, I pull myself up, stretching my hands over my head, yawning. Seconds later, I'm greeted with little wet licks on my cheek. Bobby. I pull his warm body close and bury my face in this furry neck, snuggling him.

Stroking his head, I glance at my bedside clock, the display reads 6:57 a.m. And why am I up this early? Bobby swipes his tongue over my nose, nuzzling my face.

Oh, right. Someone needs to go outside. Bobby doesn't seem to care that I just got home five hours ago. For a second, I contemplate rolling over, throwing the covers on my head, and going back to sleep (and with any luck, dream of Thor), but

I've got to study, and I don't want Bobby leaving me any "gifts" in my bedroom. Besides, I can't let one amazing date get in the way of something I've worked for years to achieve. The end is almost in sight, I can't lose focus now.

But there won't be any focus without coffee.

I pat my leg and Bobby leaps off the bed, landing at my feet. Opening the door, we shuffle down the hall to the staircase. The living room is dark, except for the light spilling from the kitchen doorway—Chloe must be up. I hop off the last step and head to the back door before I sneak into the kitchen.

Unlatching the sliding door, I yank it open, and Bobby runs outside. I turn toward the kitchen, and walk in to see it's been transformed into a baker's wonderland. Mixing bowls, pans, a standing mixer, and a variety of different size spoons cover the countertops. On the other side of the kitchen, Chloe's camera is perched on a tripod. *Sweet Nothings* filming day.

What is the date? Looking across the room, my eyes land on the giant dry-erase calendar hanging on the wall. Chloe always films on the second Saturday of the month, and sure enough, there's a cupcake magnet sitting in the square. I need to make my coffee and get out of her way, the last thing I want is to be roped into being on the show. I've been on my fair share of *Sweet Nothings* webisodes, but I don't have time today. Nothing is going to keep me from reviewing case studies of neonatal treatment plans. I had my wild and crazy last night, now it's time to get back to reality.

I empty a mug of water into the reservoir tank of the coffeemaker and slide my cup under the spout. I toss a coffee pod into the machine and press the button. The Keurig trembles to life under my palms and the scents of coffee and vanilla beans swirl around the kitchen. The smell alone is enough to jolt my tired eyes open a little wider, anticipating that first sip of caffeine nirvana.

Chloe rounds the corner and stops short when she sees me. She's wearing a short, black chemise with gold embellishments adorning the plunging neckline, and see-through lace that outlines the delicate curves of her breasts, showing just a hint of skin. As usual, her hair and makeup are flawless.

Hands fisted, I shimmy and run them from my shoulders to my waist, wagging my eyebrows, *"Sexy. What are you baking today?"*

Chloe glances downward, rubbing a hand over the shiny, black satin clinging to her frame and brings her eyes back to mine. *"Not sure I like this."* With a halfhearted smile and one-shoulder shrug, she isn't oozing her usual, bubbly self-confidence.

"Why not? You look amazing. It's sensual and tasteful all at the same time. Perfect combo."

Joining me at the counter, Chloe opens the cabinet and pulls down a mug for herself. *"I'll take your word for it, but if my comments are terrible, I'm blaming you."* She smirks, pulling my coffee cup from the machine and gently thrusting it in my hands.

"Okay. I accept full responsibility." Whatevs. I don't think Chloe's ever gotten a negative comment. Shaking my head, I press the edge of the mug to my lips. The heavenly liquid washes over my tongue, and my eyes slip closed, allowing my taste buds to have their moment. I know it's not logical,

chemically speaking, for caffeine to diffuse into the blood-stream the second it hits my tongue, but that's exactly what happens. Coffee, the perfect blend of chemical bonds and magical serum.

Chloe bumps her shoulder into mine and I'm forced to open my eyes. How dare she interrupt my thoughtful media-tion on the mystical properties of the glorious Arabica bean? Wrinkling my nose in annoyance, I sign, *"What?"* and take an-other sip of my coffee.

"I'm making smoky bourbon chocolate cupcakes with bacon bark this morning. Something new. Getting all the practice I can before Cupcake Wars. *I could use an assistant."* This time, she wags her eyebrows.

I shake my head vigorously. *"No, thank you. I am studying today and nothing is going to keep me from that."* Images of my body pressed against Thorin's pop into my head. I'd like to think I'm strong enough to say I'd even turn down the op-portunity to do that again, but that would be a bald-faced lie. Bacon cupcakes earn an easy no…Thorin, not so much.

Chloe hugs her coffee mug to her chest and bats her pretty cinnamon-colored eyes.

In front of her face, I pinch my index and middle fingers to my thumb, quick and to the point, then turn on my heels to make a quick escape before her sad puppy-dog face has me changing my mind.

A hand comes down on my shoulder before I'm even two steps away. Dammit, I was so close. I cringe, keeping my thoughts to myself. I turn around slowly, preparing for the on-slaught of "pleading best friend" eyes.

"Hey, not so fast. How did last night go?" She raises her eyebrows, expectantly.

A smile creeps to my face until I can't hold it back any longer. *"He's really great."*

Chloe beams and tugs my arm, dragging me over to the table. Pulling out a chair for me, and one for her, she sits, eyeing me, then the empty chair. *"Don't you have a show to film?"*

Her lip quirks up and she shakes her head, waving away my question. *"I'm giving my bacon bark more time to chill. Start talking girl."*

Two words I never thought I'd see in the same sentence, "bacon" and "bark." That doesn't even sound appetizing, but I'll give Chloe the benefit of the doubt, her creations, as odd as they are, end up being quite tasty. *"There isn't much to say, we had dinner, then he took me to the place where he writes his music."*

"Really?" Chloe slides to the end of her chair, ready to catch every morsel of information I toss her way. *"That's cool. You two hit it off then?"*

I nod. *"We did. He's not the arrogant, cocky musician I thought he'd be. He's thoughtful, and cool, super sweet, and—"* I stop signing midsentence, but the words carry on in my head…*You were right about him, Chloe. He's someone I could see myself falling for.* But with graduation so close and Thorin's band thinking about signing a recording contract, our lives are headed in vastly different directions. I can see the disapproving looks on Mom and Dad's faces, telling me now is not the time to be jumping into a relationship, especially when there's no way you'll ever be able to overcome the language barrier.

And the fact that he never went to college, is in a band, and has some seriously badass tattoos, that's three strikes against him and he's never even gotten a chance to bat.

But last night was amazing. Thorin and I communicated better in one evening than I have with either of my parents over the course of the past twenty years.

Chloe waves her hands, bringing my attention back to her. *"And?"* She draws the sign out, exaggerating the motion.

"And patient." I add. He was patient, all right.

"Aww!" I read her lips, as she pulls me into a hug. She pats my back three times and let's go, her hands flying in precise, animated movements, *"That's great, Harper! I so happy for you!"*

I can't help the schoolgirl grin spreading over my face. *"I'm not going to lie, last night was pretty friggin' fantastic! Thorin's the first guy I've gone out with in four years that sincerely wanted to get to know me. Never once did I get the impression that he was put off by my deafness. I didn't think there were hearing guys like him."*

"Second date?" Chloe asks.

I shrug. We hadn't made any plans for a second date. Maybe my impression of our date was more Disney, where Thor's was more Brothers Grimm. Maybe I wouldn't hear from him. That would suck, because it's been a long damn time since I've had fun with a guy.

"He'll text. I've got a good feeling about him." She winks at me.

"I hope you're right. Although, if he doesn't text, there are no rules that say I can't." I rest my lips on the side of the mug and sip my coffee.

Chloe taps her index finger on the tip of her nose and points at me. *"Damn right. Can't let him get away without a fight."* A dreamy gaze washes over her face. *"Those tight jeans he wore during the concert would be enough to make me fight. And what of his ass?"* She raises an eyebrow.

"Divine." I grin, holding in a giggle. I had seen his ass in those tight jeans…and felt other parts through those jeans. A pulse of concentrated heat runs down my spine and lands between my legs. I cross them and try to squeeze away the dull ache the memory conjures. All of Thor's good-guy qualities aside, it's been four years since I've had sex, and while my vibrator, Prince O, has never let me down, it felt damn good rubbing up against the bulge in his jeans last night. I'd be lying if I said I didn't want more. *"If I don't hear from him in a day or two, he'll be hearing from me."*

"That a girl." Chloe pats my leg and stands, taking her coffee with her. At the sink, she pours an almost full cup into the drain.

I shake my head and join her, rinsing out my empty cup. *"You are a disgrace to coffee drinkers everywhere."*

"Unlike some people"—she eyes me coolly—*"I don't need to mainline caffeine. A sip or two gets the job done just fine."*

"You are so weird." I throw my arm around her shoulder, crushing her to my side. *"But I love your brand of weird. Have fun with"*—I gesture around our kitchen-turned-baking-studio—*"all of this."*

Turning, I head toward the living room, giving Chloe space to do her thing. Taking one step, I feel a tap on my shoulder again. Socks on linoleum make spinning around an easy task.

"I almost forgot, your mom called me last night," Chloe signs.

Damn you, Mother, I curse her inwardly. I should have known ignoring her texts would backfire on me. *"I'm sorry she bothered you."*

"It's fine. No wild and crazy Friday night for this chick." She pouts. *"Anyway, she wanted me to remind you that your dad's party is at the end of the month. She went ahead and booked you a flight."* At this, Chloe presses her lips together, an air of apology softening her features. *"She wants you to text her so she can pass along your flight details."*

Over the years, Chloe has witnessed firsthand my mother's attempts to micromanage my life. As a child, my mother would always speak for me. I didn't mind when I was in elementary school; I didn't know any better. But once I got into middle school and high school, it drove me crazy. Mom, Dad, and I would be out to dinner and the waiter would ask for our orders, I'd have my menu open, ready to point to my selection. But Mom always beat me to the punch, telling the server what I wanted, and snatching the menu from my hands. The poor deaf girl, can't even order her own meal. Ugh! Mortifying!

Years later, nothing's changed. Poor deaf girl can't book her own flight home.

"Thanks. I'll text her." Filling Chloe in on the details of my date had me giddy and hopeful, now all I want to do is bang my head against the wall.

I turn to go, for real this time. The spring in my step (courtesy of Thorin Kline) is gone, replaced with a zombie shuffle... *Thanks, Mom.*

* * *

I minimize the Kindle app on my computer screen, rub my tired eyes, and pat Bobby's head. Three hours of reading and I'm only halfway through the third neonatal patient case study. Taking a break from pain management treatments, I flip to the airline homepage and try to figure out how I'm going to make a trip back east work. Mom scheduled my flight for six thirty in the morning. Without even consulting me, making sure that flight worked into my schedule, she just booked it and left me to deal with the logistics. Anger simmers in my veins.

If I remain on the six-thirty flight, Chloe will have to drop me off at the airport close to five, which I hate asking her to do; it's too early. Then there's the issue of missing an entire day of my hospital rotation—that's out of the question. Things are hard enough for me at the hospital without my interpreter; I don't need an absence to set me further behind.

Checking the other available flights, I know the two-thirty departure would work out best for everyone. Missing a half day of my rotation is easier to work around; it would be easier to prepare for.

Launching the airline's app on my phone, I get to work switching my flight. A smug grin consumes my face as I get my ticket bumped to the later time, despite the hefty service fee attached—I'll just pick up some extra shifts at the Y to cover the added expense. Mom and Dad may have bought the ticket, but I'll pay the extra to prove a point. It's not just that this new flight makes more sense with my schedule; I revel in the even sweeter victory—showing my mom that I am capable of working an app to book my own flight. Being able to hear isn't a prerequisite for that.

My phone flashes and an incoming text drops down at the top of my screen. It's from Thor. Hey, Red. You busy?

Holy shit, he texted! Me: Just studying.

Thor: Ready for your first guitar lesson?

Was he serious last night? Trading ASL lessons for guitar lessons? My heart thumps against my rib cage, images of Thorin and I curled up on my bed, trading signs and music. My Saturday night just took a turn for the better. Practice makes perfect! ;-) I hit send and my teasing response is gone.

Thor: Got rehearsal all afternoon. 6 good for you?

Yep. I smile at our conversation, scrolling through parts of last night's, too.

Thor: See you soon.

Well, there goes studying for the rest of the day, I'm too keyed up now. I glance at the clock, quarter to eleven. Five hours and fifteen minutes.

My phone flashes again and I snatch it up, my heart kicking out an extra beat. Did Thor change his plans? Maybe he can make it over earlier?

Mom: Why did I just get an email saying your flight has been changed?

Oh, shit. Not Thor.

Mom, the other flight didn't work with my rotation at the hospital. I need the later flight.

I hit send, and immediately, the little speech bubble with the ellipsis appears in the lower left corner. Mom's always been quick to fire back a text message, but ask her to use ASL and it's like the apocalypse has come. I give her credit though, when I was little and told her I hated the oral method and preferred ASL, she didn't balk at finding me a school that accommodated my preferred learning style.

Mom: You should have discussed this with me last night. Then nothing would have had to be changed. Why didn't you return my messages?

This is a loaded question. She's baiting me, wanting to know what I was doing. Biting the inside of my cheek, I run through a list of lies, ones that have put her off before. But really, I don't want to lie this time. I want to tell my mom how great Thor is. But do I have a choice? She's already having a fit over my rescheduled flight; she'd go into cardiac arrest if I told her I was on a date with the lead guitarist in a band.

Mom: Shouldn't you have been in last night, studying and getting enough rest for your clinicals? Is this about a boy?

Oh my God, Mom. I am not twelve. No, this isn't about a boy. I cringe at the thought. Thor is a man. A beautiful, hard-all-over *man.*

Me: I've been studying compulsively since classes began. Don't worry, Mom. I've come too far to let anyone derail me now.

Mom: Glad to hear it. Stay focused, Harper. You're going to need every advantage you can get.

Wow. Leave it to my mother to get in her passive-aggressive digs. It's not like I've accomplished any of my academic success on my own merit. No, that's crazy talk. Everyone knows a deaf girl can't do anything on her own. Or so my mother thinks.

I always give 110%, I type back, lifting my butt up off the mattress to yank the blanket from underneath me. Covering my legs, I watch the ellipsis flash in the left corner of the screen.

Mom: I'm proud of you, Harper. So is Daddy. Don't forget that. We'll see you for the party.

Me: Yeah. I know. You just have a funny way of showing it. At least that's one advantage I have by choosing not to speak, text messages can't convey a tone. My cynicism and disappointment are easily hidden.

I check the time again, five hours to go, and thanks to my mother, I'm exhausted.

Rolling over onto my side, I pull my covers up to my chin and close my eyes, drawing Bobby close. If she texts back, I won't know. Just another of the many talents in my arsenal—closing my eyes is the most effective way of protecting myself from her veiled insults.

CHAPTER TEN

HARPER

"How do you sign 'guitar'?" he asks, leaning against my head-board, Bobby curled up on his lap.

"That's an easy one," I sign, crossing my legs. Getting comfortable, I sit up straight, look him in the eye, and position my arms like I'm holding a guitar. My left hand holds the imaginary neck while my open, left palm strums the air, twice.

Waving my hands, I encourage him to give it a try. Together, we strum, signing "guitar" to one another in a mirrored image. It's nice to be able to teach someone my language. Lord knows Mom and Dad never wanted me to teach them. I went to so many dinner parties when I lived at home, Mom always reminding me not to sign. Since no one at the parties understood sign language, she felt it was unnecessary and distracting.

The fact that Thor wants to learn, and is eager, it's the most incredible feeling in the world, like my cells are infused with nitrous oxide—a hint of sweetness in my mouth along with a light, giddy disposition chasing away all the sad memories of my childhood. Who needs laughing gas when Thorin Kline's around?

"What about 'I'm glad you texted me.'"

My heart flip-flops in my chest, manifesting as a smile on my lips. *"I'm glad I texted you, too."* Raising my hands, I sign the phrase slowly, so he's able to copy my motions.

I repeat the pattern again, spurring him on to join me. His self-consciousness is endearing. Bobby lifts his head and licks Thor's hand, giving him an added measure of encouragement.

"He likes you," I add.

Thor glances down at the white ball of fur on his lap and Bobby's tail kicks into high gear. Lifting his head, Thor raises an eyebrow. "Hopefully, he isn't the only one."

Forget blushing, my cheeks are on fire.

Thor hits me with a piercing gaze. His eyes are wide, dilated pupils easily visible at the center of his light blue irises. He scoops my hands into his, aligning our fingertips. Pressing gently, our fingers line up, then our palms—flat against the other.

With our hands together, connected, our differences are magnified. I work with my hands on a daily basis, but nothing compared to what Thor puts his through. Being an auto mechanic and a musician has let his hands grease-stained and callused. My tiny, soft hands are dwarfed next to his palms. Yet, as he's caressing my fingers, following and memorizing each line, crease, and bend, I'm even more convinced that we need to give this a try, despite the barriers lying in our way. I like him. I like me *with* him.

My hands folded inside his, I sign his name, *"T-H-O-R"*

then mine, *"H-A-R-P-E-R."* A shiver runs down my spine, leaving me tingly all over. Warmth blooms in my core. The intimacy of signing our names together, while he holds my hands, is sexy as hell. I've dated hearing guys before, but Thor's different. He holds my words in his hands, embraces them.

I want this…for there to be an us.

Behind our clasped hands, I see his mouth move and quickly shift my eyes, trying to read the end of his sentence.

"…fucking mess compared to yours."

I pinch my brows together and shake my head, not understanding.

"My hands are a fucking mess compared to yours," he repeats. Letting go of my hands to point out the dark stains at the edges of his nails. "Working on cars leaves a permanent mark."

I trace my index finger over the discolorations, silently telling him that it's okay. My grandfather had hands like Thor's, always grease stained. I loved it when I got to tinker on cars with Papa. He didn't know how to sign, but our relationship never felt strained because of it, not like with Mom and Dad. With Papa, he'd put me to work on a car, both of us getting our hands dirty. We didn't need words, we communicated through the cars we restored. I miss him. It's been a long time since I've gotten my hands dirty.

I hope Thor understands; I like the way our hands look together.

"Beauty and the Beast," he says, moving his fingers over mine again.

We touch, our fingers brushing and twining together,

slowly at first, then more urgent, memorizing the feel of the other's skin.

The warmth inside my body ignites into a slow growing flame. My mind runs wild with thoughts of more skin-to-skin contact. He has no idea the affect he has over my libido. Dear lord!

With his hands still on mine, I sign, *"Play something?"* I point to the guitar sitting beside him, so he'll understand me better. Maybe that will take my mind off getting him naked.

Cool your jets, Harper. You just met him.

Sometimes, I really hate my voice of reason.

Glancing at the guitar, he lets go of my hand, gently lifts Bobby off his lap and sets him on the floor, before grabbing the guitar off the mattress. Settling it in his lap, he positions his hands with such care, prayerfully.

I rest my head on his shoulder and my hand on the body of the guitar, closing my eyes. I concentrate on the movement of Thor's hand on the strings. Vibrations travel through my fingertips...into my palms...up my arms, and fill my chest cavity with the most glorious music. This is so different from standing near the speaker at a concert, or guessing song titles on the radio.

The constant thrum of the guitar echoes in my chest, coupled with the rhythmic sway of Thor's body beside mine. The bed rocks beneath us, hypnotic, sensual, and intoxicatingly intimate.

His song is slow and lush, alive with heavy chords that cling to a faraway sadness. I wonder what the catalyst was for this song, why Thor felt compelled to write it. Whatever the reason, I'm touched that he's chosen to share this part of himself with me.

My analytical, science-minded brain makes the connection that his song is now a part of me; he's given me a small piece of himself. When he composed the song, he drew inspiration from some private, deep place inside him. As he works his hands over the strings, he gives life to the music. Sound waves penetrate the air, traveling out in all directions, and pass through every object in the room, including me. Inside my body, the waves produced from his thoughts, his motions, his brilliance, become mine.

Thor's hand stills on the strings and the remaining sound waves flood my system. I refuse to open my eyes until every part of his sad story is safe within me.

Our breaths move in sync, a subtle *in…out…in…out…* mirroring the rhythm of Thor's song. My heart adds a percussive beat in my chest, I'm sure Thor can feel.

Holy hell. Who knew feeling a guy play guitar could be so damn erotic? He hasn't even touched me and I'm a raging ball of hormones.

I don't move. I'm not ready to give up the heady, lustful magic swirling around us. What I wouldn't give to peel the guitar away from his chest and replace it with my body.

Check yourself, Harper. Not so fast. My celibate conscience signs in my head.

Not so fast? Why the hell not? My inner vixen snaps in response.

I want to side with my vixen, in her defense, it's been a damn long time. But, my rational side knows it's best to take things slow with Thor. The language barrier aside, our lives are complicated right now. The last thing I need is to be hopping into bed with a guy I just met. I do not have the time or energy to nurse a broken heart and jeopardize everything I've worked so hard to achieve.

Thor shrugs and my head rises with the motion. I take my hand off the guitar and sit up, giving him an embarrassed, uneasy smile. God, if he knew what I'd been thinking. I shudder at the thought.

"Want to give Lizzy a try?" He pulls the guitar away from his chest and slides it across his lap, holding the guitar out to me.

I'm pretty sure he said a name…Lizzy, maybe? *Did I read his lips right?* When he first got here, I showed him the letters of the alphabet. I form the letters with my fingers, slowly, hoping he remembers. *"L-I-Z-Z-Y."*

"Oh, yeah." Thor rubs his hand affectionately along the guitar's neck. "When I was a kid, I was obsessed with *Saved by the Bell*. Everyone loved Kelly, but I couldn't get enough of Jessie. Then, when I was thirteen, I saw Elizabeth Berkley in *Showgirls*. That was it. I was a goner. Named my guitar after Ms. Berkley. Trusty Lizzy, here. She's been with me through a lot."

"S-A-V-E-D B-Y T-H-E B-E-L-L" Thor watches my hands. Concentration lines his face as he puts a letter to each shape.

Raising his hand, he fumbles over the letters, but manages to fingerspell, *"Y-O-U B-E-T."* He nods, his right eyebrow drawing up. "Best show ever," I read on his lips.

This man is full of surprises. I would have never pegged a

rough-around-the-edges, brooding rock star for a *Saved by the Bell* fan. And the fact that he's putting forth a genuine effort to communicate with me, in my language, it's too good to be true. What's wrong with him? He's too perfect.

And that's a problem, why? my inner vixen chimes in. *Let's find out just how perfect he is!*

Good, Lord. I'm in trouble.

After the *Saved by the Bell* revelation, I want to know more about him. Favorite ice cream…vacation spot…dogs or cats…yoga pose…everything. *"What else do you like?"* I sign, mouthing the words, hoping he understands.

"What do you want to know?"

Over my shoulder, I glance at my nightstand, grabbing the notebook and pen lying there. Slipping the cap between my teeth, I bite it off, letting it drop to the page as I write. **Favorite hockey team?**

Thor takes the pen and starts to write. **St. Louis Blues, if I had to pick. Not much of a hockey fan. Love baseball, though. Go Cards!**

No hockey? ? Taking my eyes from the paper, I look at him, sticking out my bottom lip. **I love hockey! Go Bruins! Any pets? What's your roommate like? Favorite family vacation?** The questions flow from my brain and onto the page like the ink from the pen. Flipping the notebook around, he reads, yanking the pen from my hand.

As long as you're not a Red Sox fan, we're chill! Never had any pets, parents said they couldn't afford it. Now, my landlord doesn't allow pets. But, I've always wanted a pig. One day, I'm getting me a pig and I will name him Yum. My

roommate is Griffin Daniels. He's cool, like a brother.

Pen still poised at the paper, Thor stops writing. His little finger plucks at the spiraled wire like it's a guitar string as he formulates his thoughts.

Keeping time with my heartbeats, he pauses for two handfuls.

Not the vacation kind of family. You go on a lot of vacations?

He hands over the notebook. His vague answer and change of subject aren't lost on me. I recall his words from last night: *Mom's great…Dad's an ass.* I have a feeling the clocks on his arms have something to do with his dad as well. *So mysterious, Thorin Kline. Relax, open up a bit. Let me in.*

Like a kid that knows where all the Christmas presents are hidden, but still hasn't peeked, curiosity gnaws away at me. I'm tempted to press the issue, wanting so badly to know more about his childhood, the years that shaped him into the man he is today. But, the look on his face has me biting my tongue and swallowing that curiosity. He went from easygoing and laid-back, to brooding and distant faster than a 1966 Ford GT40 goes from zero to sixty.

Taking the pen, I respond. **A pig named Yum? That's ridiculous and weird! My parents and I used to go to Hilton Head every year. They have a condo there.**

"Yes. A pig is ridiculous and weird. That's what makes it awesome." He nods, winking. "Want to give Lizzy a try?" He holds the guitar out to me, effectively squashing any more family talk. *Got it, Thor. Family, a touchy subject. Believe me, I completely understand.*

I give a little nod, reading his lips.

Leaning forward, Thor shifts his body so we're facing each other, and passes the guitar over, flipping it so the neck is in my left hand. It didn't occur to me until this second that he was playing upside down to accommodate his left-handedness. I lock my eyes on his and mouth my words, *"Why do you play upside down?"*

"I saved every damn nickel I had for Lizzy. When I bought her, I didn't know that it was a right-handed guitar. Didn't know guitars were made differently for righties and lefties. But, I checked out guitar theory books from the library and taught myself everything there was to know about being a guitarist. When I found out Jimi Hendrix played his Stratocaster upside down and restrung backward, I knew I could make Lizzy work for me. And there was never really any question that I would take Lizzy back to the store. That wasn't happening. I'd already grown fond of her."

Wow. How talented is this guy? Yet another thing about him that blows me away. *"Isn't it hard to play upside down?"*

Thor shakes his head. "Nah. Learning to play the guitar, and later on the piano, came easily to me. Had school been that easy, I might have gotten better grades."

"Don't sell yourself short. What you did is pretty brilliant." Thor smiles, warmth radiating from his blue eyes, like the compliment was the sun peeking out from behind the winter clouds after months of cold, gray skies—that first hint of spring.

Focusing his attention on my strumming hand, Thor's long fingers graze over my skin, positioning my fingers on the strings over the sound hole. His hand is massive on top of mine. And hot. Heat flares through me, and I'm trying my level best to keep my mind on the guitar and not what it would be like to have his strong hands paying attention to my more sensitive parts.

Thor scoops my left hand into his palm, carrying it to the top of the guitar's neck. I wrap my fingers around wood and metal strings, and steal a glance at Thor's face. Busy placing my fingers over the correct strings, his features contort in a mask of heavy concentration. Lips parted, the tip of his tongue is pinched between his teeth. Completely absorbed in teaching me how to play guitar, he has no idea how adorable he looks right now.

A smile creeps to my face, and his eyes flick to mine just in time to catch me staring. Licking his lips, he smiles back at me, adding a panty-dropping wink. Adorable? I meant smoking fucking hot. *Gah!* He's got me so off my game.

"Ready?" he says.

I nod, pulling in a deep breath. I am so in over my head.

Thor holds up his arms, mirroring the position of mine. I can't help but notice the way his inked biceps tighten, stretching the fabric of his black Beatles T-shirt. I am the worst student ever. But, in my defense, I've never had a teacher like Thorin Kline.

Shaking his right hand, which corresponds to my left, he lifts his fingers, then pinches them to his palm, gritting his teeth, the cue for me to squeeze my fingers, I assume.

Pressing down hard on the strings, I cringe, and yank my hand away. I look down at the indentions the strings made on the pads of my fingers. The neck of the guitar falls to the crook of my elbow, as I sign around it, *"Damn, that hurts!"* For as little as they are, those strings pack a vicious bite.

Thor's eyes are wide with concern, and I catch one word of his sentence, "…okay?"

I shake my fist, *"Yes,"* knowing he understands this one, but continue my thought out of habit. *"Wasn't expecting the strings to pinch like that."*

Thor pulls his eyebrows together and shakes his head, using one of the signs I taught him last night. *"What?"*

The throbbing in my fingertips is gone, replaced by a pleasurable thump in my chest. There's no doubt Thor is hot. He could be doing a Sudoku puzzle on a Sunday afternoon and still ooze sex. But every time he communicates with me in my language, that tips the scales from hot to scorching. I will never get tired of that as long as I live.

Cradling Lizzy, I pick up the pen. **You didn't tell me that Lizzy bites! You must have fingers made of steel.**

Thor flips the notebook around and shakes his head, shoulders bouncing with laughter. Rubbing a hand along his stubbled jaw, still smirking, he holds his hand out for the pen. **The more you play, the more callused your fingers get. Can't feel a damn thing with mine.**

He gives me a second to read before circling his fingers around my left wrist. With a gentle pull, he brings my hand closer to his body, and turns it over, palm up. Supporting my left hand in his, he traces a gentle path from my inner wrist, upward, the tips of his fingers tickling over my skin.

My fingers twitch. Sensory receptors fire at will, and a blaze of sparks ignites my whole body. Closing my eyes, I give myself over to my sense of touch and Thor's skillful hands.

Goose bumps rise on my arms as his languid journey transitions from my palm to my fingers. The steady, delicate pressure of our skin-to-skin contact dissolves into a concentrated point of warmth on each of my fingertips.

Gasping, I feel the scratch of Thor's unshaven face pressing against my palm. He pauses for a beat, his lips meeting my pulse point. My heart gives away all my secrets, a loud, thumping scream against his mouth.

Exhaling, I relax against the headboard, giving myself over to him. My breaths come short and quick. I can't hide the way he makes me feel. I don't want to hide from him. His lips open and close on my skin, and the tip of his tongue dips into my palm, tasting its way upward, where he places a soft kiss on each of my string-bitten fingers.

On my pinky, he kisses, increasing the pressure infinitesimally, pulling the tip into his mouth. His tongue licks across the pad of my little finger, sending a jolt of wanting right between my legs.

At the rush of cool air on my skin, I open my eyes, and see Thor watching me, a sinful grin on his face. He brushes a few disheveled curls from the side on my face, his fingers grazing my cheek in the process. "You are…"

Shit. I didn't catch that. The end of his sentence is lost to the lipreading graveyard. *I'm what?* I sign.

I watch his mouth, his beautiful, enchanting mouth, but it remains still. Instead, he reaches for the pen and paper. **You are incredible.**

My heart beats double-time and I can't help the grin that spreads across my face. I've been called many things over the years, never incredible. I shift my shoulders, uncomfortable with such a lovely compliment, allowing my hair to fall in my face.

Thor shakes his head, his eyebrows pulling together so a small vertical crease forms right between his eyes. Bringing both of his hands up, he pushes back my hair, resting his palms against my cheeks. "Don't hide," I read on his lips.

Leaning over, the guitar pressed between us, he kisses me. Nothing like last night, where we both wanted to devour each other. This kiss is soft, vulnerable. With each shared breath, the walls we've constructed to protect ourselves start to crumble. The tips of our tongues meet between our parted lips and take up a slow dance at the boundaries of our mouths. He tastes like mint and tobacco—the boy next door and bad boy all at the same time.

His hands push back into the tangles of my hair, giving him more leverage. His lips vibrate against mine. A groan? Did he say something? He presses harder, sweeping his tongue into my mouth, his tongue caressing mine. I curse the stupid guitar on my lap, separating our bodies.

I want more, and I'm not prepared when he pulls back.

Leaning his forehead against mine, our shoulders heave in unison…*up…down…up…down…*

I can feel his light blue eyes on me, but I'm afraid to look. Why did he pull away? What will I see on his face? Doesn't he want this?

Unable to resist their pull any longer, I lift my eyes to his.

Lust, mingled with a heavy of dose of tension stares back at me. Laying his palms against my cheekbones, he presses another delicate kiss to my mouth, and lets go.

Thor's lips move as he turns his head away from me. I'm not meant to see the words on his lips, but I catch them anyway, "Why now?"

Rejection and embarrassment fall like a brick in my gut. Maybe I misunderstood everything going on between us. And with this realization, I know I'm already invested. *Dammit!* That wasn't supposed to happen. This—Thor and me—isn't in my plan.

I tap his shoulder, scared of what I'll see in his eyes when he looks at me. Lifting his chin, he turns his head, locking an expressive gaze on mine. I just wish I knew what his expression meant.

Sliding the guitar off my lap, I lay it beside us on the bed and pick up the notebook. **Why now? What does that mean?**

His lips move over the words I wrote. I search his face for clues to what's going on inside his head, but he gives nothing away. Pushing back, Thor leans against the headboard and pats the mattress beside him. I turn my body around, so we're shoulder to shoulder. Yep, this is easier. Getting lost in the crystal depths of his eyes probably isn't the best plan right now.

Thor takes the notebook from my lap and I hand over the pen. He writes fast, choppy little letters, nothing like my big, loopy cursive. One sentence jotted at the top of the page, he turns the notebook around. He didn't need to; I read the words as he wrote.

I've never met a woman like you, Harper.

My stomach twists in knots like it did last night. *"What do you mean?"* I shake my head, signing, forgetting again that he doesn't understand me. Pulling the notebook from him, I take the pen too, and underline what I previously wrote, several times to make my point.

I look up just in time to see him close his eyes and rest his head against the headboard. I'm at a loss. Trying to get a read on Thor's body language is like trying to read a doctor's signature on a script, impossible. So I take advantage of the situation, and let my eyes roam over him. With anything I don't fully understand, I've learned that serious study is the best way to glean knowledge.

My eyes trace the contours of his creased forehead. Worry lines? Tension? I wish I knew what he was thinking. Why the worry? Tonight is supposed to be easy and enjoyable, a chance to get to know each other better. At least it had been, up until now. I want to smooth away his stress written in the creases on his forehead, to lighten his mood.

I shift my gaze to his thick brow and deep-set eyes, noticing a sizable U-shaped scar on his left eyebrow. The itch in my fingers grows stronger. I want to touch it, to know more. A scar like that has to have a story. I lace my fingers together, resisting the urge to run my fingertips over the since-healed wound, letting my eyes do the touching. Moving downward over the smooth line of his nose—the end tapers, making a flawless transition to his upper lip.

Oh, his lips. Perfect. Speaking, kissing, smiling, his mouth is the one part of him I've gotten to know the best in the last forty-eight hours. I lick mine, still enjoying the lingering feel of his mouth. Outlined in a dark shadow of fine stubble, his lips are slightly parted. I could so easily climb onto his lap and resume what we'd started earlier. Where my fingers begged to touch him a moment ago, now my lips have joined the party. Everything about this man reduces me to a quivering mass of desire. With Thor, it's hard not to have sex on the brain. And having not been laid in years, Thor makes it really difficult to forget that.

A subtle bounce of the bed pulls me from my lusty fantasy, my eyes are drawn toward Thor's lap, specifically, the tapping of his thumbs against his thighs. Concentrating on the movement, I can almost feel the gentle beat all the way to my core, like he's transferring his nervous energy to me.

This time, I give into the desire to touch him, resting my hand on top of his. He stops. A beat later he doesn't lift his head, but rolls it in my direction, his thoughtful stare boring deep into my eyes. Without breaking his gaze, he pulls his hand from beneath mine and takes up the pen and pulls the notebook from my lap.

I'm scared to breathe. If even a molecule of oxygen escapes my lungs, he'll turn away and the spell between us will be broken. I've never felt chemistry like this. Ever. The need to kiss him is stronger than the urgency to draw a breath.

Thor blinks, and his eyes search my face. *One breath. Two breaths.* Then he looks down at the paper and taps the pen against the underlines I made.

Scratching furiously, he writes, **Why not now?** Looking up at me, the intensity in his eyes is almost too much. I don't know what he's trying to tell me.

His shoulders slump and he writes more. **Because when I kiss you, I feel it right here.** He beats his fist against his chest, right over his heart. **And that scares the shit out of me,** he adds to the page.

Okay, Thorin Kline, you've got my attention. All my swoony, melty attention. Seriously, I think my inner vixen just signed *Aww!*

He licks his lips and leans forward. An unsettled energy pours from his gaze, like there's a war raging inside him. I want to tell him, to show him that there's nothing to be scared on of.

I tug the pen free from his grasp and write below his words. **Scared of what?**

Taking the pen back, he scribbles, **I've been with a lot of women, Harper, and never wanted anything more than a good time. But when I kiss you, there's something there...I do want something more. And I can't want more.**

Ugh! This conversation is going nowhere! Shaking my head, I sign, *"Why?"* again. He's not making any sense. Frustrated, I yank the pen from his grasp. **Why can't you want more? I kinda figured you haven't lived the life of a priest for the last several years. I've had other boyfriends, myself. But, is that a reason to not give us a chance? Because we've been in other relationships? That's stupid. I also know that our timing sucks, your band is about to take off and I've got clinicals and graduation coming up, but I'd really like to try. I'm not going to deny that I'm attracted to you, because I am. I know we only just met, but I very much want to see where this goes.** I leave everything on the page, dropping the pen on the paper.

Thor takes his time reading my thoughts, his eyes moving from side to side, touching each word. Setting the notebook down, he shifts his body around, motioning for me to do the same. We sit cross-legged, facing each other. Thor fits his hands beneath mine and squeezes as I look up, my eyes landing on his moving lips.

"...scares me, Harper," he says.

Dammit! I missed the beginning of his sentence. I watch his perfect mouth, waiting for more, hoping to fill in the blanks. *What scares him?*

"I don't do the relationship thing."

I catch every word this time. My heart sinks, pulling my mouth into a frown as it plummets into the pit of dating hell. I knew last night was too good to be true. The first person I've connected with in a long-ass time and he has commitment is-sues. Just my luck.

I glance around, searching for the notebook—I've got ques-tions for him—but, Thor tightens his grip on my hands, forc-ing me to look at him.

"I want this," he says, the corner of his mouth pulling into a playful smirk. "I want to give us a shot." He nods.

"Really?" I sign, mouthing the word around a growing smile.

Thor lets go of my hand and mimics the sign. *"Really."* He moves his hand to my face, his fingertips brushing along my cheek. Pushing my red curls behind my ear, he gently guides me forward.

Staring into the ocean depths of his eyes, desire crashes over me. I give in, closing the distance between our mouths. The second our lips touch, Thor brings his other hand to my face, deepening the kiss, but keeping his gaze locked on mine. My heart pounds in my chest, there's something sinful and erotic watching *and* participating in a kiss, simultaneously.

When lips touch, eyes close. That's what's supposed to happen. Not this time. Thor's tongue sweeps into my mouth, teasing mine, all the while, our eyes silently beg for more, pushing and steering the both of us into uncharted territory…into a relationship.

CHAPTER ELEVEN

THOR

I've had a girlfriend for two whole weeks. How I've managed not to fuck this up is beyond me. Everyone who knows me, knows I don't do relationships, so I'm driving in the dark here. And swinging the Charger into a parking space at the YMCA is the first stop on my relationship map. I'm in over my fucking head, but when it comes to Harper, I can't say no, even if it involves playing my guitar to a bunch of kindergarteners.

I don't know a damn thing about kids. Never been around 'em. How the fuck am I supposed to entertain them? I kill the engine and pull the keys from the ignition, wiping my sweaty palms on my jeans. How is it that I'm more nervous to play a concert for a handful of twerps, than I've ever been playing in front of a packed club? "Shit," I groan, leaning over the seat and grabbing my guitar case. Harper King has got me wrapped around her slim little pinkie.

Walking across the parking lot, I push open the door and immediately, my eyes fall on Harper. I'm drawn to her like a heat-seeking missile. Separate us in Time Square on New Year's Eve and I'd still find her in record time.

Kneeling beside a blond-haired little boy, she's signing animatedly. The little guy nods his head, understanding whatever it was that she said, and throws his tiny arms around her neck, pulling her into a fierce hug. Harper returns the boys affection, a tight-lipped smile on her face. Whatever their conversation had been about, it impacted them both.

Another little kid, working over a cupcake at the table, stares at me for a beat, then stands and runs over the Harper, pulling on her shirttail. Harper and the blond boy pull apart and she turns her attention to the kid covered in frosting. The cupcake kid points and Harper twists around.

When her sea glass green–eyes land on me, her shoulders fall back, and her face lights up with a brilliant smile. My ego just got a hell of a lot larger. Fuck yeah, I put that smile on her face.

Harper ushers the frosting-coated kid toward the restroom and makes her way to me. Watching her walk, the sway of her hips, I have to keep my thoughts in check. I'm here to give a music demo, not a biology lesson. But damn, I can't take my eyes off her. I don't remember ever having a teacher that looked like Harper, if that had been the case, I might have paid more attention in school. Van Halen's "Hot for Teacher" echoes in my head. Damn right I am.

Harper waves and stretches her arms out wide as she comes closer. Setting my guitar case on the floor, I'm ready when her arms go around me. I pull her into a tight hug, taking everything she's giving. She fits me like no other person ever has, her body filling all my hollow spaces. And fuck, she smells good. With her head tucked right under my chin, wafts of coffee and something flowery and girlie floats up from her hair.

I take in another breath just as she pulls away. Dammit! I want more. I'm beginning to sound like a looped track, but I can't help it. I don't think I'll ever get enough of this girl. Still smiling, she takes her phone from her back pocket. While she types, I pull my phone out, waiting for her message.

Harper: Hey! Glad you're here! How'd rehearsal go with the new drummer? She brushes a few errant curls behind her ears and shifts her weight between feet. She's always so chill; what's got her so fidgety?

Me: Yeah, no problem. Happy to do it. Everything all right? You okay?

As she reads my text, two kids come running up behind her, throwing their bodies around her legs like magnets to metal. Caught off guard, Harper sways, arms out wide, stumbling forward.

"Whoa, Red! I've got you." Harper grabs my upper arm, her fingers pressing into my biceps, doing all she can to not faceplant in front of the kids. I dig my fingertips into the crooks of her elbows to hold her up. The kids stare in shock, mouths in perfect Os, not quite sure how they managed to nearly take out the teacher.

Finding her feet, Harper whirls around, giving the kids a stern look. She's signing fast and hard, hands smacking together in loud pops. No fucking clue what she's saying to the roughhousers, but by their downcast expressions, it can't be good.

The boys make fists and rub them in a circle on their chests. I know this sign. It's the one I'm actually good at. Dropping down to their level, Harper gives the kids a tight-lipped smile and pulls them in for a hug. She's so good with kids, why is she in pharmacy school and not teaching? I scratch the back of my head, filing that thought away for later.

Standing back up, she's already typing out a message before she turns around and faces me.

Harper: Sorry about that. Those two have been told to stop running all afternoon. Follow me, I'll show you where you can get set up.

Flashing me her come-hither smile and tacking on a wink for good measure, she starts walking, motioning for me to follow her. *Red, I'll follow you anywhere.* And kids or not, I can't help it when my eyes zero in on her ass as I trail behind her. Those skinny jeans are hugging her in ways I only hope to one day.

Harper takes me to the far side of the room where an adult-sized, navy-blue plastic school chair is front and center on a multicolored alphabet carpet. Instantly, I'm sent back to second grade, images of Miss Carmike sitting in her blue plastic chair. My butt always claimed the letter "X" on the alphabet carpet. Damn, I loved second grade, Miss Carmike was the fucking best. I never wanted to go home.

Harper taps my shoulder, pulling me out of my second-grade time warp. Scooting the chair back an inch, she gestures from me to it. Catching her drift, I sit and place my guitar at my feet. I give her a reassuring wink just as she bends down, kissing my cheek. It's a quick peck, but enough to take my mind off the task at hand. *Children, Thor. There are fucking children in the room.*

Shaking off my naughty thoughts of Harper and what she can do with those lovely lips, I lean over and unlatch my guitar case, taking Lizzy from the velvet-lined interior, cradling her in my arms. I settle myself on the chair and get to work tuning her up.

While I pluck away at the strings, in twos and threes, the kids start gathering on the carpet at my feet. One little girl in particular catches my eye. She situates herself, crossing her legs, and stares up at me with the saddest dark brown eyes.

I know this girl. Not really, but I know that look in her eyes, like a puppy that's been kicked one too many times.

She watches my fingers moving over Lizzy's strings, shifting her eyes from my fret hand to my strumming hand. Her head starts to bob with the beat of the song while her lips pull into the ghost of a smile, like she's trying to remember how to do it.

This kid...

A hand touches my shoulder, and I stop playing. Looking up, Harper stands beside me. She gives me a smile, then turns her attention to the ten kids who are all waiting for me, the rock star, to wow them.

Harper signs fast. The kids smile and wiggle, excitement taking over. What is she telling them? It's not like I'm SpongeBob, or whoever gets kids excited these days.

The group raises their hands, shaking them wildly just as my phone vibrates in my pocket. Fishing it out, I glance at the text message. Relax! They don't bite...well, not as hard as Lizzy, anyway. ;-) Just tell them a little about the band, how the guitar works, and play a song or two. You'll be great and the kids will love it! I'll be here to interpret, just look in my direction when you speak.

I glance over my shoulder. A huge, crooked grin lights up her porcelain face and she pats me on the back as she sits to my right, angled enough to see me and the kids.

What's the most fucking terrifying thing on the planet? Ten kindergarteners. No question. Twenty pairs of innocent eyes staring up at me like I'm some kind of role model.

Never in my life have I been thought of as a role model. If Griffin could see me now, he'd shit himself.

"Okay," I mumble, pocketing my phone. "I can do this."

Slipping Lizzy back into place on my lap, my left hand grazes over the strings, strumming, while my right hand holds down the chord. With any concert, no matter how big or small, when my fingers find their home on the strings, I know I can tackle any problem. Hell, if it hadn't been for Lizzy, I might have never gotten through school myself.

My eyes roam to the back row of kids, to the little brown-eyed girl. I focus on her. Maybe Lizzy can help her too.

"Thanks for having me, kids." I clear my throat. "I'm glad to be here."

Harper beams at me, signing my words for the group. It's her smile that reminds me why I'm here...seeing how happy I've made her. I don't think I've ever been the reason for someone's happiness. It's awesome and head-trippy.

Confidence bolstered, I dive back in. "This here is Lizzy." I hold up my guitar, facing it outward so each of the kids can see the front. "Who wants to hold her?"

Ten heads turn to Harper. They watch her hands, then snap their attention back to me, hands fly upward, waving in the air, all saying, *Choose me.* I keep my eyes on the brown-eyed girl in the back. She doesn't raise her hand.

"Okay. How about you"—I point to one of the boys that almost knocked Harper over earlier—"and you...and you." Two girls sitting front and center pop up from their spots on the carpet and join the little boy at my side.

Passing Lizzy to the little guy, I help him get his fingers settled on the strings, and motion for him to give the guitar a strum. He follows my lead, dragging his hand downward over the sound hole. Lizzy responds with a weak, tinny sound. The kid repeats the motion with more confidence this time, grinning toothlessly at the girls beside him.

Out of the corner of my eye, I see Harper holding up her hands and shaking them, just like the kids did when she introduced me.

Bobbing his head, the little guy strums my guitar like he's Paul McCartney playing Shea Stadium with Beatles. I hate to be the one to squash his rock-star dreams, I've been where he is; it's a feeling like nothing else, but I have to give each kid a turn.

Tapping his shoulder, he freezes. Biting his lip, the little man opens his eyes and glances around the room. The kids raise their hands in silent applause and Little McCartney hands Lizzy back to me, taking a bow.

For fifteen minutes, I cycle through the group, giving each kid their turn at being a rock star. When it's the brown-eyed girl's turn, I point, waving for her to join me. "Come on up, little lady."

Harper walks over to her, crouching low, signing. The girl shakes her head, letting her scraggly, dark blond hair fall in front of her face. Glancing back in my direction, Harper frowns and shakes her head too.

Oh, hell no. I know that look...I've *worn* that look. I refuse to let this pint-sized darling be scared of me. I'm not the person who's broken her spirit, but I'll be damned if I don't want to be the one who fixes it...even for just a little bit.

Getting up from my seat, Lizzy in hand, I step through the mass of kids, careful not smash tiny fingers under my giant feet. Coming up beside Harper, I lay my right hand on her back, and sit down, crossing my legs. Crammed between Little McCartney and the next Eddie Van Halen, I smile at the little girl on Harper right. "Hey, sweetheart."

Harper signs my words, adding something at the end. I recognize the letters "Z" and "Y." She must be fingerspelling Lizzy. The little girl watches from beneath long, tangled strands of hair, inching her way closer to Harper's side.

As a peace offering, I hold the guitar out to her. "It's okay, cutie. Go ahead, give it a try."

Harper takes Lizzy from my hands and passes it to the girl. The other kids watch as the girl brings her head up all the way, showing off her big, brown, gorgeous eyes. Brushing her tiny hand over the blond wood, across the strings, she almost smiles. Almost. It's still there, I can see it in her eyes, it's just buried under all the shit she has to endure at home. I want to fucking punch the asshole that makes this sweet little girl cower behind her unwashed hair. Thank fucking God she has Harper and a safe place to come after school...that's more than I had when I was her age.

The girl hands the guitar back to Harper. Turning her head in my direction, Harper's green eyes shine and she smiles gently—soft, like a flower petal. With just one look, she makes me believe I'm some sort of superhero. How did a screwup like me end up with her?

Touching her fingertips to her chin, Harper signs, *"Thank you."* She places Lizzy in my hands, her fingers grazing over mine—another "thank you."

I smile at Harper and the girl, holding up three fingers and circling them against my chest. I think that's the sign for *"You're welcome"*…at least I hope so.

Harper nods, her face lighting up. Nice! Yep, that's it!

As I stand up, the little girl lifts her head, catching my eye. Bringing her fingertips to her chin, she lowers her open palm. *"Thank you."*

Never in all my life has a kid almost made me cry. I don't even like kids. But this little girl is one in a million. With a lump in my throat, I crouch back down so I can look her in the eyes. "What's your name, sweetheart?" I ask, hoping Harper will interpret for me.

Without missing a beat, Harper signs.

Hesitantly, the girl brings her right hand up and finger-spells her name. *"P-E-N-N-Y."*

I'm glad Harper taught me the ASL alphabet. "Well, Penny. It was lovely to meet you." I offer her my hand to shake.

She watches Harper sign, then looks back to me, slipping her tiny palm into my hand. We shake hands and this time, she really smiles. Two missing front teeth and eyes that reflect a moment of pure happiness; she melts my heart.

Standing back up, I notice the letter Penny's sitting on...my letter..."X." I wonder how Griffin would feel about sharing an apartment with me and a five-year-old, because right now, I want to fucking adopt Penny.

I make my way back to the seat in front, the kids shifting so I don't step on them. Settling Lizzy in my lap, I swallow the lump and pull myself together. "How about a song?" I place my hands on the G-chord and strum downward, transitioning to C, then back to G—the opening chords of Van Morrison's "Brown Eyed Girl."

The kids like the song...I think. Their little heads bob in time with the beat of my strumming hand. I get a kick out of the air guitars that Little McCartney and Little Eddie play. Their parents need to get them lessons.

Belting out the chorus, I stand up, kicking the chair backward. The kids cheer and holler in excitement, popping up from their letters on the carpet, dancing and swaying to the beat.

Harper works her way through the crowd, grabbing kids' hands and spinning them around. I've never heard giggling like this, unadulterated happiness. My childhood didn't sound like this, that's for sure.

Watching Penny, I make my move, singing and playing as I travel through the lively bunch. Penny's standing, swaying timidly on her feet, scared to death to let loose and have fun. Harper meets me at Penny's side, scooping up her hands. Together, they swing their joined hands back and forth.

The more I sing, the wider Penny's smile grows. Harper spins her in a circle and Penny laughs. A full on belly laugh.

For the rest of my life, that sound will echo in head...*I will remember when she sang.*

Okay. I take it back. Concerts for kindergarteners are the easiest. And by far my favorite.

While I'm busy giving Lizzy a workout, my phone vibrates in my pocket. Slowing down, I end the song, and pull my phone out, wondering what Harper sent me. *Shit.* Did I get carried away there at the end? Have I worn out my welcome?

Glancing at the screen, my eyes scan over the words. Mom: Your dad's back. He's at my place and he won't leave. Can you come over? I afraid he's going to bust his way inside.

Nine months of worry-free days and nights screech to a halt like a needle over vinyl. My head spins in two different directions, trying to keep my rage locked up, and a lighthearted smile on my face. If he hurts her, I will fucking kill him. I send Mom a quick response. On my way. Keep the doors locked.

Slamming my thumb down on Harper's name, I type out a message: Sorry, Red. I have to go. Emergency at my mom's. I'll explain later.

Without a second thought, I walk back to the front, lay my guitar in the case, and snap it shut. Standing up, Harper's beside me, a worried look in her eyes. I plant a hard, fast kiss on her lips, and book it to the door.

Shoving my way out of the Y, my blood boils. That man has crossed the line. No fucking way does he get to terrorize my mother at her new place.

* * *

Forcing the gas pedal down, the Charger growls and speeds up. I feel the exact same way. With each tick on the speedometer, my heartbeat picks up the pace, a kick drum against my ribcage. Why the hell hasn't she gotten a restraining order? Weaving in out of lanes, I scream by the Sunday drivers who didn't get the memo: Hurry the fuck up!

Pulling into Mom's apartment complex, the Charger fishtails on the pebbled parking lot, kicking up a cloud of dust in my rearview. Dead ahead, Dad's beat-up Chevy is parked in front of Mom's place and he's on the porch, nursing a forty.

I turn hard, whipping into the spot next to the Chevy. Killing the engine, I pull the latch, and step out. "Yo, Pop," I holler, slamming my car door.

He looks up. Drunk piece of shit.

I want nothing more than to plant my fist in his bearded face…break his nose like he did mine so many years ago. He has no fucking right to come here and terrorize my mom. Hitting him won't help her, though. I won't cause more of a scene in front of her neighbors.

"Whatcha doing here?" Gravel crunches under my boots.

"Need to talk to your ma. Don't see how that's any of your business, though." He lifts his chin, acknowledging me.

It's more of my fucking business than yours, old man. I glance up at the building, studying each of the windows. The blinds are drawn and everything looks quiet. *Good. Stay hidden, Mom.* "Don't think she's home."

Dad looks over his shoulder, toward the front door. "Bullshit," he groans, turning back around. "I know she's here."

"She's not. Time for you to leave, Pop."

Grunting, Dad shuffles to his feet. At his full height, the top of his head only comes to my chin. He sucks in a breath, takes a step in my direction, and nails me with his dark eyes. "You don't tell me what to do, boy." His breath reeks of stale beer and cigarettes.

There used to be a time I cowered and backed away, fearing his right hook. A lot, actually. Not anymore. Not since my eighteenth birthday—the night he broke Mom's jaw and blackened both of her eyes. At 4:27 that afternoon, I learned that a drunk, sorry excuse of a man is nothing when pitted against his stronger, taller, sober son. I beat the shit out of him. I would have killed him if Mom hadn't pleaded, sobbing for me to stop.

I promised Mom that Dad wouldn't hurt her anymore. Raymond Kline would never lay a fucking hand on her again, because if he did, I *would* kill him.

Looking down at the man that gave me half my genes, I say, "Leave."

He watches me, trying to pick up on any sign of weakness he can latch on to and manipulate.

Minutes pass, I'm sure. I don't back down despite the awful stench each time he exhales. When was the last time he brushed his fucking teeth?

"You tell that bitch she can't leave me. I own her. That pussy belongs to me!" He thrusts his hips and grabs his crotch, licking his lips. "Mmmm!" He shakes his head. "She always was a good fuck."

I ball my hands into fists at my sides and bite my tongue, fighting the urge to close my eyes. I can't stand to look at this worthless piece of shit. But I don't back down. I show no weakness. My stomach rolls, acid churning with one-quarter disgust and three-fourths pure hatred. I loathe this mother-fucker with every fiber of my being. My self-control is nearly maxed out. I'd give anything to beat him to a bloody pulp.

"Leave." The word falls from my mouth in a menacing whisper. He knows I'm not joking, and he loves the fact that he can provoke me, get under my skin.

A smug grin on his face, he bends down and picks up his beer can, throwing back a swig. He stares me down and I do the same. "Some man you've turned out to be. Fucking mama's boy." He turns his head and spits.

Stepping off the porch he walks around me, clipping my shoulder with his as he makes his way back to his truck. I keep my feet planted where they are, holding my breath. Oxygen will only add fuel to the fire burning through my veins. If I move…breathe…his life is over.

"Nice chatting with you, son. Be a good boy and pass along my message."

Like hell I will. And I'm not *your son.* The word burrows into my skin like a flesh-eating parasite.

A door slams.

When an engine roars to life, I exhale, letting my eyelids close. I can hear his truck crushing gravel beneath its tires, then a loud screech as he pulls out onto the road.

Mom peels back the front door, peeking her head around the side. "Is he gone?" she asks meekly.

I nod, still too angry to say anything.

"Come inside," she says, opening the door wider.

Crossing the threshold, Mom steps aside, giving me room.

"Thanks for getting him to leave, Thor. He'd been pounding on the door for fifteen minutes before I sent you the text."

Mom closes the door behind me; it whines and creaks in protest. I need to grease those hinges for her. "Two words, Mom"—I whirl around—"'restraining order.' Now that he's back, you need one."

Wrinkling her nose, she waves my comment away. "Nah. Leaving him and getting that legal separation was hard enough. I'm tired of making a fuss."

Making a fuss? My brain hurts trying to keep up with her small-minded reasoning. "What the hell, Ma. That man just made a huge damn fuss on your front porch. What if he would have gotten in? What then? Leave me to pick up the pieces after he beats the shit out of you, or worse, kills you? Isn't that a fuss?" I shout, but hold back most of my outrage for her sake. I hate yelling at her. Lord knows she's had enough of that in her lifetime.

I can't fucking see straight. The urge to drive my fist through her wall is overwhelming, but I rein it in. I won't let my anger and frustration take over…I'm *not* him.

Mom comes closer, her eyes locked on mine. Reaching for me, she rests her palm on my cheek. "How was I lucky enough to get a son like you?" Her features soften, diffusing my anger like she clipped the wires on a ticking bomb.

"Mom—"

"Shhh," she cuts me off, shaking her head. "It was a big step for me to leave him. I've been with your father over half my life. Being his wife is all I know, it's all I'm good at. You've got to cut me some slack. Let me get used to being alone." She chuckles, tears pooling in her eyes. "I've never been alone. I'm a forty-three-year-old woman who's never been alone."

I shake my head. "Mom." Wrapping my arms around her, I pull her to my chest, and hold her. I hate it when she talks like this. She's so smart and talented. "You're not alone. I'm here."

Guiding her to the kitchen table, I pull out a chair so she can sit. I do the same. The silence between us lingers, both of us trying to work our way out from under Dad's heavy shadow. Even when he's not here, he is.

"Why the hell did he come back?" she mutters, staring at the wall across the room.

"I'm worried." I don't pull any punches. She needs to know. "I fear the day that I don't get here in time."

Leaning over, she puts her hand on my leg and meets my eye, nodding.

"If a restraining order's too much, then let's get you a gun. Or enroll you in a self-defense class. Now that he is back, I've got to know you can protect yourself."

She laughs. "Oh, baby. Not a gun! I could never." Shaking her head she leans back, wiping her eyes with the sleeve of her shirt. "I'll look into a self-defense class, though. I think I could do that."

Why is this funny to her? Why doesn't she understand how dangerous that man is? "I'm serious." Right now, I'm convinced she's all talk; that she'll say anything to get me off her back.

My phone vibrates in my pocket. Leaning to the side, I pull it out and glance at the screen. Harper: Everything okay? Worried about you. Please text back.

Her radiant smile flashes in my head. An hour ago I was rocking out with a handful of smiling kids and a smart, beautiful woman at my side. My life is so fucked up. Who am I kidding? Harper's world doesn't mesh with mine at all. I can barely keep my mom safe, how am I supposed to keep Harper away from all this shit?

"Who's that?" Mom asks, startling me back to the present.

Turning my eyes on her, I shake my head. "No one. Not important."

Harper deserves more than what I have to offer. Standing up, I slip the phone back in my pocket, ignoring the message…remembering why I've stuck to one-night stands all these years.

CHAPTER TWELVE

THOR

Dropping my cigarette in the grass, I press my heel into it and tear back the ripped fence, calm already seeping into my veins. The air's different here. Can't explain it, but it's clearer, or lighter, some fucking scientific reason, I'm sure. Whatever it is, no matter what kind of mood I'm in, this place can Zen me out.

And Lord knows I need some serious fucking Zen right now.

Making my way to the deep pool on the other side of complex, Dad's skeevy-ass words echo in my head. I wish to God I could forget them. I could have gone my whole life never knowing that my mom is a good lay. Bile rises in my throat and I choke it down, grimacing.

And don't get me fucking started on Mom's comment about *"making a fuss."* Did I drop acid and forget, because I'm seriously tripping. I love my mother, but she makes me fucking crazy.

Even after an hour at Mom's place, I'm still seeing red. I'm damn lucky my car knows the way here, because I remember fuck all of the drive over.

Tight grip on my guitar case, I climb down the rusty ladder, and into the empty pool, thankful for my dank piece-of-shit safe haven. It's a fucking mess, but it's quiet and dark. And it's all mine. This whole night has been nothing but the loudest fucking mic feedback ringing in my ears. Too many voices in my head. It feels nice to escape life.

Foregoing the last two rungs, I let go and drop, my boots hitting the ground with a loud *clomp*. I readjust my grip on Lizzy's case and stalk toward my spot under the diving board. The itch in my fingers gets stronger by the second, craving a workout on the six-string.

I plant my ass on the ground, directly beneath the diving board, and snap the latches on the case. Folding back the top, Lizzy gleams, nestled into the black, velvet lining. "Come to papa," I croon, lifting her out of the confines at the same time my phone vibrates against my ass cheek.

Settling Lizzy on my lap, I lean to one side and pull my phone out of my back pocket. I glance at the message. Harper: Freaking out here. Worried.

"I'm freaking out too, Red." I don't know what to do. I want to be the guy that gives Harper everything she wants. The boyfriend she deserves. Hell, I even bought into the fairy-tale bullshit, thinking I could pull it off. But, I know enough that the princess doesn't end up with the trailer park trash. Prince fucking Charming I am not.

I stuff my phone back into my pocket and tune up Lizzy.

Plucking out some chords, I wait for the sound waves to ricochet off the side of the pool. This place has great acoustics. Even at my shittiest, I can rival Clapton or Slash. When there's no one around to hear, I can be whoever the hell I want.

My slow, steady strum, grows into something rich and heavy. A monster waking up. Standing. Stretching. I feed it more of myself, giving it strength. Sweat runs down the side of my face. *Motherfucking bastard.*

I thrash the strings. Slap my hand against the wooden body. Pummel Lizzy with all I've got.

Black eyes. Bloody noses. Gashes. Snapping bones.

Blow after blow.

The monster strains at its leash, and I keep going, my fingers biting into the strings. Taking hit after hit. Adrenaline courses through my veins until I finally release the harness, and set the monster free. Hunched over, rocking out, I scream.

For Mom. The little boy trapped inside, cowering in the corner. For Penny who sits on the letter "X."

And For Harper, because I know she isn't safe with me.

"Fuuuuuuuuuck!" I roar. Anger claws and scrapes at my throat until I'm spent.

Beaten.

Broken.

I drop my hands to my sides, sucking in air, chest heaving. Lizzy collapses on my lap. The grandfather clock from my childhood flashes in my brain, and I zero in its face. It's not 4:27. I didn't win this fight.

My phone vibrates again.

I'm scared to look. Six damn years since fear rattled its

chains in my chest, reminding me of how weak I am…*who* I am—*"You're my son, boy."*

The message is from Harper, I feel it in my marrow. I can't face her. I won't put her in danger. What if I snap, lose my shit, and it's not Lizzy in my hands next time, but her?

What if it's Mom? What if he came back? Round two. The voice inside my head weighs in—the voice of reason. *Priorities, Thor. Suck it up. She needs you.*

Shifting to the side, I push my hand into my back pocket and take out my phone. I hold my breath, and bite down on my lower lip, drawing strength from the sting, preparing for what I'm going to see on the screen. No matter what it is, it's going to hurt like hell when I read it.

With the metallic tang of blood in my mouth, I push the home screen button.

Mom: Thanks, baby. How'd I get lucky enough to have a son like you?

She's safe. I let go of the air in my lungs, my chest burning.

I reach for the pack of cigarettes in my shirt pocket, draw one out, and shove it between my lips. Striking the lighter, the yellow and blue flame dances in the light breeze, a pinprick of light surrounded by a whole lot of darkness.

Bringing the lighter to the end of my cigarette, a cloud rises, filling my nostrils. The paper and tobacco crackle, dying in the fire. I pull in a long drag, feeling the smoke land heavy in my lungs. Closing my eyes, I lean my head back on the cold concrete, and pretend to enjoy my smoke and the illusion of serenity it provides. I know it's just the nicotine fucking with me. But for now, it's enough…at least until Harper texts again.

I have to end things. I can't put her in the crosshairs. The damn fairy tale was nice while it lasted, but it's time to live in fucking reality again. She's too good for me.

* * *

"That her again?" Griffin asks, pulling a beer out of the fridge.

I nod, trading my phone for my guitar, plugging into the amp. "Grab me one, will you?" Adjusting the volume, I strum a chord.

"Here." Griffin shoves the Budweiser in front of my face.

Yanking it out of his grasp, I raise an eyebrow and pull the tab. "Switching things up?" I take a long swig. It's not the microbrew Griffin usually has on hand, but it'll do.

"All there is, man." Griffin takes a drink and sets the can on a stack of *Sports Illustrated* magazines. "Dad's garage. He stocks the fridge how he wants." Grabbing his bass, Griffin throws a punch into my shoulder. "What the fuck did she do to piss you off?"

I dampen my strings and glare at him. "Nothing. She did nothing. Just had a moment of weakness. I slipped up. I should have never chased her down. It's what happens when I let a pretty face seduce me. Lessoned learned." I'm sick of talking. There's nothing to be done. Harper's safer with me out of the picture. Thanks to my dad's timely reappearance, I've got my head on straight again. Fairy. Tale. Fucking. Over.

I take another long drink and set my can down so I can pick out a rhythm on the strings. "We gonna play, or what?" I shout over my guitar. I like getting in touch with my feelings as much as the next guy, but I don't have all night for a Dr. Phil session with my roommate. I want to practice and stop in at Ma's place before I head home

Griffin adds his bass to my guitar, and just like old times, we rock out. Countless hours in his parents' garage, or mine—when Dad wasn't home, of course—we'd hone our craft and learn to play off each other. Jam sessions are the fucking bomb.

After our drummer, Adam, broke his wrist, Griffin and I haven't had any time to squeeze in an extra practice. All our free time has been caught up in finding a temporary replacement for Adam. But this, pounding out a month's worth of stress, it's exactly what Griffin and I need before heading into the lair of the corporate music machine next week. A return to our roots. Just Griff and me. How it all started.

"Sweet riff," he shouts, pointing at me. "Keep it going, I want to try something."

Like I did at the pool last night, my fingers rip over the strings. I keep my muscles tense, my biceps strain, burning as I give my guitar a workout. The tune seethes with anger, driving and hard, yet, buried beneath the hatred and discordant tones, a rhythm emerges…the ghost of a melody.

Griffin hears it too, adding a groovy bass rhythm. We play off one another for what seems like eternity, our song shifting and changing, following an unknown path.

It's cathartic, my temper mellowing with each note. And as I complete the cadence, slow my strum, and dampen the strings, all my anger and anxiety are spent, for the moment.

Griff stops playing and tweaks a knob on his amp. "We were

in the zone. That rocked. Think we could do it again?" He glances in my direction.

"He's back," I blurt out. Griff should know. In case something happens to Mom, or I get pulled away from the studio. I've got to be upfront with him. "I was with Harper yesterday when Mom called. The douche bag was pounding on her door, trying to bust his way inside. No sign of him for nine months and now he's back like a fucking plague."

"Shit." Griff lifts the shoulder strap of his bass over his head and sets it on the couch. "Your mom all right?"

I nod, picking up my beer. "Peace of mind is rattled. I got there before anything happened. Made him get lost." Taking a long drink, I'd love nothing more than to get piss-ass drunk and forget the last two weeks ever happened. Mom and I both got lazy and complacent as fuck.

"That why you're ghosting her?" Griff asks. "Also explains why you just pounded the shit out of that song, which was awesome, by the way."

"Harper and I haven't been together that long, man. Two weeks and some change. It's better this way. If we're not together, I can't fuck things up. Like you said, I pounded the shit out of that last song. What will stop my temper from pounding the hell out of her?" Leaning back in my chair, I prop my feet up on the little table beside the couch. I know Griff's dad wouldn't care, not with the countless rings covering the surface, each marking the spot a cold one kept him company during a football game.

"Bullshit. You know as well as I do, you're nothing like your old man." He drains his beer, squeezing the can into a twisted heap of aluminum. Chucking the empty in the direction of the recycling bin by the door, he bricks it, and the can goes skittering in the opposite direction. I'm glad he plays the bass better than he sinks shots from less than five feet away. Griff is to organized sports what the Pope is to the dating scene.

"You don't know that. There was a time when that d-bag didn't beat the shit out of his family. Mom loved him. Sad thing is, I think she still does. After the hell he's put the both of us through, she still fucking loves that prick." I shake my head, trying to wrap my head around the enormity of that statement. *How?* How could she still love him? Beating her was one thing, but how can she still love him after he beat the shit out of me, too? I love my mom, and I will always be around to protect her, but where the fuck was she when I was little and needed protection?

"I can see it in her eyes when I mention getting a gun, or bring up a restraining order. God forbid, an actual fucking divorce. She'd rather live in fear, than get him out of her life for good, and it's because she's still loves him." I crunch my empty beer can and fling it toward the bin. Two points to the guitar player.

"There's nothing rational about love, man. It's not an on-off switch."

I hit him with a pissy scowl. Somehow, I think we stopped talking about my mother and moved onto his complicated love life. He's been in love with his best friend, Jillian, for years. Everyone who knows the two of them can see the attraction, yet, they ignore it and spend their days in denial. And let's not talk about the weird-ass relationship he's got going with another chick. *You're the master at the on-off switch, brother.*

Griffin runs his hand through his hair and stands, walking over to the fridge. He pulls out another beer, pops the top, and drinks deeply. Hauling it away from his mouth, he stabs me with a heavy look. "You have to call her."

I raise a questioning brow. "My mom? Why?"

He cocks his head and glares. "Your girl. What's her name?"

"Harper. And why should I call her? The point is to stay away, so I don't end up using her as a punching bag."

"Do you like this chick?" he asks, plopping on the couch with his beer.

Walking around the other side, I flop onto the other cushion, propping my feet up, one on top of the other. Staring at my filthy work boots. I nod. "Yeah. But I haven't figured out why she wants me. She's out of my league."

"That's when you know it's something. When you figure out you'll never be good enough for her, but she doesn't see it that way. Give it a shot, dude. See where it goes. Trust me, you'll only regret it if you don't."

Regret. It's already digging its claws into my gut. I haven't talked to Harper since I ran out on her.

"Shit." I wipe my hands over my face. "Fucking relationships, man. Makes me crazy. Why I've avoided them all these years."

"She's worth it?" Griffin asks, turning to look at me. "Worth all this frustration? All the crazy?"

I don't even hesitate. "So fucking worth it."

"Then you have your answer. You and Harper are not your parents. You guys do you. Don't let someone else's relationship bullshit dictate yours."

Maybe I can make this work. I want to. I'll just have to keep my family shit under wraps. The less Harper knows about me, or where I come from, the better. The safer she'll be.

And Griffin's right about knowing what I have with Harper is something different...special. With every woman I've been with, never once have I thought of them above myself. It was always, *"What can she do for me? How can she get me off?"*

With Harper, it's the complete opposite, and I'm left hoping and praying I'll get the chance to show her exactly what I can do for her.

CHAPTER THIRTEEN

HARPER

Are you busy tonight? I leave for New Hampshire tomorrow. I'd like to see you before I go. Pressing send, I let my head flop against the back of the couch. This rerun of *Parks and Rec* can't even hold my interest, and I love that show. *Come on Thor, give me something.*

For three days, I've mulled over reasons why he ran out of the Y and has evaded my text messages with veiled excuses why he can't (or doesn't) want to see me.

I understand that life is complicated right now. I get it. But, I wish he'd let me in. He's always so guarded, keeping me at arm's length every time I ask him about what's going on in his life.

It's hard to keep my mind from traveling to darker thoughts. *He can't deal with your deafness, Harper. You've read too much into the way he feels about you. He's not attracted to you. He's ghosting you. It's over.*

My phone vibrates in my hand. Lifting my head, I glance down at the message. Thor: On my way over.

My heart shifts into overdrive. *Holy shit!* I wasn't expecting him to actually come over. Giddy, I throw my classic car blanket off my legs and run to the bathroom. Flipping on the light, I stare at my reflection. My hair is sticking up in every direction—red curls with minds of their own. Under my eyes, mascara and eyeliner smudges set against my pale skin make me look like a corpse, or an extra on *The Walking Dead*. I'm a mess.

Turning on the water, I wash my face, brush my teeth, and try to tame my curls. Two out of three isn't bad—Thor will just have to live with my hair channeling its inner Carrot Top.

Decent enough for a Thursday night at home, I go back to the living room and await Thor's arrival. I'm surprised to see Chloe and Megan sitting on the couch. Chloe pulls on her knee-high black leather fuck-me boots.

"Where are you two going?" I gesture to Chloe's outfit—a fitted black dress and killer boots that add at least six inches to her five-eleven frame. *"You look stunning!"*

Chloe pulls the zipper on her boot and stands, smoothing out the wrinkles from her dress. *"Megan is in town visiting a friend. She asked me if I wanted to go clubbing with them. Want to come with us?"*

I shake my head. *"Thanks, but T-H-O-R is coming over."* I'm glad Megan's here. Since Chloe and Trey broke up, all she does is bake and watch Netflix. Chloe needs her sister right now. *"You and Megan have fun. Be safe."*

Megan stands up and holds her arms out wide. "It's been a long time, Harper." I read her lips.

"It has. Chloe's missed you." I see Chloe's lips moving, interpreting my response, as I pull Megan in for a hug.

Stepping back, I ask, *"What club are you headed to?"*

"The Cave," Megan says.

Chloe bites her lip. *"Don't freak out, okay?"*

I cringe. *"That place is rough."* I never did like going to The Cave. The place is aptly named, most of the guys that frequent that dive are cavemen. And it's always in the news for all sorts of awful crap. A shiver runs up my spine at the thought. *"Why are you going there?"*

"To check out this new female alt-band, S-W-Z-Z-I-L-E S-T-I-X. Heard of them? They're really great."

I shake my head. The only band on my radar at the moment is Mine Shaft, and whatever the hell is going on with their lead guitarist. *"Why would an all-girl band want to open at The Cave? I hate that place."*

Megan taps my shoulder. "Chlo and I will stick together, Harper. Don't worry."

I move my hand up and down, pointing out their gorgeous outfits, impeccable makeup, and beautifully curled hair. *"I do worry. You're both too gorgeous for that place."*

Chloe grabs my arm, yanking me close. *"We'll be fine."* With a quick, tight hug, she lets go and grabs her black clutch off the couch. *"I'll text if we need anything."*

"I'm not going to pretend that I like this, and you better text me if anything goes wrong. Please, be careful." Chloe and her love of new bands is going to get her into trouble one day. The Cave is the last place two women should be going to alone. It sucks that the world is like that, and it worries me that Chloe isn't more responsible when it comes to self-preservation.

In my peripheral vision, the LED light above the front door

flashes, and I pull away, looking over my shoulder. Bobby runs to the door, sniffing and pawing, tail waving like a white flag.

Chloe taps my shoulder and spells, *"T-H-O-R?"*

I nod.

"Finally got ahold of him?" Her eyebrow quirks up in question.

"Yeah. But I still don't know what's going on with him. Hoping we can resolve things before I leave in the morning."

The light blinks again.

Chloe walks to the door and bends down to pick up Bobby before pulling it open. Thor's on the porch, hands shoved in the pockets of his dark jeans. Chloe waves him inside and turns around, depositing a wriggling Bobby in my arms. Megan walks over and stands next to her sister, not even hiding the fact that she's checking Thor out. Both girls' eyes flick to mine; Chloe's are wary. She mouths, *"Good luck,"* giving me the "be careful" look we've perfected over the years. Megan's eyes scream, *Yum!*

With a tight grip on the dog, I flash Chloe the same look as she grabs her sister's hand and drags her out the door.

Thor waves to Megan and Chloe on their way out, then turns his attention to me. Lifting his hand, he makes a fist, circling it over his chest—a silent apology. He takes two steps and scratches Bobby behind the ears before putting his hands on the backs of my arms, staring into my eyes.

More than anything, I want to step into him, snuggle up to his warmth. But, my heart is too invested at this point and I need to guard it. Taking a step backward, I set Bobby on the floor and grab my phone off the end table beside the couch. Thor crouches down to pet Bobby while I type. When I'm finished, I hold out the phone.

Grabbing it he reads as he stands. Thought you might have wanted to end things.

Thor's eyes land back on me, ice-blue and intense. His shoulders move up and down with each breath and he shakes his head, stepping closer, he invades my personal bubble. Both hands on my cheeks, he leans down and kisses me, hard.

My eyes widen, caught off guard, but the second Thor pushes his tongue into my mouth, every nerve ending in my body blazes to life. I close my eyes, throw my arms around his neck, and kiss him back.

Wild, our lips move in a frenzy as our hands grope one another. Raking my short fingernails over his close-cropped scalp, Thor bites my bottom lip, drawing blood. A metallic tang lingers in my mouth and his tongue roams deeper. He cups my ass, pressing me against his hard-on. I want to climb him, meld my body to his.

Unrelenting in his desire, still caught up in his touch, he walks me toward the couch and we collapse together. I open my legs to accommodate his body, wrapping them around the backs of his thighs, locking him to me.

Thor tears his mouth from mine, licking and kissing his way over my cheek…along my jawline…my neck. Goose bumps rise on my skin when the tip of his tongue glides over my skin, leaving a cold trail in the wake of his hot breath. I shiver, feeling a vibration on his mouth, humming over the skin on my collarbone. I love that, the hum in his throat, sending those vibrations up to his mouth and over my skin.

Oh God, Thor, don't stop. I lift my hips, a hint that I want so much more.

He moves his nose along the path of kisses he just left on my neck, working his way back up. His tongue laps at my earlobe before he sucks it into his mouth with a sharp nip. My hips buck beneath him, and I exhale.

Thor captures my breath with his mouth, tightening his lips over mine, and I spiral into a haze of lust. Our bodies move in sync, a blessed rhythm. I meet him thrust for thrust as he grinds his hardness between my legs like we're naked, not fully clothed. And I can't help mourn the fact that we are fully clothed, goddammit!

Tugging at the hem of his shirt, I take the initiative to put an end to the "fully clothed" conundrum. My fingertips meet skin and I sigh, opening my mouth wider. Thor takes advantage, his tongue stroking mine, drinking me.

Yanking the shirt higher, I pull hard, wanting it gone. Catching my drift, Thor breaks his mouth away, rips the shirt over his head, and crashes his lips back on mine. He doesn't miss a beat and my hands revel in the feel of hot, sweaty flesh and rippling muscles beneath my fingers.

Thor kisses me like I'm air—greedy, wanting, and strong, like each kiss is another infusion of life-preserving oxygen. Running my hands down his spine, I reach the small of his back, working my fingers under the waistband of his pants. Thank God his belt isn't very tight, both of my hands slip inside. I keep going, working my way downward, sliding my hands along his skin…under his boxers…caressing his ass.

Squeezing, guiding his rocking hips, I tilt my head, offering my neck to him again.

I'm waiting, panting, anticipating the next bite or suck, but nothing happens. He stops grinding.

Oh my God. Why did he stop? My eyes flick open. Thor's looking down at me, his mouth pink and swollen, but smiling. He brushes my hair off my cheek and tilts his head.

Drawing my brows together, I mouth, *"What's wrong?"* along with the signs.

He shakes his head, his eyes thinning to narrow slits, scrutinizing me even more. Adjusting himself so that his weight is held in his hands, he pushes up, forcing my hands out of his pants. Thor sits up, pulling me with him.

Looking around the room, he points to something on the floor and gets up to retrieve it. Turning around, he holds up his phone, and flops back down on the couch. Unlocking the screen, he opens the Notes app.

While he types, I rearrange my disheveled clothes, twisting my shirt back into place. Bobby, being the good boy he is, has curled up in his bed on the other side of the living room, oblivious to what Thor and I had been doing. Out of the corner of my eye, Thor's shirtless torso captures my interest. I enjoy the view, taking in all his sexy ink.

Thor passes me the phone. Red, I'm really sorry I ran out on you the other day and that my messages have been so vague. I've just been dealing with some family shit. I didn't mean to worry you.

I write: What happened? Is your mom okay? What can I do to help? I hand Thor the phone. While he reads and types his response, I resume my perusal of the artwork covering his skin. I've seen his arms on plenty of occasions, but the artwork on his chest is something I haven't had the pleasure of seeing yet. I can't help but stare, taking in all of his body art.

The dark lines of the ink on his arms swirls and blends, morphing into handfuls of timepieces. Some large, others are small, each bearing a different time. The largest one, the one I traced with my finger on our first date is set at 4:27.

Still typing, he flexes, drawing my attention to the ink covering his left pectoral muscle, along with the silver gleam of a nipple piercing.

I glimpsed the flash of something shiny when he stood up earlier, but couldn't make out what it was. Up close, I can see it's at the center of some sort of circle with eight tangents radiating outward, each line ending with a symbol, all under a giant hammer.

His body is a study in Thorin Kline hieroglyphics. I wish I knew what each pictograph meant. Why he chose to have these images etched onto his skin forever. What is the significance of 4:27? Why an eight-pointed star? None of these tattoos are something someone would get on a whim. I want to know this part of Thor.

He passes the phone back to me. There was a disturbance at her place. Had to make sure she was all right. She's fine. Everything's good.

I write back: Glad she's all right. Anything I can do?

Taking a second to glance at the screen, he cranes his neck in my direction and lifts an eyebrow. "I'm sure I can think of something for you to do."

I didn't catch all of that, but enough to understand his innuendo. A smirk tugs at my corners of my lips. *"Oh, Really?"* I mouth.

He nods, abandoning the phone on the cushion beside him, and shifting his body in my direction.

I did want a better look at that piercing but I'm not close enough, yet.

Angling my body, I throw my leg over his lap, straddling him. Moving my hands to his chest, I trace the outer circle of the tattoo, working my way to one of the lines, stopping before I reach the silver barb. I've never seen a nipple piercing. It looks good on him...really good.

Thor's chest moves up and down, as I caress the tines of each fork radiating out from the center of the star. He watches my finger as I draw over the next ray, still too shy to touch his nipple. What if it hurts?

He breathes in. And out. Faster and faster.

I match my breaths to his, inching my finger closer to the center of the circle...closer to the piercing. He shifts his hips, pressing the hard bulge in his pants against my apex.

Gasping, I hold his gaze. Our eyes locked together, I bend down and flick his nipple with my tongue.

"Fuck." I lip-read the word as he bites down on his lip, staring at me.

I lick again, enjoying each reaction my roaming tongue elicits. I love the way the hard metal feels in contrast to his warm flesh.

Wrapping my mouth around his whole nipple, I lick and suck at the piercing. Thor's heart pounds inside his chest. His head falls back against the couch, while his hands work at my waist, balling the fabric of my shirt in his strong grasp.

Pumping his hips, I bounce on his lap as he removes my T-shirt, forcing me off him.

Eyes locked again, both of us catch our breath. He is so friggin' sexy. His stormy eyes push me over the edge. I want him now. Can't wait.

Standing up, I grab his hand and pull him off the couch, leading him toward my bedroom.

Inside my room, I don't waste a second, crushing my mouth to his as I kick the door shut. He doesn't hold back, kissing me hard. Touching his chest, I finger both of his nipples. I can't keep my hands off his piercing; it's such a turn-on. *Oh my God!*

Thor flips the hooks on my bra and it drops to the floor. He spins us around, pushing me onto the bed. Stalking toward me, he forces my legs wider with his knee, covering my body with his. Bending over, he licks across my nipple, just like I had done to him, and a wicked grin spreads across his face. With a playful bite, he sucks me into his mouth.

And I'm dead.

A wave of desire crashes over me, igniting a blaze of wanting between my legs. My head falls back, absorbing the sensation of each nip and suck. No one has ever made me feel like this. I've wanted this since the night we met.

I give myself over to him, welcoming the release building inside me.

CHAPTER FOURTEEN

THOR

"I want to touch you." I lean in and kiss her, caressing my tongue over her swollen lips. I know she needs to see my mouth when I speak, but goddammit, I have to kiss her, too. It takes everything thing I have to tear myself away. Pulling back, I stare down at her. "Show me where to touch you, Harper?" I ask, hoping she can read my lips. I want to watch her come undone from just my touch before I slide inside her.

My hand grazes the inside of her thigh, climbing higher and higher, meeting the lacy edge of her purple panties. I've wanted to rip them off and bury myself balls deep between her legs ever since she shimmied out of her leggings a moment ago, but watching her squirm under my fingers is satisfying in its own right.

From what I've learned about Harper in the weeks since we've been together, she isn't shy about what she wants, and I fucking love that. So damn sexy.

Not missing a beat, Harper takes my hand, guiding it over

her smooth stomach. She has got the most gorgeous body, soft and curvy in all the right places. Her stomach isn't completely flat, but rises to a tiny hill just below her belly button. *Fucking hot as hell.*

I grab hold of her waist, pressing my forehead to the perfect pooch of her stomach, breathing in her sent as I kiss my way down. Harper moves her hand from mine, placing it at the top of my head, pushing me lower. *Fuck yeah, Red, show me what you want.*

She's going to kill me. And I want her to.

Hooking my fingers into the sides of her panties, I pull them down. Drawing in a deep breath, my eyes roll to the back of head. She smells divine. I want to bottle this scent—sex and longing and nothing but Harper.

She guides my head all the way between her legs, lifting her pelvis in offering.

Pushing my hands between her ass and the mattress, I hold on tight, bring her pussy to my mouth, caressing her slick folds. Fuck me. She's so wet.

Licking over her clit, I suck her into my mouth, flicking my tongue over the sensitive bundle of nerves. Harper arches her back, a sighing breath escaping from her mouth. She presses closer, begging for more. And I give it to her, loving the way she moves her body against my mouth. She tastes so fucking good. My cock aches, so jealous.

I kiss the inside of her thighs, loving the gasps coming from her mouth. She's close…so close. I want to watch her come.

Rising, I cover her body with mine, my fingers taking over where my mouth left off.

My thumb traces circles over her clit, while I press two…three fingers inside, fucking her. Eyes closed, she rides my hand, chasing her release. One of many I'm going to give her tonight.

Fuck, she's gorgeous. Wild red curls splayed out over the pillow, fingers white-knuckling the comforter, hips grinding against my hand. I slide my fingers in and out, giving her what she wants. "That's it, baby," I breathe against her ear, biting her earlobe.

She clenches around my fingers, body shaking. I rub my thumb against her clit and she shudders uncontrollably, legs straight, toes pointed. Letting out the longest breath, her body relaxes, and she opens her brilliant green eyes.

Her hand clawed, she waves it in front of her face. *"Amazing."*

I see the word on her lips, wishing so much that I could hear her say it. "We're not done yet, Red," I promise.

She smiles, leaning up and pressing her mouth to mine.

While I kiss her, I get my fly open, tugging on my pants, not getting very far. *Shit!* "Hold that thought," I say against her mouth. Standing up, I take my wallet from my back pocket and pull out a condom before my jeans and boxers hit the floor.

Harper shimmies the rest of the way out of her purple panties, completely naked, and fucking beautiful. It's time. I've got to get inside her.

Ripping open the condom wrapper, I roll it over my cock, and climb back onto the bed, Harper beneath me.

Poised at her opening, I press against her. She opens wider, an invitation.

With one thrust, I'm in, buried from shaft to hilt. *"Fuuuu-uck!"* I growl, savoring the way her pussy tightens around me. I almost afraid to move, worried that I'll come the instant I work up some friction.

But, my body takes over and it moves of its own accord, pumping slowly at first, until Harper joins in the rhythm, her hands on my ass, driving me farther into her.

Now I'm thrusting at the exact moment her body rises to meet mine. We fit together, our bodies moving in unison—like we're made for each other and no one else. It's never felt this good.

Dragging her fingernails up my back, she cups my face in her hands, pulling me down, her tongue sweeping into my mouth. Bodies rocking, we kiss.

I peel her fingers off my cheeks and force her hands above her head, locking our palms together. Kissing over her mouth and along her jaw, I revisit all those sweet spots that made her pant earlier.

Our sweat-slicked skin rubs together, and I can feel her beaded nipples, hard against my chest. I want to lick every inch of her skin, even if it means I have to last all fucking night. I'd do it for her.

Harper's breaths come harder. I can feel her heart pounding inside her chest…and against my cock. I pump faster. She's close. So am I.

Letting go of her hands, I touch her face, needing her to open her eyes. "Talk to me, Harper. I want to hear you come."

She watches my lips and frowns slightly, shaking her head.

Fuck. What did I just do? I slam into her, wanting her to

know how much she means to me. "It's okay, baby." I kiss her deeply, giving her everything I am. Trying desperately to erase the frown I put on her face.

With everything I've got, I thrust and thrust until her body quakes under mine, and all her breath leaves her body. Only then do I let go, ass clenched, my balls pull up and stars burst behind my eyelids. I spill into her, pumping until I'm empty and spent, collapsing in a boneless heap on top of her.

Harper's gone, riding the high, her body soft and satiated.

Rolling off her, I slide the condom off, and lay it on the wrapper on the floor, careful to keep the mess contained. I'd take it to the bathroom, but I don't want to leave Harper's side.

Lifting my arm, I pat my chest. Harper takes the bait and snuggles into my side, resting her head on my shoulder. Bringing her hand up, she traces lazy circles over my Viking compass tattoo—a Vegvisir.

"Why?" She taps my chest, tracing her finger over the lines of the compass.

I lift my head, eyes straining to see what she's pointing to, like I forgot what my own tattoo looks like. Slowly, I pull my arm from under her head and roll onto my side, facing her.

"Got it when I was sixteen. Saved my pizza delivery money for a year and a half to afford it. Worth every damn penny."

She glances down again, resuming her exploration with hesitant fingertips. Each stroke is feather light, like she's afraid she'll smear the ink if she applies too much pressure.

Flicking her eyes back on my face, she brings her hands between us, and signs with a furrowed brow, *"Meaning?"* I like that she mouths the words when she signs, it helps me pick up on the language.

"It's a guide, helps the bearer find his way even during the darkest, stormiest weather. It was a good reminder when I was a kid: life's shit now, but I'll get through it."

Harper moves her hand to my eyebrow, touching the scar at the side. My eyes close and I pull in a deep breath. We're dancing so close to things I promised I would keep far away from her. How Dad hit me so hard, I flew right into the corner of Mom's coffee table, and it took eight stiches to patch me back up. Hair never did grow back over the gash, my eyebrow's split in two on the left side.

"What happened?"

"Let's just say, my father and I didn't see eye-to-eye." I've already told her my father's a prick. She doesn't need to know more than that.

Stretching her neck, she reaches up and kisses my scar, laying her palm against my cheek. Lips pressed near my temple, her breath is warm, her kiss, tender. Not like a kiss I've ever had before. It's…? Not sure what it is. Caring? Loving?

I cringe at the last thought. There's no fucking way. She's too good for me.

Sliding her hand down the side of my face, my stubbled cheeks prickling beneath her gentle fingertips, she touches my neck…shoulder. With the fingernail of her pointer finger, she draws figure eights around the edges of two clock faces, her eyes lifting back to mine. *"And these?"*

I can't tell her. But I want to. I know I should tell her.

"Reminders." I mumble, my stomach churning. Lies are

heavy in your gut and leave a bad taste in your mouth, like chowing down on week-old takeout that you find shoved in the back of the fridge. It's sketchy, but you eat it anyway, because that's all there is to eat.

My lies are the only way to keep her from knowing the real me, and the bastard I share blood with.

I want to drop the subject, but I know my one-word answer won't appease her. She wants more…all of me. *I want to give you all of me, Harper. But then you won't want it.*

What does a wealthy, smart, fucking gorgeous-as-hell woman like Harper King want with a grease-stained auto mechanic turned musician? She could have the pick of the litter, and here she is, slumming it with me.

"Battles lost. And a war won," I add, cracking open the door to my past a little wider. One of these days, she's going to get her foot inside, and throw it wide open, revealing everything about me that I never wanted her to know.

And then she'll close the door on us.

Shoving the unknown, depressing shit into the dark corners of my mind, I concentrate on the languid figure-eight path she's still tracing on my chest, her unruly hair moves right under my nose. With each inhalation, a corkscrew curl pushes against my nostril. Exhaling, the curl blows away. I bite back the urge to sneeze, concentrating on the flowery scent of her shampoo.

My pulse has returned to normal, but the more I think about the reasons why I shouldn't be with Harper, anxiety kicks it back up. Harper's everything I've ever wanted in a woman, and I didn't even know I was looking until I saw her at Mississippi Lights that night. She's so much more than the barflies I've hooked up with in the past, she's not even in the same fucking galaxy.

Tightening my arm around her, Harper shifts, lifting her head. Smiling an easy, satisfied grin, she yawns and continues her lazy trail over my chest.

You're too good for me, Harper King. You deserve so much more than the trash I come from.

I smile at her, working one of her curls around my index finger. I lied when I said playing a room full of five-year-olds was scary. Holding this amazing woman in my arms is the most frightening thing in the goddamn world.

Harper's hand stills. Turning her body, she puts both arms on my chest and rests her chin on top of her folded hands. Staring at me she smiles again, but this time, it's not the smile of a well-pleased woman; there's mischief and playfulness in her eyes. Biting her lower lip, she draws a line down my chest, right smack down the middle. Lifting her finger, she places it next to my left nipple and drags it to the right in a horizontal path. My skin tingles at her touch, goose bumps prickling across my arms and chest.

Her movements are deliberate, repeating the motion again, only with a subtle variation. Letters. She's drawing letters over my skin.

"T-H-O-R."

She takes my fucking breath away.

Smiling, I grab her hand and bring it to my mouth, kissing the tip of her forefinger.

Stretching her body against mine, she leans up to kiss me, and resumes her spelling on my chest. I could get used to communicating like this, a gorgeous, naked woman writing letters across my body, fuck yeah. My dick twitches his sign of approval.

Concentrating on the feel of each letter and the motion of her finger, it's easy to pick up what she's writing: *"W-h-a-t u t-h-i-n-k-i-n-g?"*

Harper flicks her eyes up to me, awaiting my answer.

"How hot it is when you write on me," I say.

Pinching her eyebrows together, she looks down, readying her finger on my chest. *"H-o-w d-o-t- w-r-i-t-e-s m-e?"* Green eyes back on me, she shakes her head, confused.

Laughing, I trail my finger down her back, *"U"*—I point at her for emphasis, wagging my eyebrows— *"h-o-t."* With each letter, my finger travels lower, sliding into the dip of her lower back and grazing the top of her ass cheeks.

Her face is still flushed, but I love that they get a little pinker at my words…or is it my touch? Whatever the cause, I fucking love the effect.

Harper scoots up, draping her body over mine as she reaches for her cell phone lying on the bedside table. Her tits press against me, claiming my dick's full attention.

Flipping onto her back, oblivious to my now raging hard-on, she unlocks her phone and opens the Notes app, typing.

I watch the words, reading as she types. You think I'm hot?

What the hell kind of question is that? I don't need a phone to answer that one. I raise a questioning eyebrow and point at my dick. "What do you think, Red?"

She bites her lip and writes some more. Did you…umm…like it?

Is she serious? Again, I point to my dick, still hard—and getting harder by the minute—ready for round two. But, I take the phone and give her the reassurance she wants.

What we just did, fucking amazing, Harper.

A look of relief washes over her face. What is this look? Why was she worried? She grabs the phone from me.

I just thought you might not have enjoyed it as much since... She stops typing.

"What?" I sign, urging her to continue, pointing to the screen.

She finishes her thought, I wouldn't talk to you.

I sit up, forcing her to follow suit. I pluck the phone from her hands. Red, I'm not lying when I say that was the best sex I've ever had. Fucking hot as hell. Can't wait to do it again! ;-) So don't worry about that. I think you're perfect the way you are, but can I ask why you don't talk?

She waves her fingers, wanting the phone. Oh, good. As long as you enjoyed it. I was worried. It's been a long time since I've spoken out loud. I was nine. I wasn't very good at it and I hated going to speech class. My teacher was awful. Out in public, when I tried to talk, strangers stared at me, kids would point and laugh, etc... You know how cruel kids can be. When I told my parents about the bullying, they suggested that maybe I shouldn't speak, save myself the heartache. I was devastated. I thought they'd back me up, support me, build up my confidence and self-esteem. Nope. Although they never said anything negative to my face, I always felt like they sided with the bullies. If I didn't talk, I couldn't embarrass them. No talking, no heartache, no embarrassment.

Wow. Just wow. Emotions pummel my heart like fists on a punching bag. The urge to grab Lizzy and head to the abandoned pool hits me hard. Images of a young Harper, looking very much like the little girl, Penny, I'd met at the YMCA, flip through my brain. I'm sad and angry for Harper, having had endured ridicule from strangers. And it makes me ill to think that little Penny is struggling with her own set of monsters at home.

Fuck them. Fuck them all for not making this world a safe, happy place for those young girls.

I want to make Harper feel safe with me. I want to seal her in my arms and protect her from all the shit in the world. I don't ever want to be the cause of her pain.

I hold my hand out for the phone. Harper drops it onto my palm. I shift, angling my body toward her. Pinching her chin between my thumb and index finger, I lift her head, needing her to see me. "I'm sorry you had to put up with that. It's not right. In the short time we've been together, I've never met anyone as strong and brave as you." Bringing my right hand to her face, I brush my fingers over her cheeks, cradling her head, hoping she understands every word I'm saying. If not, I pray my touch will convey the message. "I can't imagine what it's like for you, but if people can't get past the fact that you can't hear, so what. Fuck them. They're missing out on getting to know a brilliant woman." I lean in for a gentle kiss, brushing my lips over hers. I can still taste her desire from earlier, lingering on both our mouths. And it's so goddamn hot. My cock throbs, remembering how amazing she tasted.

I drag my tongue over her lips, savoring the taste of *her*.

Harper kisses me back, her tongue teasing mine until I can't take it anymore. I plunge deep into her mouth. My hands at her sides, I lift her body, bringing her onto my lap. My cock presses against her, desperate to slip inside. I want to devour her.

Harper rocks her hips, my dick rubbing against her clit.

I'm going to fucking explode if I don't take her now. Tearing my mouth away from hers, breathless, I say, "Baby, don't stop." I love that she's getting herself off on my cock. Not taking my eyes from her, I lean to the side, groping for my wallet on the floor. Damn condoms. Annoying as shit, but necessary.

Harper throws her head back, pure ecstasy on her face. So beautiful. I keep guiding her rhythm with my right hand, helping her grind away, wanting her to get there. "That's it, Red."

Seconds later, my fingers touch leather. Latching on to the wallet, I pull it up, flip it open, and grab the corner of one of the foil packets with my teeth. Ripping it open, I take out the condom, and drop my hands between us.

Lifting her head, Harper glances down, as I'm about to fit the condom over my cock. Wrapping her fingers around mine, she grabs the latex from my hands. My eyes flick to hers. A sultry, crooked smile grows on her face and she winks, wrapping her hand around my dick, rolling the condom into place.

"*Uhhh…*" A sigh rips from my mouth and my eyes close, succumbing to the overload of sensations. So many nerve endings firing at once.

Harper positions me at her opening. Before I can open my eyes, tight warmth engulfs my dick. Holy…fucking…shit. Blinking, I watch as she lowers herself on me. A sight I will never forget.

I wrap my arms around her back, tugging her close. In turn, Harper does the same as she circles her legs around my waist, melding our bodies together.

Pressing my palms under her hair, I work my fingers upward through her tangled strands, lowering her head to mine. I kiss her deeply while she rides me.

Faster and faster, Harper bears down on me, rolling her hips. Neither of us can manage to sustain a kiss any longer, so we've given over to pressing our open mouths against each other's, panting wildly. I lick her tongue, tasting, bouncing her on my lap.

"Harper," I groan, "I'm gonna come." I try to hold off, not sure if she's found her release. "Come for me, Red," I say against her mouth.

She tightens around me, every inch of her. Riding out her pleasure, she throws her head back with a breathy sigh. I'm right there, light bursting behind my closed lids as I let go.

Our rocking slows, coming to a halt. I drop my sweaty forehead to hers, catching her gaze. "Fucking perfect," I say, shoulders heaving.

And it is. More perfect than ever before.

* * *

"Hungry?" Harper signs and leans over, pulling on a pair of leggings. I didn't know that sign, but seeing the word on her lips, I catch the drift.

"How do you sign, 'starving'?" I ask.

Smiling, she repeats the sign for "hungry," only slightly

more dramatic. I make a C shape with my left hand and replicate her motion, facial features and all.

Harper raises her hands in the air, shaking them.

Grabbing my hand, she fits her fingers between mine, and opens her bedroom door. Bobby pops up from his post, tail wagging, happy to see us. "Hey there, little guy. Did you get locked out?" I bend down and scratch behind his ears. Immediately, he falls and rolls onto his back, needing a few belly scratches.

Harper crouches beside me, ruffling Bobby's fluffy ears, smiling contentedly.

Standing, I grab her hand, and we walk down the stairs, Bobby trailing behind. I can't remember the last time I held hands with a girl. *Becky Lambert in the fourth grade, maybe? I know she's the first girl I kissed. Or did I kiss McKenzie Swanson and hold hands with Jessica Oliver? What the hell did I do with Becky Lambert?* Shit. My left eye starts twitching. Too many fucking girls.

Making a sharp right into the kitchen, I stop in the doorway. There are cupcakes everywhere; the counters, the table, the stove, the top of the refrigerator, even on a couple of the chairs. I throw a look at my feet. This is a dog's wonderland, but Bobby obediently sits just outside of the kitchen, recognizing his boundary. Such a well-trained dog. If I were him, this kitchen would be a chocolate cupcake murder scene, and I'd be dead, because, you know, dogs and chocolate.

Tapping Harper's shoulder, she spins around, piercing me with her green eyes. "You didn't tell me you had a cupcake fetish?" I joked.

Finger-spelling and moving her hand in a wave motion away

from her chest, Harper signs and mouths, *"C-U-P-C-A-K-E fish?"* Eyes drawn tight, she looks very confused.

I shake my head, laughing. *"No."* I pinch my fingers together, signing the word. I can't get enough of the look on Harper's face when I sign—like someone's thrown a switch for a spotlight, she glows like she's in the goddamn sun. Not wanting that radiance to dim, I clumsily shape my fingers into the letters she taught me. *"F-E-T-I-S-H."*

"Oh," she mouths, nodding. Turning on her heel, she walks across the kitchen and pulls open a drawer. With a brown crayon and a Post-it in hand, she scribbles on the paper and hands it to me.

My roommate's a baker.

Giving Harper a thumbs-up, I snatch a cupcake from the counter and peel the paper off. I'm not as well mannered as the mutt.

Even though it's chocolate, and not butterscotch, which my favorite, it'll do. Popping the whole thing in my mouth, it's an instant chocolate overload, with a hint of something else. What is that flavor?

I chew, trying to place the weird, savory tang mixed with the chocolate. *"What?"* I ask, pointing at the empty wrapper. Swallowing, I can still taste the odd flavor. It's not bad, but, the jury's still out on whether it's good.

She writes on the Post-it and flips it around. **Bacon bourbon cupcakes.**

Bacon and bourbon. She's right, that's what it is. "Chocolate bacon bourbon cupcakes? No offense to your roommate, but I'm sticking to butterscotch."

"Wine?" She pulls out a bottle from the fridge.

"O-K-A-Y." I shrug. I'm more of a tequila or beer kind of guy, but wine'll do. Mind-blowing sex, wine, and cupcakes; lord knows I've had worse combinations.

Taking two glasses from the rack under the counter, she grabs the bottle, and nods her head in the direction of the kitchen table.

Catching her drift, I slide a handful of the bacon cupcakes to the side just as she sets everything on the table.

"Thanks."

I wink, hold three fingers to my chest, and move them in a circular pattern. *"You're welcome."*

There's that glow again. Her eyes shine like sea glass sparkling in the sunlight.

Sitting down at the table, Harper goes to work, pouring the white wine. I keep thinking about the sea glass, and how much her eyes remind me of a time when life with my dad wasn't so fucked up...before he was a drunk asshole.

Sliding a cupcake-free chair next to hers, I take a seat. Smiling she passes me a glass. Harper points to me and then to herself, winking. A toast? To us, maybe? Whatever her meaning, I'll drink to anything that involves the two of us, together.

I take a hefty sip, wincing. Spinning the bottle around, I read the label: Angel's Wings. Riesling. A better name would be Syrup of Hell, or Diabetic Coma. Think I'm sticking to beer from now on.

Setting the glass down, I hold up a finger, "Be right back." Standing, I jog out of the kitchen and to the sofa in the living room. I rub a hand over my chest, remembering how Harper was driving me mad, playing with my piercing not too long ago.

Glancing around, I look for my phone. It's got to be here. I pat the cushions, shoving my hand between them. *Aha!* Grabbing hold, I pull it free. "Gotcha." Now I can talk to Harper.

Turning around, I see her standing in the kitchen doorway. "Found my phone," I say, holding it up, walking in her direction.

Someone distracted me earlier. ;-) Couldn't remember where I left this, I type, handing her the phone.

She types her response and flips it around. Sorry, not sorry.

She sticks out her tongue, smiling coyly. Too damn sexy for her own good. And I'm hard again. Before I can make my move and pull her tongue into my mouth, she glances back down at my phone and types. I pull on the crotch of my jeans, adjusting my hard-on around the seam while she's not looking.

I'm leaving town tomorrow, had to give you something to remember me by.

I read the rest of her message. Dread pools in my gut like I just got sucker punched. Not only did I forget she was leaving to go back home, I sure as hell hope she doesn't think I slept with her *because* she's leaving. She must think I am the biggest fucking douche bag. I yank the phone from her grasp and type quickly. Harper. Fuck. I'm so sorry. Please don't think that's the reason I let things go as far as they did. Shit. What you must be thinking of me right now. I run a nervous hand over my head, acid churning in my gut. I hand her the phone.

She scans over the words, then flicks them back to me. I can't read the expression on her face as she types.

What do you mean? I don't understand. Do you regret sleeping with me?

I answer: God no! I just don't want you to think you had to do that so I would remember you. I may have been an asshole like that once upon a time, but not with you. Even without sex, I would still be here when you got home. Never think that you have to do something you don't want in order to "keep me around."

I step closer to her, my heart aching. I've never felt like this before—caring more for the woman I'm sleeping with than for myself. Her body radiates warmth, I crave it more than my fingers crave the bite of Lizzy's strings.

That was supposed to be a joke. I trust you. I know you won't hurt me. Frankly, I WANTED you. Badly. I had to have you before I left. Please don't think that I felt pressured in any way. You're a gentle, kind man, Thor.

As I read her message, Harper closes the gap between our bodies. I can feel her tits beneath her flimsy tee, brushing against my chest. She puts her hand over my heart.

"Kind" and "gentle" in the same sentence as my name? What kind of *Twilight Zone* have I entered? All the reasons why I never get involved with a woman come rushing back. What the hell happens if I turn into my father? I do share half a gene pool with him.

Harper touches my cheek, forcing me to look at her.

"Talk to me," she mouths, her hands making words I wish I understood. *"What's wrong?"*

I back away and fall onto the couch. Harper follows my lead, sitting beside me.

When's your flight? I show her the message, hoping to change the subject. I hate talking about my dad.

Taking the phone from my fingers, she replies. Early evening. I'll be at the hospital half the day, then I'm heading straight to the airport.

Harper types fast, faster than I do. My thick fingers always manage to hit letters that even confuses autocorrect. Backspacing, I try my answer again. How long will you be gone?

She answers: Just the weekend. That's about all the parent time I can handle at once. I get back Sunday night.

My weekend's busy too. I have to work. And the guys and I hit the studio on Monday. We've got nonstop rehearsals planned.

Passing the phone back and forth, I avoid the hard questions—the ones lingering in the space between us. The questions I know she wants answers to. Even though I've never heard her voice, in my head, I can hear her speak, *What are you so scared of, Thor?*

The house is quiet. I've never really contemplated it before, but this is what normal sounds like to Harper. And even still, if I concentrate, I can hear the hum of the fridge, cars passing by outside, and the faint tick of a clock somewhere upstairs.

She stares ahead, captive by a world of thoughts I'm not privy to. Hidden away in her secret world.

Her secret world…

My brain works over the rough edges of a song, carving and molding it into…*something.*

Hidden away in her secret world.
Measuring time with the beat of her heart.

When to stay? When to leave? When to hold her
   in my arms?
Can't hear the thoughts she plays in, can't see
   what makes her smile.
It's only when her eyes light up she lets me in for
   a while.

I watch her from my periphery, content in her thoughts, lovely green eyes focused on the dark TV. Glancing down at my phone, I type, compelled to let her into my world, just a little. I've got one good memory of my dad. The memory she stirred up weeks ago when she asked me about our family's favorite vacation spots. That, coupled with her sparkling eyes, I haven't been able to get that beach vacation out of my head.

When I was little, four or five, my parents took me to the beach. One of our only family vacations. It's a vague memory, I don't remember much about most of it, but I remember watching it storm from our hotel room. The lightning would crash down on the ocean, followed by ear-splitting cracks of thunder. I wasn't scared, just pressed my face against the glass and watched like it was Saturday morning cartoons.

Harper rests her head on my shoulder watching me type, patient as she waits for my words.

Once the storm passed, Mom and Dad took me down to the water's edge. Dad got down on his knees and started sifting through the wet sand, until he pulled up a handful of col-

ored pebbles—so many different shades of blue and green.
He plopped the mess into my hands. The polished rocks were
nothing like I'd ever seen. He called them sea glass.

I've never forgotten that moment. It's clear as day in my
head. And the only good memory I have of my father.

Your eyes are the same green as the sea glass my dad gave
me that day. A shiny, bright green, with a whisper of ocean
blue.

Pretty much the only happy memory I have of my old man.

Thumbs stiff and cramped, I hand Harper my phone. I
crack my knuckles and run my sweaty palms along my pants
leg, nervous. I've never told anyone that story. And I know it's
going to open up a slew of questions about my family that I'd
rather keep buried. But she went out on a limb, was brave, and
opened up about something painful in her past, I needed to
give her something of mine. I need to trust her the way she says
she trusts me.

Harper angles her body so she's facing me. Now I can read
the expression on her face. So much concern and tenderness
softening her features. I've never been scared of much in my
adult life, but hurting this woman has me scared shitless.

She signs. Not short phrases like she usually does. This time,
she speaks her mind. Turning up the volume. I only wish I was
tuned into the same frequency. I'd give anything to live inside
this part of Harper's life, to really *hear* her.

With each motion, each new word, her expressive face
dances over so many emotions: pain, sorrow, devotion, bold-
ness, determination. I want to know the thoughts and words
that bring her to life like this. Simply reading her words illumi-

nated on a phone's blue screen is so impersonal, so far removed from the intensity and passion her hands capture with each word she signs.

Lifting my hands, I cover hers, stopping her midsentence, or midword, I don't know. Her shoulders heaving, she watches me. "Teach me." I squeeze her hands. I'm tired of being left out. "Please. I don't want to rely on phones, or notebooks, or lipreading. I want live here." Folding her hands completely inside mine, I hold on tight. "And here." Letting go, I brush my fingers over her left temple. "And here." I lean in and kiss her. It's a simple kiss, just my lips on hers, but there's weight to it, words and thoughts and actions being spoken from my mouth to hers. A promise and a plea.

I close my eyes. "I want to hear you," I whisper, holding her tight in my arms.

CHAPTER FIFTEEN

Harper

Walking out of the terminal, Lance is waiting for me, just like he does every time I come home, or need a ride anywhere. Sixteen-year-olds, if they're lucky, get a car. I got Lance. I don't know if my parents didn't think I could drive, or they felt I needed a driver because they didn't want me driving, they've never said. But, like every red-blooded sixteen-year-old on the planet, I wanted a car, not Lance. When it came to my well-being, I didn't have a voice...I mean choice.

My parents had hired him, so I was stuck with him.

But, Lance was cool. He knew how much I hated being chauffeured around. Instead of driving me in the limo, he'd choose one of my dad's many sedans. When we were far enough away from the house, he would pull over, and let me get behind the wheel. Like in the *Princess Diaries,* I was Mia Thermopolis to his Joe.

It's thanks to Lance that I can drive, he taught me how. Yep. My chauffeur taught me how to drive, not my parents. Hell, I didn't get my license until I was eighteen, when I went away to college. That was an argument and a half. Both of parents were so resistant to the idea and to this day, they've never told me why. But I put my foot down. I refused to move halfway across the country and not be able to drive myself around. That wasn't happening.

And look at me now; I have an impeccable driving record. Not so much as a parking ticket to my name. It's a proven fact that deaf people are better drivers, fewer distractions to pull our eyes off the road. I love my parents dearly, but sometimes their ignorance blinds them.

Lance flashes me a smile and holds out his hand. On cue, I latch on to his fist and we fall right into our secret handshake, ending with Lance pulling me in for a big hug. Lance always gives the best hugs.

Stepping back, I pull out my phone and type. It's good to see you, Lance. I've missed you. Flipping it around, I hold it up, so he can read my pleasantry.

"Good to see you to, Miss Harper. Glad you're home."

"Yeah." It is good to be home, if only to see Lance and Mrs. R. Like any visit home, I know it will lead to some sort of argument between my parents and me. Even though I'm twenty-six, and have successfully taken care of myself for a long time, they will inevitably do or say something that will make me feel less than, or not as good as their hearing friends' kids. I do believe that Mom and Dad have my best interest at heart. I mean, they've always provided for me, given me all the best tutors and newest tech when it came out. But, emotionally, they detached themselves. Sometimes, a hug would have been more precious, *louder* even, than the world's best hearing aid.

And even then, the best hearing aids in the world couldn't make me hear. I could see the disappointment on their faces. Was it disappointment in the tech, or disappointment in their daughter? I've never been able to tell.

Take me to your leader, I add to my message, flipping it around to show him.

Giving me a sidelong glance (Lance is well versed in the continuing saga of *Harper vs. Samantha and Charles King*), he reaches for my Kate Spade carry-on (I packed light to keep this visit short) and ushers me toward the parking garage.

Lance opens the door to the backseat of the limo and I slip inside, sinking into the deep bucket seat. The small pull-down table between the seats is stocked with my hometown favorites: cider doughnuts and Polar brand seltzer water. It's been a thorn in my side since I moved to Missouri, haven't been able to find Polar seltzer anywhere!

Twisting off the cap, I press my lips against the mouth of the bottle and tip it back, savoring the elixir inside. *Oh, refreshing raspberry Polar, how I've missed you!*

Glancing at Lance, I hold up my bottle of Polar in thank you. He smiles and winks, gently closing me inside.

Resting my head on the high back of the plush leather seat, I let my eyes fall closed, yawning. The car purrs to life and we're moving. Dad's limousine rides so smoothly, it's hard not to fall asleep. Early rounds will be the death of me. And it certainly didn't help that Thor spent the night. Not that I'm complaining about the second part; that was a welcomed change of plans to the otherwise uneventful Netflix romance movie marathon I had on the docket.

I shiver at the memory, recalling in vivid detail, how amazing Thor's body felt next to mine. It's not like my experience with men is through the roof—there have only been two, and Thor is one of them. But somehow, when I'm with Thor, everything feels so much…more…amplified.

His fingers seared my skin. The way he kissed me, sometimes like a whisper or a prayer, other times, it was like he was belting one of his songs to the last row of a concert venue. I don't remember being able to hear, but with Thor, and the way his body hummed with each spoken word, it was like I could hear him…his every thought. Our bodies were tuned into a different frequency, one that only the two of us could hear. I've never felt so connected to someone.

Not even David.

Thoughts of David surface. My high school sweetheart and the boy I lost my virginity to. We were together for four years, a long time, at least by high school standards. Oh, who am I kidding? Four years is a freaking long time, longer than some Hollywood marriages last.

A smile creeps to my lips. I haven't thought about David in a while. He was a great boyfriend. And from what I've seen from Facebook posts, he's happily married and going to be a father.

When David and I graduated, we wrestled with the notion of a long-distance relationship, but in the end, mutually decided it was for the best to call it quits. It killed us both. We were each other's firsts. But, we needed to spread our wings and see what the world had to offer. He was off to Gallaudet

University, where I chose Washington University in St. Louis. His roots were firmly planted in the Deaf world, where I straddled the line between the Deaf community and the hearing world—the defining characteristic that overshadowed our relationship from the very beginning. David came from a Deaf family, I came from a hearing family. We respected each other's differences, but in the end, we knew our relationship wouldn't work out. We made better friends than lovers.

I'm happy for David. I will carry him in a special place in my heart forever. But Thor, in a very short time, has touched my heart in a way no man ever has.

Lance makes the sharp turn onto the long drive and takes the limo up the steep incline of my parents' circular drive.

I'm home.

A year. That's a long time to be gone. And I'm not going to lie, I wish another six months had been tacked on. It's going to be a long weekend.

Lance stops the car and turns off the ignition. Five seconds later, he's at my door, pulling it open. Offering me his hand, I put my palm against his and climb out of the limo.

Cold and impersonal, the King mansion stands before me, every window lit up like a beacon in the dark world. It's funny how the little clapboard house Chloe and I rent from her aunt has more character and is far more inviting than Mom and Dad's twenty-five thousand square feet of luxury living. Sometimes bigger isn't always better...at least when it comes to houses.

Climbing the polished white marble stairs leading to the front door, I glance over my shoulder to see Lance following behind, my leopard-print Kate Spade carry-on in his right hand. I love Lance, but Kate Spade leopard print doesn't suit him.

Stepping to my left, he grabs the latch on the front door and pushes it open, waiting for me to enter the foyer. The pristine Brazilian cherry hardwood floors and trim work stand in contrast to the light cream-colored walls. The only splash of color comes from Mom's prized Afshar rug that is proudly displayed to the right of the open foyer, in the sitting room. Not that anyone actually sits in there, because come on, you can't walk on an antique Afshar rug that's made with wool foundations instead of cotton, like the newer oriental rugs. *Everyone knows that.* I can see Mom's reproachful glare in my mind's eye.

In my periphery, a flash of hot pink catches my attention. Twisting in the direction of the pink blur, I'm just in time to intercept a hug from Mom. She crashes into me, squeezing hard. I can't hug her back because my arms are pinned to my side.

In a situation like this, I'm at her mercy. I'm free when she decides to let go. Mom's not much of a hugger, so it shouldn't be too much longer.

Any day now.

She smells like fermented grapes. A red. It has a heavier fragrance than white.

Seriously, why is she still hugging me?

After an unusually long hug, she pulls back and looks me in the eye, smiling. "So glad to see you, sweetheart," she says. "You look beautiful. And looky here"—she touches the side of my nose—"you got a…piercing."

I read her lips effortlessly, just like old times. It makes me miss Thor and the clumsy way he signs. He may not be good at it yet, but at least he tries; that's more than I can say for my parents. Even with all their money, and everything they provided me, they never did give me what I really wanted…parents who communicated in my language.

I take a step back, brushing a light finger over the small, diamond stud in my left nostril. I forgot she hadn't seen it yet.

"Well." She smiles, her shoulders, dropping. "Let's get you settled in upstairs." Mom takes to the staircase, her shapely butt sashaying in a rhythmic side-to-side motion as she ascends. Glancing down at my drab blue hospital scrubs, I sigh and pick up my carry-on, trailing behind her.

She opens the door to my old room. It's been eight years since I officially inhabited this room, and nothing's changed. The walls are still the same latte brown, and the quilt on the antique four-poster bed has the same yellow and orange sunbursts shining in each panel. Mom's all about the antiques. Even the bathrooms have claw-foot tubs with vintage Wolff faucets. It's all in the details, she always says.

Tossing my suitcase on the bed, I turn around. Mom is waving her hands, trying to get my attention.

"Did you catch that?" she says.

"No, Mom, I did not." I sign, not even bothering to move my lips. *Did you understand me?* Still, after all these years, she can't manage to look at me when she talks? A surefire way to piss me off.

"Harper, you know I don't understand you when you only use ASL. I have to be able to read your lips to understand you."

Patting my shoulder, she gives me a half smile. "Why don't you get out of those scrubs and come downstairs. I found this fabulous centerpiece on Pinterest and had to give it a try. Pauline, Sophie, and I have a bottle of wine open, and the glue guns are hot. They'd love to see you, and we could use the help. Come on downstairs."

Biting my tongue, I nod. Pinterest crafts were not on my list of things to do tonight. I'm tired. Yet, sleep remains the best friend I never hear from but wish would call and check in sometime, maybe even stay for a slumber party. A girl can dream...well, *day*dream.

"Good." Mom pats my cheek, sweeping me into another hug.

The minute she's gone, I fall face-first onto the bed, burying my head in a pillow. I want to scream, but I hold it in, opting for deep breaths instead. Pulling in a lungful of air through my nose, the scent of freshly laundered sheets and pillowcases calms me.

Exhale...in...out...

After an hour flight to Chicago, then another two to Manchester, not to mention that I lose an hour coming east, I'm beat. The last thing I want to do is change clothes and hang out with my mother's socialite friends, who are most likely on their second or third bottle of wine.

I wonder what Thor's doing? Sitting up, I grab my purse and pull my phone out. Made it to NH. What are you up to? Pressing send, I set my phone on the mattress and unzip my suitcase. Riffling through folded clothes, I take out a pair of black leggings and a long dark green and blue plaid button down. It's comfy and cute enough to pass Mom's scrutiny. (I knew the scrubs wouldn't. And let's not even talk about my nose piercing.)

My phone flashes with an incoming message. Thor: Glad you made it. Have a great time. Thinking about you.

Me: No way, Mr. Busy Rock Star. Not buying that line for a second. I'm sure you're at some important rehearsal, too busy to be thinking about me.

Thor: You're kind of right and kind of wrong. I am at some important rehearsal, but that birthmark I found on the inside of your thigh this morning, when we were in the shower...haven't been able to get it out of my mind all day. And when you took me in your mouth. I can still feel your lips wrapped around my cock.

Blood pools in my cheeks, remembering how hot that shower was—and it didn't have anything to do with the temperature of the water. I run a hand along the inside of my thigh, wishing it was Thor's.

Me: Two days. I'll be home in two days.

Thor: I'll be extra dirty in two days. A shower will be a must. ;-)

Along with the heat of my blushing cheeks, I press my legs together, mourning the emptiness at my apex. Thor pressing me against the shower wall with his wet body, my legs wrapped around his waist as he filled me so perfectly, has me hoping I remembered to pack Prince O. Not the same by a long shot, but I'm going to need it if Thor keeps sending me text messages like this all weekend.

My phone flashes again. I'm gonna bite that birthmark when you get back. That's a promise.

The lights in my room flash. My eyes flick to the door just in time to see Mom peeking around the corner.

Holy hell! I slide the phone under the pillow and am off the bed in 2.3 seconds, heart thumping wildly. *"You scared the shit out of me!"* I sign fast, mouthing the words. I doubt she understood anything, which is for the best. She hates it when I let expletives fly. I don't know how many times I've been told that swearing isn't ladylike. Naturally, those were all the signs I learned first.

Mom, shoving the rest of the way into my room, says, "What's with you? You're so jumpy?" She raises a perfectly manicured eyebrow. "Are you coming down?

I nod, bringing my hand up, signing, *"Yes."* I hope the exasperated look on my face hides the blush Thor put there. *"I'm coming down."*

"Well, don't dawdle. We could use your help." She winks, closing the door again.

Spinning around, I pull my phone out from under the pillow, another two messages light up the screen: And the things I'm gonna do to you with my tongue. Want me to tell you or let your imagination run wild?

Harper? You okay?

Oh, dear God. My boyfriend is sexting me at the same time my mother is begging me to hang out and make Pinterest crafts.

Sorry. My mom needed me. I have to go help her with something. I pout, hitting send. Picking through my suitcase, I find Prince O, snuggled inside his carrying case. *Oh, thank God. Boy, am I going to need you later.* I pat the case, a sensual ache already growing between my legs, thinking of all wonderful things Thor's tongue is capable of.

Thor: Thought I scared you off.

Me: You don't scare me. We'll continue the dirty talk later. Why don't you get yourself warmed up? You paid close attention to my birthmark while we were in the shower, remember what I paid special attention to? I'll text when family time is over. ;-)

Thor: You've got my attention. I'll be waiting.

Smiling, I lock my phone and toss it onto the bed. Swapping my scrubs for leggings and a long, comfy shirt, I head downstairs. Walking toward the dining room, I peek inside. Mom and her friends, Sophie and Pauline—women I've known my whole life—are sitting around the massive table gesturing wildly, enormous smiles on their face. Three uncorked bottles of wine sit in the midst of wineglasses, fake flowers, ribbon, and tulle. Why bother with the glasses when you can have the whole bottle? There's one for each of them.

Oh, hell no. It's too late for this. You couldn't pay me enough to walk into that room.

Tiptoeing past the dining room, I hold my breath and turn down the hall, toward the kitchen. The closer I get, the more fragrant the hallway becomes. Fresh fruits: strawberries, apples, blueberries, their sweet, earthy scents permeating the air. Whatever Mrs. Rutherford is baking, it smells heavenly.

Like when I had seen Lance at the airport, my heartbeat picks up in anticipation of seeing Mrs. R. I've missed her equally as much, if not more. When I was a kid, if I had a problem, Mrs. R was the one person I'd run to. She always had all the answers. And if she didn't, she'd still offer sound advice.

Strolling into the kitchen like I live here all the time, I walk right up to Mrs. R and tap her shoulder. Whirling around, the plump older woman stares at me with wide eyes. *"Harper!"* She signs, pulling me into a warm hug.

When my mother hugged me earlier, I was held captive in her grip, unable to participate. With Mrs. R I'm able to squeeze her back with the same fervor.

I close my eyes and let Mrs. R's scent wash over me. For my whole life, she's always smelled the same way, like warm buttered croissants, fresh out of the oven. Or homemade pound cake. Years of time spent in the kitchen, her skin and clothes radiate *home*.

Pulling away, I offer her a sunny smile. *"I've missed you, Mrs. R."*

"It's never the same around here when you're gone." Besides Chloe, Mrs. R is the only other person close to me who uses ASL. But, unlike Chloe, who learned ASL so she could communicate with me, Mrs. R was already fluent in the language, having learned years before she took the job with our family, in order to communicate with her mother. I think Mrs. R's ability to sign was one of the reasons my parents hired her in the first place.

"Are you hungry? Peanuts and pretzels on the plane is no dinner. Let me make you something."

At the mention of food, my stomach rumbles. What was the last thing I ate? I don't even remember. *"I don't know if I should. Mom wants me to help her with the centerpieces."*

"Give her another twenty minutes and the wine will kick in. She won't be finishing those centerpieces tonight. You need to eat.

You're too skinny."

I glance down at my C-cup chest and poke my soft tummy, shaking my head in disagreement. With the demands of school, stress eating peanut butter cups has become my new favorite pastime. Those mini ones are the perfect size to tuck into my lab coat's pockets. *"I've actually gained a few pounds since I've been home last. But that's okay. Food and I have a good relationship."* I give her a thumbs-up. *"A sandwich would be amazing. Thank you."*

"You got it." Mrs. R winks and shuffles off to the refrigerator abandoning her tart shells and bowls of fruit. Pulling out several varieties of deli meats, mayo, mustard, tomatoes, lettuce, and cheese slices, she keeps piling the ingredients on her ample chest, using it as a table.

Skirting the island, I jog up next to her, and take jars and containers of meat off her hands, lightening her load.

Both of us spin around, depositing the makings of the world's greatest sandwich on the island's granite countertop. *"Grab the bread."* Mrs. R instructs, pointing to the other side of the kitchen. At least a dozen loaves are stacked on the far end of the counter, in preparation for Dad's party tomorrow, I assume.

I swipe a loaf off the top, not even bothering to see what kind it is, I'm so famished. At this point, I might not even mind a little mold growing on the crust. Plopping the bread next to the jar of mayo, I take a quick look at the edges, just to make sure there is no green fuzz, though. *Yeah, don't think I'm hungry enough to share my sandwich with mold spores. Not wanting to channel my inner Alexander Fleming tonight.*

Twisting the bread tie, I pull out two slices of rye, loving the earthy scent. I reach for the knife sitting beside the bread bag and Mrs. R. slaps my hand away. I look at her, sticking out my bottom lip. *"What was that for?"*

"You, go sit. I'm making this sandwich." She points to the barstools on the other side of the island with the table knife.

I give her my best pouty face. *"Okay, but I was just trying to help."*

"You can help by telling me how you have been. What have you been up to?"

"Oh, goodness. I'm so busy. I feel like I'm always a step behind at the hospital, so I work twice as hard to make up for it. And when I'm not at the hospital, I'm working at the YMCA. I'm in charge of the Deaf Youth After School Program. I'm beat, Mrs. R."

Folding slices of turkey, roast beef, and salami on top of each other, Mrs. R layers sharp cheddar between them—just the way I like it. Topping it off with lettuce, a couple of slices of tomato, and a thick coating of mayo and mustard on the top piece of bread, she puts the cap on and slides the plate across the counter. *"Dig in."*

"This is a work of art." Lifting the sandwich, I bring it to my lips. It's so tall, I can't fit my mouth around it. I smash it down with my fingers, biting off a small corner of the crust, the bitter taste of mustard hitting my tongue first.

I move in for a bigger bite, foregoing any modicum of manners. Mouth full, my eyes roll to the back of my head, savoring Mrs. R's handiwork. Holding the sandwich with my left hand—refusing to give it up—I sign with my right, *"This is amazing. So good."*

"Glad you like it." Mrs. R. busies herself, cleaning up the sandwich mess. Restocking the fridge, she turns around and asks, *"Sounds like you're working hard. Any time for fun? Got yourself a fella?"*

Midbite, a smile creeps to my face.

"Oh, so there is a man." Mrs. R. shimmies her hips, eyebrows wagging.

Chewing, I set the remaining one-fourth of my sandwich on the plate. *"His name's T-H-O-R. He's in a band."*

"A musician." She nods her approval. *"Nice."*

"He's got such a kind heart. You should have seen him play his guitar for the kids at the Y. He was a natural with them." I pick at a corner of cheese poking out from between two pieces of salami, popping it into my mouth. *"And he's so protective of his mother."*

"Any man that's good to his mother is a keeper." She nods, carrying a bowl of raspberries and a cookie sheet of tart shells over to the island, resuming her work.

"Yeah." I agree as I watch her assemble one cute little tart after another. My mind replays bits of last night, when Thor shared his sea-glass story. I pressed him for more, wondering why his relationship with his father had gotten so bad, but he got quiet. Changed the subject. *What happened between you and your dad, Thor?*

Every time he opens up, even just a little, the second I push for more, he shuts me out. I've gathered that his dad wasn't the best, and Thor pretty much hates him. *But why? Why won't you tell me? Why won't you let me in?*

Mrs. R drops another raspberry into the pastry, drizzling

melted white chocolate on the top. I want to steal one, but I know better than to take one of her creations without invitation. Chloe gives me the evil eye when I steal her food but Mrs. R is ruthless. She won't hesitate to smack your hand, and it *will* leave a mark.

"Looks like you've got it bad for this guy." There's that eyebrow waggle again.

Who am I kidding? I really do. *"I think I'm falling for him."* I keep my signs small, hesitant to confide that tidbit of information.

"Oh, Harper!" Mrs. R signs, her smile beaming. *"I know that look."*

I roll my eyes, trying to hide the look Mrs. R is referring to. The one that makes my cheeks burn with heat and heart skip a beat, pinching tight in my chest, and stealing my breath away. The feeling that scares the shit out of me. I've never felt *this* before.

Risking a bruised hand, I pick up on of Mrs. R's tarts and take a bite. I need the distraction. The sharp tang of the berries floods my mouth, along with the sweet, white chocolate drizzle. It's a delicious combination. *"This is fantastic!"*

Mrs. R eyes me, contemplating her next move, a sly smile lifting one side of her mouth. *"Thank you,"* she signs, bring her palm down from her chin.

I pop the rest of the tart into my mouth, savoring the bite. And just when I thought I was safe, Mrs. R smacks the back of my hand, leaving an angry, red outline where her fingers made contact.

"Ouch! That left a mark!"

CHAPTER SIXTEEN

HARPER

Who knew stealing one of Mrs. R's desserts warranted onion duty? I've chopped onions all morning and shed approximately two cups of tears in the process. I'm sure this is some form of cruel and unusual punishment.

Mom hustles through the kitchen, waving and most likely shouting. I've got to hand it to her, she was up before me this morning, and has been working her ass off ever since. She's determined to make sure Dad's party goes off without a hitch. She's even called in the troops: her friends on the New Hampshire Women's Foundation board of directors, the ladies she golfs with at the country club, and anyone who was available to pitch in from the National Society of New England Women. Mom does have loyal friends...well, except for Sophie and Pauline, who were too hungover to put the finishing touches on those centerpieces.

Mom and Mrs. R discuss something while I pick up a pile of onions and drop them in a bowl. Glancing at the microwave clock, I see it's well past three o'clock. Shit! I've got to start getting ready.

Walking over to the sink, I run my hands under the water, working the soap into a good lather. I turn off the water and dry my hands on a paper towel, still reeking of onions. Great. I'm going to be the only one at the party wearing eau de onion.

Twisting the hot water back on, I repeat the process, sudsing up again. Drying, I press the back of my hand to my nose, taking a hesitant sniff. *Ugh!*

Ready to whirl around and give Mrs. R a piece of my mind, she plops a giant, metal serving spoon in my hands.

I glare at Mrs. R's retreating backside, then at my hands. What am I supposed to with a big-ass serving spoon? Does she want me to wash it? Turning the spoon over in my hands the words "stainless steel" are etched into the handle.

Stainless steel. Of course. An image of my interpreter signing a lecture from my first-year undergrad general chem course flickers in the back of my brain.

Onions contain a high level of sulfur molecules, which give them their distinctive odor. Rubbing your hands with stainless steel under running cold water for a minute or two neutralizes the sulfur molecules when they come in contact with the chromium in the steel.

Pouring soap on my hands and the spoon, I rub, making sure the metal comes in contact with every inch of my skin. When my fingers are pink and raw, I drop the spoon, and turn off the water, patting dry. I give them the sniff test.

Chemistry for the win! And Mrs. R.

This time I do whirl around, but instead of giving Mrs. R

a piece of my mind, I give her several *Thank you*s, and plant a kiss on her cheek as I waltz out of the kitchen.

Upstairs, my dress is laid out neatly on the bed. Mom took a shopping trip into Hanover last week and found this amazing royal-blue Shoshanna. One of my mother's best qualities is her giving heart. Gifts, service projects, manning crusade after crusade—from collecting school supplies for underprivileged children, to lobbying politicians for better healthcare for the elderly—my mother loves to give back.

She's always wanted to save the world. Even more so after I got sick. And being married to New England's most sought after neurosurgeon, she had the means to do so.

Mom's not a bad person. Far from it. I just wish she accepted me for who I am, instead of pretending I'm not deaf, or wishing I were hearing. There's nothing wrong with being deaf. I'm proud of who I am. Why can't she be?

Climbing in the shower, I ponder this question, knowing I won't ever find the answer.

* * *

Coming down the stairs, the handkerchief hem skirt of my dress swings at my knees. My parents wait for me at the bottom of the staircase. Dad looks so handsome and distinguished in his tailored Ermenegildo Zegna power suit and striking red tie that matches the dress of the beautiful woman on his arm.

Mom's a knockout in her sleek Ralph Lauren number. Her jet-black hair touches her shoulders, curls softening her look.

In her heels, she's just about the same height as Dad. No one would ever know, not with Dad's full head of silver hair and Mom's well-maintained color, but Mom's actually older than Dad by a year. She doesn't look a day over forty-five, but she's sixty-one! And if anyone asks, she'll deny it until she's blue in the face. But I've seen her birth certificate. I know the truth.

It dawns on me that I'm two years older than Thor. Like mother, like daughter? Going for the younger men?

As I make the last step, Dad raises his arms, shaking his hands in silent applause. Between the two of them, Dad is more likely to bust out a sign—a *"yes"* here or a *"thank you"* there. Nothing too complicated, but he tries.

"Darling, you look breathtaking." Kissing both of my cheeks, he pulls me in for a hug. He smells like mint, as always. Still using the same aftershave he did when I was a kid.

I step out of his embrace and smile. *"Thank you."*

"Glad you're here, Freckles. It means a lot."

Giving him a sidelong glance for the old nickname, I tuck my clutch under my arm and sign, *"Wouldn't have missed it, Daddy. Happy birthday."*

Dad touches his fingertips to his chin, lowering his palm. *"Thank you."* And just like when Thor signs, my heart gives and extra beat. God, I love that!

Offering me one elbow and Mom his other, Dad escorts us from the foyer and into a room that's used for all her epic parties, the great hall.

The room is packed, wall-to-wall people. All here to celebrate the life of Dr. Charles King. Mom waves at a couple near the back of the room, nodding her head for Dad to follow.

Towing me along behind him, we weave in and out of clusters of guests, Dad shaking hands with many of them as he passes by.

Mom stops short, air-kissing a woman I've never met. I glance around. I'd be surprised if I know a handful of people in this room. Nothing like being a stranger in your own home.

Isn't that the way it's always been? my internal pessimist weighs in.

Mom grabs my hand, jerking me close to her side as she speaks to the woman. Both of them carry on their conversation while Dad kisses Mom's cheek, leaving us.

And just like old times, he works the room, Mom chats with friends, and I fade quietly into the background.

As a child, I won the role of the "adorable little girl." I had the Little Orphan Annie thing going for me, with my curly red hair. Mom's friends couldn't help fawning over me. I don't know how many cheek pinchings I endured over the course of my childhood. Too many to count.

As I grew up, the adorableness gave way to a "womanly grace," as Mom called it. When that transformation occurred, the cheek pinching stopped, thank God. But a new kind of attention started. Mom's guests didn't have that "Aww, isn't she adorable!" look on their faces anymore. It was more of an "Oh, I'm so sorry." expression. Like they knew that the adorable little deaf girl had grown into a beautiful deaf woman that would never be able to make anything of herself.

They felt sorry for me.

I know my parents spoke of my academic accomplishments, but that never changed the sad expressions cast in my direction.

And no matter how many of these parties I've attended in my life, my function has never changed: stay quiet, smile, nod, and look pretty. And don't sign. It draws unnecessary attention and no one understands it anyway.

It makes Mom and Dad's life easier if I don't rock the boat. Can't lose my temper. Ever.

"Let people think what they want. Prove them wrong later." Dad's words to live by.

The woman Mom's been chatting with turns her attention toward me. Oh God. Did she say something? To me? I couldn't see her lips. She tries again, this time, opening her mouth wider with each word, overenunciating.

Mom told her I'm deaf.

Happens every time.

When most hearing people find out I can't hear, they do one of three things: speak like they're a star in an iPhone slo-mo video, shout, or a combination of the two.

I want to scream: *News flash! None of those options make lipreading any easier!*

You know who got that without me telling him? Thor. Never once did he alter his speech pattern to "help" me out.

The woman chatters away, turning her head to the right. Left. Down. Up. Side to side. Stuffing her mouth with crab cakes. Sipping wine.

Never once looking directly at me, yet, still speaking to me.

Be polite, Harper. She doesn't know any better.

I nod and smile, putting on the nice act. Don't rock the boat. Lord, I hope I'm not agreeing to some sadistic cult ritual. Staying away from the Kool-Aid tonight.

Crab Cake Woman hugs Mom, then me, and moves off through the crowd, grabbing another hors d'oeuvre for the road.

Without missing a beat, Mom strikes up another conversation, keeping me in tow.

And another.

And another.

Smile and nod, Harper. No signing.

I miss Thor.

I run the fingertips of my right hand over my left palm, twice, giving this woman a pleasant grin. *"Excuse me,"* I sign anyway. I'm twenty-six years old, for goodness sake. Every one who knows my parents, knows I'm deaf. Who cares if I sign?

I touch Mom's shoulder and point across the room, pretending there is someone I must speak to over there. Swiveling her head in the same direction, she stands on her tiptoes and scans the room, a light of recognition dawning on her face, like she knows exactly whom I'm scurrying off to see. It takes every ounce of my self-control to rein in the eye-roll I so desperately want to unleash.

Over the years, I've gotten good at holding things in, and escaping. It's all I can do to get rid of all the…noise.

Snaking through the crowd, I press my fingertips into my temples. A waiter passes by with a tray of full champagne glasses. I snatch one and down the bubbly, hoping it will help my thumping head. So much focus and concentration on people's mouths, trying to decipher words that aren't in my language, I'm exhausted. And my cheeks hurt, not from pinching, but from too much fake smiling.

Tucked safely in the corner, on the opposite side of the room, I welcome the silence. Embrace it, actually. Setting the empty champagne flute on the windowsill, I wrap my arms around my shoulders and turn my back to the stifling crowd. The large picture window in front of me overlooks the west side of the grounds. The bright lights from the party spill into the dark yard below, casting an eerie yellow hue on the lawn. But, in the distance, it's the pool house that catches my eye, dimly lit by the silver moon.

I remember the night Thor took me to the abandoned pool and showed me the place where he goes to think, to write his music. There's a fire in my belly to retreat to the pool house—to be alone in a place that might make me feel closer to the person I want to be with right now.

Keeping along the perimeter of the room, I slip my heels off, carrying them and my purse in the same hand as I dash down the back staircase leading to the kitchen. Thankfully, Mrs. R is busy filling empty serving trays with stuffed mushrooms, crab cakes, fruit tarts, and a dozen other kinds of finger foods. She doesn't even bat an eye as I tiptoe through the kitchen and out the back door.

A harsh, frigid wind whips my hair into my face as it sends fallen leaves skittering over the grass. *Holy crap, it's cold out here!* The chill of the concrete soaks into the bottoms of my feet. Setting my Louis Vuitton heels on the ground, I slip my feet back inside and wrap my arms around my body, hunching over to keep warm.

Freezing, I run across the lawn, toward the pool house. I did not think this through. It won't be much warmer in there, but at least I'll be out of the wind.

Coming to a stop at the front door, teeth chattering, I try the doorknob. Locked. *Come on, Harper, did you really expect it to be open?*

Key? Where did Daddy hide the key?

Searching the landscaping for the hide-a-key, childhood memories flood my thoughts. As a kid, I'd come out here and watch my dad swim in his small lap pool, the kind where the swimmer has to swim against a current. That pool always fascinated me. He would swim and swim, and never go anywhere, just stayed in the same place.

I always enjoyed swimming…in the pool outside. The one that allowed me to move. I never understood the appeal of swimming against a current; feeling like you can't ever break free.

A small chuckle escapes my lips. Battling a current that you can't break free of. Sounds a lot like my life. I've endured an uphill battle with just about everything—my parents, school, romantic involvements (with the exception of Thor), my future career. Nothing has been easy.

Tilting a flowerpot, I peer underneath. Sure enough, there's a small compartment in the bottom. Working the latch open, the lid swings free, and the key falls to the ground. Scooping it up, I set the flowerpot down, and fit the key into the lock.

Pushing open the glass door, I'm hit with a wall of hot chlorine-scented air. *Ohhhh!* I welcome the unexpected warmth. Stepping inside, I shut the door quickly, sealing off the blasting wind. Shivering, I walk around stacked chairs and a few tables pushed together—Mom's outside pool accessories brought inside for the winter.

Plumes of steam rise off the surface of the gently swirling water in the lap pool. Dragging a chaise lounge closer to the pool's edge to soak up its heat, I plop down and stretch out. Crossing my ankles, I lay my head back, and close my eyes.

Deep breaths. I pull in lungfuls of chlorine-rich oxygen, feeling my body relax. It's not Thor's pool, but it's peaceful nonetheless.

Minutes drift by. The tension in my shoulders and head subside, and my mind wanders to Thor. What's he doing right now?

Lifting my head, I flip open my purse and pull out my phone. Me: Thank you for wanting to learn ASL. He doesn't know it, but it means so much to me. If there's anything this weekend has taught me, or reminded me, it's how much I yearn to be able to communicate with my loved ones. How much I've always wanted that. The fact that Thor wants to learn, it's everything.

My phone flashes, lighting up the dark pool house like a bolt of lightning. Thor: For you, Red. Anything. I want every part of you.

Tears sting my eyes. My own parents never wanted that part of me. Me: I miss you. What are you doing? My heart hurts with how much I miss him. My heart feels like a lead cannonball lodged in my chest; something I've never experienced before, not even when I left David and moved to St. Louis.

Thor: Miss you too, babe. At work. I'm sitting in the break room putting away some Taco Bell. How's it going there?

My stomach growls at the mention of Taco Bell. I love Mrs. R's food, but some greasy tacos would go down easy right about now. I slide my fingers over the keyboard. Oh, Taco Bell. That's sounds divine. Things are going. Mom and Dad mean well, but the language barrier has always been a gigantic hurdle we've never been able to get over. My brain physically hurts from trying to be a part of the conversations at Dad's party.

Thor: Taco Bell. Got it. Filing that away for later. ;-) Hopefully, I don't make your brain hurt.

Smiling, I type back. Never! You hear me just fine. :-)

Out of the corner of my eye, I see something waving in the dark, and then the lights come on. Turning my head, I see Dad making his way around a stack of tables. He grabs a chair and drags it over to mine, plopping down. "Hey, Freckles. Everything okay? I noticed you disappeared."

I squint against the light, trying to focus on his moving mouth. The tentacles of my headache return, creeping up the back side of my skull.

My cell phone lights up with an incoming text. Holding up my index finger to Dad, I glance down at Thor's message, careful to angle the phone away so he can't see.

Thor: Loud and clear. And when you get back, I'll show you just how much I hear. ;-)

Me: Can't wait! I've got to go, my dad's here. See you soon!

Shoving my phone back in my purse, I give Dad my undivided attention; after all, he did notice I wasn't at the party. That's got to count for something, right?

I sit up and kick my legs over the side of the pool chair, facing him. It's easier to "chat" if we're facing each other. *"What's up, Daddy?"* I sign, mouthing the words for his benefit.

"Haven't seen my favorite girl in a year. Wondered where you disappeared to."

Sighing, I sit up, grabbing my purse. I love my dad. The last thing I want to do is disappoint him on his birthday. Opening my purse, I dig my phone back out. I want to be sure he understands why I needed a break from the party. Too many people inside. Sorry I bailed. I flip it around so he can see.

Lifting the phone from my fingers, he types a response. Sorry. Your mom goes a little overboard with these things. I don't need to tell you how she gets. To be honest, I would have preferred a quiet dinner with my two favorite women. But, I learned a long time ago, your mother does not take no for an answer.

Reading his words, silent laughter shakes my shoulders. Dad's so much like me. Quality time over quantity always wins out. What's the point of sharing your time with a couple hundred people if they only get a handful of minutes with you? I prefer spending my time with one or two people and giving them all my time. Time is so precious anyway, why sever it into so many inconsequential little bits?

Since I have my dad's ear and it's been on my mind so much—with Thor and everything, it's time I asked the question I should have asked so long ago. Why didn't you ever learn ASL?

Handing the phone to him, I watch his eyes move over my short sentence. The jovial, lighthearted expression he usually wears falls, sadness making the wrinkles at the sides of his eyes more pronounced.

He shrugs, passing the phone to me. For several minutes, he's quiet, refusing to meet my eye. I rest my palm on his knee and he looks up. I can see his sixty years, now. My dad has always been handsome, he still is. But, he's carried the lives of all his patients on his shoulders for so long, the gravity is wearing on him. Neurosurgery is one of the hardest surgical subspecialties to get into, and the fact that my dad is still practicing, albeit, on a case-by-case basis, it says a lot about his character, how much he cares.

"I love you, Daddy," I sign. He knows this one.

"Love you, too, Freckles," He signs back and my heart threatens to explode. "I'm sorry, Harper." He doesn't sign this time. I'm forced to read his lips. "Can I tell you a story?" he asks, scooting closer to the end of his chair.

I nod.

"Good." He pats my knee and smiles. "When you got sick…lost your hearing. I couldn't fix you. With all my knowledge and skill, I couldn't put my own daughter back together." Pressing a fist to his mouth, his shoulders rise as he takes a breath. He turns his head away from me, but signs, *"Sorry."*

Nice, Harper. You've made him cry on his birthday. Daughter of the year award coming your way.

I pat his leg, trying to console him, not knowing what else to do. Turning his attention back to me, he moves his fist in a circular pattern over his chest again. *"Sorry."*

Unlocking my phone, I type quickly and turn it around so he can see the screen. I'm sorry. You don't have to do this. I didn't mean to upset you, especially on your birthday.

He waves away my apology and pats my leg again. "You

didn't. I can't recall a time when you've ever upset me. I've been upset with myself for the last twenty-four years. I performed countless surgeries, restored so many patients to health, but I couldn't save my own daughter's hearing."

I type. My fingers move over the keyboard, the words in my brain moving faster than I can get my hands to work. So many thoughts and emotions are bottled up inside me. I hate that he thinks I'm damaged, someone that needs put back together. Shaking my head I flip the phone around so he can see what I wrote. I'm not broken, Daddy. Being deaf isn't some illness that needs to be treated. It was never your job to "fix" me. I don't need to be "fixed." All I've ever wanted is for you and Mom to accept me the way I am, for the both of you to want to be in my world. But, you've never wanted that. I'm your greatest disappointment, the one medical case that bested you. You distanced yourself from me, and all things "deaf" because that would mean having to concede, accept defeat.

Swiping a tear off my cheek, I know I shouldn't have unleashed all my anger in that message. But, dammit, I'm so sick and tired of the charade my parents put on when I'm around them, the stupid avoidance dance we've perfected over the years—*Sure, Harper's deaf, but if we get her every gadget imaginable, we can pretend she's as normal as all the other children.*

If there's one thing I've learned since Thor came into my life, the language barrier isn't an obstacle that can't be scaled. Yeah, it's hard, but not impossible. The only difference between my parents and Thor? He doesn't want there to be a wall between us...my parents like the wall, it protects them from their own guilt.

Tears pool in my eyes and a lump sticks in my throat, but I

choke it back. My parents aren't the only ones who are safe on their side of the barrier.

"Harper." Daddy signs my name and a tear slips down my cheek. The dam is crumbling.

"What?" Twisting my head away, I suck my bottom lip into my mouth and bite down, hard. Holding my breath, I let the wave of emotion pummel me, but I refuse to give in. I. Will. Not. Cry.

Daddy's warm hand rests against my knee, patting gently. It's when I feel his other hand touch my upper arm that I know he's trying to get my attention. Steeling myself, I face him. Tears are running down his face. He's not even trying to hide them, or wipe them away.

"I know you're not broken, Harper. I've let my own inadequacies come between us. If I'm being honest, I never learned ASL because I'm afraid."

Tugging my eyebrows low, I shake my head, confused. Afraid? Why would learning my language scare him?

"In my mind, if I gave in and learned ASL, I'd be giving up. I've always held out hope that you would hear again." His shoulders shake and he buries his head in his hands.

Some of my own tears breach the dam and roll down my cheeks. I've never seen my dad so upset.

I scoot to the edge of my seat and put a hand on his shoulder, running it toward his back in slow circles. All these years, I thought I was the disappointment—that signing somehow embarrassed him—and that's why he never learned.

He looks up, his eyes red and glassy, he points to my lap. My phone.

Unlocking it, I pass it to him. "I want to be sure you get every word of what I need to tell you. You need to know this." Looking down, he types.

As his agile fingers—surgeon's hands—move over the screen at the same time I see Mom walking up behind him, her face pinched in exasperation. Uh-oh, we're busted.

Dad tosses a quick glance over his shoulder, but returns to the message he's typing.

Mom stands at the end of Dad's chair, hands on her hips. "I saw the light on down here. What are you two doing? We have a houseful of guests." Her hand flies off her hip, gesturing in the direction of the house.

"Too much lipreading. I needed a break." Dad presses the phone into my hands the moment I finish signing. He stands, pulling Mom's hands into his, calming her, putting out the fire our absence caused.

While they talk, I read the message. I'm so proud of you. Against everyone's loud advice, telling you pharmacy was a career choice that would be too far out of your reach, you didn't listen. You did your own thing, looked every challenge in the eye, and shoved them out of your damn way. You're stronger than I've ever been. Don't think for one minute that you've ever been a disappointment or an embarrassment. I got so caught up in mourning the loss of your hearing that I stopped hearing you. I'm so sorry, Harper. All I can do is beg your forgiveness and hope to do better. I love you. You are my greatest accomplishment in the sixty years I've been given. Don't ever forget that.

Dropping the phone on the chair, I stand and throw my

arms around his waist. Eyes closed, I block out anything that can detract from this moment. I've never questioned my parents' love for me, but knowing I'm not an embarrassment, or disappoint in my dad's eyes is beyond amazing. I've lived with that notion for so long, sometimes I think it's held me back, like I'd been swimming against an unrelenting current and not gone anywhere.

His words just turned off the current. I'm in a calm pool and I can go wherever I choose.

Dad brings his arm up, wrapping it around my shoulder. Looking up, I open my eyes and see him smiling down at me. Mom's circled in his other arm, smiling at me, too. Did he tell her what we've been talking about?

"I'm proud of you, too, Harper," Mom says, pinching my chin between her thumb and forefinger.

Yep. He must have.

"But can we continue this heart-to-heart later, we do have a houseful of people here to see your dad. You can't keep him all to yourself." She winks and Daddy gives me a conspiratorial smile that leads me to think he disagrees.

"*Sure.*" I sign with a nod. Daddy squeezes me tighter and leads Mom and me to the door. I know things with my parents aren't going to change overnight, but at least this is a step in the right direction, all of us together.

CHAPTER SEVENTEEN

THOR

Stuffing my phone back in my pocket, I ball up the Taco Bell wrapper and shoot it into the trashcan clear across the break room, sinking the shot. *Nothing but can!* Slipping a Camel between my lips, I give the lighter a stroke and bring the flame to the end of the cigarette. A few puffs and I can already feel the nicotine seeping into my veins. I close my eyes, savoring my smoke and thinking about how I'm going to welcome Harper home tomorrow night. Taco Bell and an invitation into my bed. My dick twitches just thinking about her. Damn, I miss her. Never thought I'd be the kind of guy to miss a chick, but Harper is one of a fucking kind.

"Boss ain't gonna like you lightin' up in here," Doug says, crunching into his seventh taco and killing my nicotine buzz.

Opening my eyes, I take a long pull. "He won't know unless someone opens their fucking mouth." I blow a cloud of smoke in his direction. Leaning back in the chair, I rest the heels of my steel-toed boots on the table. "With any damn luck, I won't need this job once the music gig starts to pay off." Don't get me wrong, I love working on cars, but if I have to change the oil in one more crossover SUV for some soccer mom that doesn't know the difference between a windshield wiper and a dipstick, I'm going to lose my shit.

Reason number 111 why Harper is the perfect chick: I can talk cars with her and she understands, and is genuinely interested. Who would have thought a rich girl from New Hampshire would share my love of automobiles? Unreal. She's always full of fucking surprises.

Chewing, Doug continues the small talk. "You still in that band?"

I take a long drag, nodding. "Contract signed. We hit the recording studio on Monday."

"Cool. I can say I knew you before you were famous." Draining the last of his Pepsi, Doug lets out a huge belch and stands, rubbing prominent beer gut. "We better get back out there. Wouldn't want Wyatt to come looking for us. Then you're busted."

"Shit." I kick my feet to the floor and sit up, glancing at the clock—8:32. Two minutes over our break time. "That thirty minutes went by too fucking fast." With one last pull on my cigarette, I drop it on the floor and ground my boot against it. Picking up the butt, I toss it into the trashcan on my way back out to the floor.

"Thor, I've got a CR-V in bay two. Standard oil changed," Wyatt shouts from the computer at bay one.

"On it." Walking over, the driver, a beautiful blond woman, lowers her window.

"What brings you in today?" I ask, turning on the charm. It's a well-proven fact that charm can lead to more services rendered than just an oil change. And in years past, it could have led to something beyond the One Stop Lube Shop's premises. Ladies can't resist a man in navy-blue coveralls popping their hood. But these days, I'm keeping my skills strictly vehicle related; Harper gets the off-premises services.

"I just need an oil change, thanks." She flashes me a wide smile and snaps her gum.

"Mom! Mason took my iPad! Tell him to give it back!" A shriek rises from the backseat.

The woman whirls around. "Mason! Give your sister her iPad. It's not her fault that you didn't charge yours. Behave yourself! We're in public!"

Turning her attention back to me, she flashes an even wider smile. I know this smile. *I'm so mortified. Please excuse my children's behavior, or better yet, let's pretend it never happened. Please.*

My mother has worn this smile before, albeit, for different reasons. *I'm so mortified. Please excuse my husband's behavior. You didn't just hear him threaten to hit me, or better yet, let's pretend it never happened. Please.*

"I'll get you taken care of. Go ahead and shut off the engine, put your keys on the dash, and pop the hood."

The engine dies and the hood shutters with a loud *pop*. I scan the vehicles VIN number and pull up the diagnostics on the computer.

"Yo, Thor," Doug hollers from the office. "You got a phone call." He's got the office cordless in his hand, waving it out the door. "Whoever she is, she sounds pretty upset."

She? Upset? It can't be Harper, she'd text me.

Mom.

I abandon my post at bay two, hustling toward the office. Seizing the phone from Doug's grip, I shout breathlessly, "Ma?"

"I just got home from the grocery store and he was here. I'm scared, Thor."

"You fucking bitch!" I hear Dad's slurred growl muffled in the background.

Running a hand over my head, I pace the office. I am utterly fucking helpless here. Looking out the window, I see Doug under the CR-V hood, taking over where I left off. "Where are you? Are you in the car? Get the hell out of there, Ma!"

All I hear is sobbing on the other end.

And glass shattering.

Fucking shit!

"Raymond, no!" Mom shouts, still crying.

"I'm coming, Mom." I press end on the call and put the phone back on the charger, racing out of the office. I've got to get to her. "Wyatt. Doug," I yell. "I've gotta go. My mom's in trouble." Without waiting for a response or an all clear to leave, I run to my car, digging my keys from the pocket of my coveralls. Wyatt can fire my ass for all I'm concerned. I've got to get to my mom.

Driving like a bat out of hell, I speed down the highway, hoping no cops get in my way right now. Although, if one tailed me, it might not be a bad thing, I could lead him to my mom's place. In my other pocket, I yank out my cell phone, fumbling to unlock it. Hitting Mom's name in my contacts list,

I slip the phone between my shoulder and ear, listening to it ring over and over again.

No fucking answer.

I tear it away from my ear and throw it onto the passenger seat, pounding out my frustration on the steering wheel. "Fuu-uuuuuck!"

Fifteen minutes later, I skid over the gravel, and pull up alongside her empty car. I'm not quite sure if I'm going to find my mother's lifeless body in the parking lot of her apartment building. A cop car sits on the other side, blue and red lights flashing.

My stomach drops, sending bile rising in my throat.

Killing the engine, I step out of the car. The second my feet hit the ground, glass crunches under my boots. I survey the scene. Mom's window is busted out and Dad's truck is parked a few spaces down, but no sign of either of them.

"Sir?" A deep voice calls from behind me. Whirling around, a cop approaches. "Are you a resident in this complex?"

I shake my head. So many words pile up in my brain, but I can't get them to come out of my mouth. What did that fucker do?

"I'm sorry, sir, but if you're not a resident, I'm going to have to ask you to leave."

"My mom." I point to her car. "That's her car."

"Your Linda Kline's son?" the cop asks.

I nod. "Where is she? Is she okay?"

"Can I get your name, sir?"

Ignoring the police officer, I bend down to peer into the broken driver's side window of Mom's Corolla. There's blood and tufts of blond hair on the jagged pieces of glass still left in the frame. I round on the cop, needing some fucking answers. And if I don't get them, I'm going to fucking lose it. "What happened?" I'm trying my damnedest to be respectful, but his lack of useful information is quickly becoming a thorn in my side.

"I need your name and identification, sir. I cannot disclose any information until I can confirm your identity."

Fucking red-tape bullshit. "Thorin Kline." Sticking a hand in my pocket, I pull out my wallet, yanking my driver's license free. I hand it to Officer Protocol. "My mother, Linda Kline moved into this complex about nine months ago. That's her car. I need to know if she's all right."

The officer eyes my driver's license, then me. My hair was longer in the picture, but other than that, my features haven't changed much. With a nod, he hands back my ID. "A neighbor called when they heard shouting and glass breaking. According to the woman who phoned in the disturbance, an older man busted out Mrs. Kline's window and attempted to drag her through it. When we arrived on the scene, the perp had already fled."

"Is she okay? I need to see her. Where is she?" Turning in circles my brain races over all the places she could be.

"Your mom's fine. She had some superficial cuts to her face and neck, and she was pretty shaken up. The paramedics took her to the hospital for observation."

Fuck me. This is bad. "Shit!" Shoving my license back into my wallet, I drop it in my pocket, and jog back to my car. I've got to get to the hospital. But, before I climb behind the wheel, I point down the row of cars. "That's his truck. The beat-up Chevy."

"Wait, you know the man who did this?" Pulling his eyebrow low, an air of suspicion clouds his features.

"Raymond Kline, my dad." I slam the door shut and start the engine, not bothering to give the cop any other information. His name is enough. *Find the bastard before I do. I won't show him any mercy.*

* * *

The bleached, fluorescent lights of the emergency room sting my eyes. Squinting against the brightness, I run over to the nurses' desk, heart in my throat. "Was a woman brought in? Cuts and scrapes, maybe in shock?"

"I need her name, sweetie," the nurse says, lifting her warm, dark eyes off the computer screen to look at me. She has a comforting smile, too. She gets an A-plus for bedside manner, but I'm so keyed up right now, nothing can calm me down. I just want to find my mom.

"Linda Kline. She was brought in about ten or fifteen minutes ago."

The nurse taps on her keyboard while I beat out an impatient rhythm on the counter. "A Linda Kline was brought in at 9:05." She stares up at me, delivering the information.

"Can I see her?" My patience is wearing thin. I don't want to go off on this nice lady, but if I don't get back there, I will.

"I can only allow family in the exam rooms." Still smiling sweetly, she blinks.

I want to plant my fist through the fucking wall, but it's hard to be angry with this woman. She's just so nice. I rein in my anger. It's not her I'm pissed at. I'll have enough time to hunt down the fucking animal that did this to my mom, later. I have to make sure she's all right, first. "I'm her son, Thorin Kline."

"Wonderful. She's in exam room four. Go down the hall, make the first right, her room will be the fourth on the right."

I smack the counter, and for the first time in the last forty-five minutes, a smile blooms across my face. Fucking answers, finally. "Thanks."

Running down the hall, my boots clomp on the polished tile. I skid to a halt in front of her room, hesitant to go in. A fireball of anger and fear roils in my stomach. Knocking, I push open the door.

Inside, Mom is lying on the small bed, her eyes closed. "Mom?" I whisper. The last thing I want to do is frighten her.

Her eyes flutter open. It's now that I get a good look at the aftermath of hurricane Raymond. Her cheeks are covered with scrapes, extending down her jaw, and onto her neck. Patches of dried blood run along her hairline, and a faint purple shadow is visible over her left eye.

Pulling the chair over to her bed, I sit, fitting my hand beneath hers. "I'm here, Ma."

Guilt, hatred, fury, outrage, weakness, sorrow, all of them slash at my insides like the claws of a raptor, ripping me to shreds. I was too fucking late. He got to her. I couldn't protect her.

"Thor," she croaks, her voice heavy. "I'm sorry, baby."

"You have *nothing* to be sorry about," I growl, hating that she thinks this is her fault. She always does this, takes all the blame. Covers for him. "What happened?" No one's been able to give me a straight answer.

"I got home from the store and was unloading the groceries. He came up behind me. I dropped everything—the groceries, my purse, keys. I got away and ran back to my car. Locked myself inside. Luckily, I had my cell phone shoved in my back pocket. That's when I called you. When you didn't answer your cell, I called the shop."

"I'm here now. Sorry I didn't get there sooner." I brush my hand over her matted blond hair, careful to avoid the cuts at her hairline. "You gotta call the cops in situations like that, Ma. When you can't get ahold of me, or I'm too far away."

"I know. I just panicked. When he busted out my window, I didn't know what to do. He punched me, grabbed handfuls of my hair..." She pauses for a second, breathing heavily. "Then he tried to pull me through the broken window. That's when the cops got there." She touches the cuts on her jaw, eyes glisten with unshed tears. "The jagged pieces in the frame cut me pretty bad. Doc says I'm going to need stiches for some of them."

"They'll get you put back together." It's all I can say. "Just rest. I'm gonna go talk to the doctor. I'll be right back." I pat her hand and bend down, placing a kiss on her forehead.

My hand poised on the door handle, Mom says, "Thor, my purse. I dropped it at my door. If he gets it..." her voice trails off at the thought of Dad getting his hands on the contents of her purse. Her life. Money, credit cards, license, keys. Everything.

"Don't worry, Ma. I'll find it." And so help me God, if he has her things, I will end him. Even if it means spending the rest of my life in prison for manslaughter, I will get her purse back. That piece of shit doesn't deserve to draw another fucking breath.

"And Thor"—she stares at me, one eye swollen shut—"promise me you won't go looking for him. I don't want you hurt or in trouble."

I hold my breath. Goddammit. She knew exactly what I had planned. Track the son of a bitch down and mess him the fuck up.

"Promise me, Thor." Her shout is strangled.

"Yeah," I growl, throwing open the door, anger burning up my insides.

CHAPTER EIGHTEEN

THOR

Harper: Just landed. It's nice to be home.

Thor: Come over. I need to see you.

Harper: On my way!

I lay my phone on the table beside my bed and plant my feet on the floor. Standing, I stretch, the sore muscles in my back scream in protest, and the knuckles on my hands have seen better days, but other than that, I'm no worse for the wear. Can't say much for the speed bag I beat the shit out of this morning. Had to work out my aggression somehow. The cops recovered Mom's purse with everything accounted for, but they still haven't found Dad. They put a warrant out for his arrest and had his truck impounded. He can't hide for long, especially since he has no ride. A small bit of karma coming to bite him in the ass, but not nearly enough in my opinion.

But, most of all, I'm just glad Mom's all right. A night in the hospital for observations and she's back home, safe. After spending the better part of my day over at her place, installing a security system, the both of us will sleep easier, knowing he won't be able to get to her without the whole fucking neighborhood hearing. And all the residents of hell; that system will wake the dead.

Slipping on some jogging pants, I pick up the other clothes strewn across the floor. Don't want Harper to think I'm a total slob, but in my defense, I've had a lot of shit to deal with in the last twenty-four hours.

Damn, it's gonna feel nice pulling her in my arms. I can almost smell the flowery shampoo she uses. I wish I knew more about flowers, so I could figure out which one it smells like.

Tossing my dirty laundry in my closet, I slide the door closed. Out of sight, out of mind. I make quick work of stripping the bed, depositing my dirty sheets in the hamper in the bathroom. Pulling out clean sheets from the linen closet, I slip them over the mattress while visions of Harper spread out on top pop into my head. The only thing better is when my imagination has me climbing on top of *her*. Going to give her a proper "welcome home," then I'll take her out to Taco Bell, as promised.

With my bed made, and no other domestic jobs that need attention, I pull *Signing for Dummies* off my nightstand and flip to a dog-eared page. As a surprise for her, I want to sign a whole phrase. Needless to say, I didn't get much studying in last night, so I've got to cram now.

"I missed you." I practice it, touching my index finger to my chin and then point at my reflection in the mirror across the room. It's an easy enough sign. I can remember this.

"Glad you're home." I move my open palm up and down in front of my chest, point to my reflection again, and then sign

"home" pinching my fingertips together, touching my cheek and moving my hand toward my ear.

I repeat the two phrases over and over again, perfecting my fluidity. I love the way her face lights up when she watches me sign. I crave that light more than fucking cigarettes.

Running through the phrases, I tack a third one on at the end, a little dirty talk. Watching that playful light in her eyes morph into something sexy will be well worth the time I spent scouring YouTube and Vine videos on dirty sign language.

When I think I've got the hand movements down, I toss the book aside and grab my phone off the nightstand. Typing out a quick message, I hit send. Checking in. You okay?

I wait for a response, hoping she has her phone nearby. Downstairs, there's a knock at my door.

Harper's here.

Like a giddy preteen boy with his first girlfriend, my heartbeat ratchets up a notch and a goofy smile spreads across my face. I feel like I'm eleven and a girl just said hello to me. I'm a bumbling idiot.

Still no message from Mom.

Dropping the phone on the bed, I head downstairs, fucking glad that I've got the place to myself tonight.

There's another knock, more forceful this time. Banging. Maybe it isn't Harper. The cops? Did they find him?

Picking up the pace, I get to the front door and tear it open. Harper's standing on my porch, her arm raised in a fist, ready to pound again.

Her wild, red curls stick out in every direction, the perfect accompaniment to the mischief dancing in her eyes. Despite the jacket and scarf she has on, my eyes roam over her body, remembering how every curve fits against me. I fucking missed the shit out of her.

Lowering her hand, she circles her fist over her chest. *"Sorry."* Sucking her bottom lip into her mouth, I want nothing more than to kiss that sheepish grin off her face.

Grabbing the end of her scarf, I give it a swift yank, drawing her to me. My arms are around her waist, hands sliding toward her ass, as my lips find hers.

I don't hold back. I bend my head and kiss her deeply. It's been too fucking long. I need her. With everything that's happened with my mom, I need to get lost in her. Have her take away my pain, remind me what's good in life.

Harper returns my fervor with the same urgency, running her hands over my shoulders and down my shirtless back.

Kneading her ass, I pull her against my erection, letting her know how much I missed her. Feeling her tongue lapping against mine, I'm not even sure I'm going to make it upstairs to the bed. I want to bury myself inside of her right here, against the fucking door.

I take a step backward and let go of her waist to kick the door shut. I walk us forward until her back crashes into the door, and I slam into her. She gives a soundless gasp, and sucks my tongue into her mouth. I lengthen my body, pressing all of my hard edges against her soft peaks and valleys.

Tearing at the scarf around her neck, I unknot it and yank it off. Kissing the corner of her mouth, I work my way over her jaw, and to the hollow at the base of her ear, getting in a good nip of her lobe while I'm at it.

She smells fantastic. Flowers everywhere. Her scent blooms around me. I'm going to find out what kind of flower this is and buy bouquets by the dozens.

"Fuck, Harper," I moan, pulling her shirt down so I can taste the dip between her collarbones. She lifts her chest, her tits brushing against my chin. I didn't think it was possible to get any harder, but I just did. My hips move against her, dick aching, ready to fuck. "I forgot how good you feel," I say, my hands roaming beneath her shirt.

I run my hands up her ribcage, moving north, filling my palms with her heavy tits. Through the lacy fabric of her bra, I rub circles over her nipples with my thumb, sealing my mouth over hers. Drawing her nipples into hard pebbles, her breath picks up, and I've got her panting, wanting more.

She fits her hands into the waistband of my jogging pants and keeps going, slipping them beyond the boundary of my boxer briefs. While our tongues dance, her hands smooth over my backside, journeying to the front. *Dear God, yes.* "That's it, baby, keep going."

The second her fingers graze the sides of my dick, my balls tighten and pull up, begging for more attention. She's got me so keyed up. My speed bag workout this morning may have helped release a lot of my pent-up rage, but this fucking promises to set my world back on its axis. Make things right again.

She wraps one hand around my dick and cups my balls with the other. I'm fucking dead. I wrench my hands from her shirt, slamming them against the door, pressing my forehead to hers, my eyes slide closed, absorbing every sensation.

She pumps me. And I want to come right here and now.

But, I put a heavy hand on my crotch, silently telling her to stop. As much as I want to take her against this door, I refuse to fuck Harper like I would have any of the faceless girls in my past. I want inside her head and heart, first. To find out how her weekend was, how things with her parents went, what's her favorite place in New Hampshire, how many peanut butter cups she indulged in, and steal a kiss or two when she least expects it, because those are the best fucking kind. The sweetest.

Harper, still gripping me, doesn't move. Her eyes, like green lasers, try to get a read on the situation, scan my face for an answer as to why I stopped her. Lowering my left arm, I grip her right elbow and give it a gentle, upward tug. *Please let go, Red. Two more seconds of you holding my cock and all my resolve will be shot to fucking hell.* My dick throbs in her hand, loathing my brain with a passion.

"Not like this." I shake my head, and pull up on her arm again.

She lets go, taking her hand out of my pants. I'm in for a serious case of blue balls. *Fuck.*

"What's wrong?" She signs, worry clouding her features. *"You okay?"*

"Perfect. Now that you're back."

She scrutinizes me, her eyes becoming slits. Taking her hand, I lead her to the couch, determined to give this gentlemanly thing a fucking chance. The raging hard-on in my pants has other notions, involving her pinned beneath me on said couch. Honestly, how serious of a conversation can we have if my dick is pitching a tent between us?

I plop onto the black leather, pulling Harper down beside me. She's still wary. I can see it on her face. Twisting around, she rummages through her purse, withdrawing her phone. Unlocking it, she types. When she finishes, she turns it around, shoving it in my face. Thor, what's going on? Why are you acting so weird?

Lifting it from her fingers, I add my response below her questions. Working my thumbs over the tiny keys, I feel Harper's fingertips graze over the backs of my hands, across the scabbed over cuts on my knuckles from the speed bag.

With a little shove of my arm, she forces me to meet her eye. *"What happened?"* Furrowing her brow and shaking her head, she waits for an answer.

What can I say? I want every detail of her weekend, the mundane, the exciting, anything that she'll give me. I want *all* of her. Yet, I can't do the same. I can't tell her what happened yesterday, what my dad did to my mom. There's not much I fear in this world, but to have Harper look at me like I'm trash, because the man who fathered me is trash. That's the worst nightmare I can think of.

I hold it in. She can't know about my dad…about the other half that made me. If she did, she'd head for the door and never look back. I finish typing and hand the phone back.

Not weird. Just missed you. Wanted to know how your weekend went. Hands are fine, babe. Did a little boxing workout this morning, speed bag tore me up.

Not exactly a lie.

She lays the phone on the coffee table and cups my hands in hers. Bending down, she kisses the backs of my hands; her lips pressing gently over each cut, scrape, and busted knuckle. What did I do to deserve this woman?

Pulling back, she yanks her phone off the table, types, and turns it around. My weekend was actually pretty great. I did not expect it. Had a heart-to-heart with my dad, worked some things out. It was nice to understand him, and for him to understand me for once. Mom is going to take a little more work, but things are good. Besides work and sending me dirty text messages, what did you do?

Me: That's awesome, Red. Glad to hear it. Trust me, you just nailed the highlights of my weekend. Oh, with the exception of one thing...

When I finish typing, I hand the phone back to her, waiting for the quizzical look I know she's going to hit me with.

And there it is. The head tilt, half smile, squinty eyes. *"What?"*

Holding up a finger, I straighten my back and clear my throat, shaking out my hands. I swipe my open hand, fingers together, in an upward motion on my chest. Continuing the phrase, I point to her and then pinch my fingers together at the corner of my mouth, moving them up and inch or two toward my ear. *"Glad you're home."*

Her smile brightens. No. It fucking glows. Raising her hands, she shakes them. Pushing her palms outward, twice, she signs, *"Wonderful!"*

I read the word on her lips, but the sign makes sense. The more she uses them in front of me, the more I understand. I do think another ASL-guitar lesson is in order. I need to know more. I love talking to her in her language...seeing how happy it makes her.

"Wait," I say, wishing I knew the sign. Holding up my index finger again, I sign, *"More."* and *"I miss you."*

"T-H-O-R!" Scooping the phone off her lap, she types, and passes it over when she's finished. You have no idea how much I love it when you sign! It's like a shot of adrenaline right to my heart! You learned those phrases this weekend?

Oh, I just might have an inkling about how much you love it, Red. I feel it in my chest, too.

I nod. *"Yes."*

"Thank you." She leans in and kisses me quick before pulling away. Sitting back, she taps out another message. How did practice go? You guys ready for tomorrow? How's your mom?

We're ready. Tomorrow will be kick ass. Mom's fine. I hesitate to turn the phone around. Again, another half-truth. Yes, technically, Mom is fine. But, really, she isn't. It's not fine when your estranged husband beats the shit out of you.

I hate lying to her. But, if I'm going to keep her around, it's what has to be done. She doesn't need to know about my father. Period. End of story.

I drop the phone in her hands, hating my lie, but knowing it's the lesser of two evils. Keeping Harper as far away from my fucked-up family is the safest thing I can do for her.

Harper: When do I get to meet your mother? You speak so highly of her, I want to meet the woman that raised such a great guy. ;-)

Stitches, a scabbed-over scalp where he pulled out tufts of her hair, a bruised and swollen eye, scrapes, and a broken soul. This is not the mom Harper needs to meet. She's getting over a cold. Not a good time. Another lie. I fucking hate myself.

Harper: When she's better then.

Handing the phone back to me, I read her words and nod. I don't know if it's my guilty conscience, or if she knows I'm hiding something, whatever it is, a shadow passes over her face, dimming the light in her eyes.

She runs her fingers over my busted knuckles, her eyes like X-rays, seeing right through me. Harper's superpower. She knows I'm full of shit.

And she's still here, Thor. Tell her what happened.

That little voice in my brain loves to play head games. One minute it's, *Tell the truth, Thor.* And the next minute it's like, *Shut the hell up.*

I wish I could flip the switch and turn it off completely.

The doubt in Harper's eyes fades, turning into a coy smile. She snatches the phone from my hand, types, and flips it around for me to see. Umm . . . I'm really horny. Wanna help me out with that?

Holy. Fucking. Shit. I did not see that coming.

My eyes flick to hers. Smiling her lopsided grin, she bites her lower lip and shrugs.

Is she for real? And how did I end up with her? Girl next door and sex kitten all rolled into one. I am the luckiest bastard on the planet.

Standing, I whip out the phrase I did not learn in the *Dummies* book. *"Let's fuck."*

Her eyes go wide and her jaw drops. *"Did you learn that, too?"*

Proud of myself, I shake my head up and down, wagging my eyebrows.

"Let's fuck, then." Her silly grin widens into a full-fledged megawatt smile, shoulders bouncing in silent laughter.

My heart thumps an extra beat and my dick stands at attention. *Hells yeah!*

Holding out my hand, Harper puts her palm against mine, and I yank her to her feet. My lips are on hers faster than Jimi Hendrix played his "Red House" solo. Bending my knees, I lift her up and she locks her legs around my waist in an instant, hugging me tight.

Burying my lying guilt deep in the pit of my stomach, I focus on her body and how good it is to have her back in my arms. Opening her mouth with mine, I taste her. Chocolate and peanut butter, sin and pure heaven. I'll never be able to eat a peanut butter cup without getting hard.

My hands on her ass, pressing her to me, I kiss her like tomorrow's the fucking apocalypse and all we have is tonight, because if she ever finds out my family's secret, this may be all we have.

I carry her down the hall, eager to get her to my bed. Taking to the stairs, Harper moves her mouth to my neck, planting kisses over my skin. "Almost there, babe." I tilt my head, giving her better access. She kisses my Adam's apple and I groan. Racking her fingers over my throat, she kisses the same spot. "Do you like when I talk to you, Red?" I ask.

She exhales, her breath cool against my damp skin. Thrusting her hips upward, I readjust my grip on her. My arms shake, biceps burning, but I flex harder, bringing her closer still, giving her whatever she wants.

"I love it when you tell me what you want." My vocal chords

vibrate in my neck and chest, and I know Harper can feel it. As I speak, she presses her lips to my Adam's apple, drinking in each vibration.

My bedroom door is open. Walking inside, I kick it shut, and step up to the bed, lowering Harper onto the clean sheets.

Leaning over her tiny frame, she begs me to come closer. I press my body weight into her and she tightens the vise grip her legs have around my waist.

Pulling my lips away from hers, I stare into the sparkling depths of her eyes. There's so much life inside her, it blazes, burning up everything in its path. I'd give anything to be consumed by her wildfire, her passion.

I stroke my hand over her forehead, pushing back a tangle of untamed curls. She smiles and it crashes into me. I don't ever want to forget the way she looks right now. I want to remember everything. Her racing heart, the light in her eyes, the pink flush of her cheeks. The way her hair springs in every direction because I can't keep my hands out of it. I've had so many women in this bed, but not one of them has forced me to pause and take stock of each little feature.

I rest my fingertip at the bottom corner of her left eye, against a dark freckle. Leaning down, I kiss it and I feel her eyes close. The whisper of her eyelashes brush against my lips.

Slowly, I pull at the bottom of her sweater, working it upward. Harper lifts her shoulders, rising up just enough that I can remove her top. I throw it away, keeping my eyes on her breasts, full and beautiful, committing each inch of her skin to memory. The sexy way the black lace of her bra hides her nipples, but not quite.

I touch her. Running a hand from the base of her neck and over the rise of her chest. She breathes in, filling my hand even more. Reaching for me, her fingertips graze over my piercing. I gasp, sucking in air between my teeth. Shaking my head, I smile and pull away from her roaming fingers. "It's my turn, babe. I'm going to touch you. And I'm going to watch your beautiful body fall to pieces as I make you come. And then"—I slide my hands to her waist, tugging her leggings down—"I'm going to slide my dick inside you, real slow." I rub my hands up the insides of her legs, my fingers stopping just shy of her panties. She's hot; I can feel it rolling off of her in waves. Lifting her hips, she tempts me closer as she watches my mouth, licking her lips.

"I'm going to stretch you, and fill you, and commit to memory the way your tight, wet pussy"—I hook my index fingers into the sides of her panties and drag them down, too—"clamps down around my cock."

Lifting up beneath me, she reaches around her back, unhooks her bra and rips it off, tossing it to the floor with the rest of her clothes. A second later, she wraps her arm around my neck, and kisses me deeply; bring me with her as she falls back on the bed.

Now it's time to put all my talk into action.

I pull away from her mouth, breathless, moving to her chest. I flick my tongue against her nipple, watching it tighten into a hard pebble before I suck her into my mouth. "Jesus, Harper. You have…" I suck harder and tug her nipple between my teeth. "The most gorgeous tits." I move to the next one, making sure I give both equal amounts of attention.

While I play at her top, I feel Harper's hand move between us, dipping between her legs.

I stop what I'm doing to get a better look as she touches herself. "That's it, babe. Show me how you like it."

With her eyes closed, she rubs circles around her clit, grinding her hips for added pleasure. I put my hand on hers and she stops, eyes popping open. Nodding my head, I urge her to continue, "Keep going. Teach me what to do." I move my fingers over her sensitive bundle of nerves.

Continuing her sultry ministrations below, she guides me over each slick fold until she gives her body over to me completely. And just as I promised, I watch her fall to pieces as she comes around my fingers, her body quaking with pleasure. She's so goddamn beautiful.

I kiss her, tasting bliss on her mouth, and wishing so desperately that I could *hear* her come.

* * *

Harper's sprawled out on the bed beside me, sound asleep. Tangled in my sheets, her ass is covered, but the speckled, porcelain skin of her back needs to be touched. My fingers hover inches above her spine, remembering how smooth and silky her skin feels. I want to draw constellations over her back, make pictures from her freckles.

I drop my hand on the mattress between us, instead. I don't want to wake her. I want to savor even the sleeping moments we share. Is this really what a relationship is supposed to feel like? I can't imagine Mom and Dad ever having this. Peace, contentment…happiness.

Remembering the dark purple bruise covering Mom's left

eye, I'm sure as shit she's never felt this way. My chest constricts, suffocating my newfound serenity. I can hear Dad's drunken growl in the back of my head, "You're still my son, boy."

Harper's the first woman I've allowed to spend the night. *Was that a mistake? What if I do end up just like him?*

I shake off the nightmare thought. I can't. I won't. I'll remember what this feels like, waking up beside her. The warmth of her body, the scent of our lovemaking and her flower shampoo lingering on my sheets.

Between the slats of the shade on the window, the sun chases away the darkness, just like Harper's presence scares away my dad's voice in my head. Pulling the sheets over my legs, I slide in beside her, touching the tip of my nose to hers.

Heavy with sleep, her eyes flutter open, and she smiles. I kiss her, throwing my arm over her bare shoulders, drawing her close. I've never needed someone to protect me, but Harper does, even though she doesn't know it. She's my safe place.

Today's going to be insane. First day in the studio. Probably should have gotten more sleep than I did, but I'm not complaining. In spite of all my apprehensions and fears, I'll take an eternity of sleepless nights if it means I get to spend them with Harper in my bed. And wake up with her at my side.

Rolling toward me, she scoots closer, slinking her leg over mine. No words are exchanged, but we understand what the other needs, loud and clear.

CHAPTER NINETEEN

HARPER

Sitting at the computer, I record Xavier Bexworth's prescription information onto his patient chart. At rounds this morning he did not look any better, whooping cough and pneumonia taking a toll on his little three-year-old body. His worried parents hadn't looked much better than their son, both sick with worry.

Midsentence, there's a tap on my shoulder. Abandoning the detailed list of antibiotics and nutrient fluids Xavier's being administered through his IV, I swivel my chair around. Pharmacy manager, Mr. Ellis, the man that holds the fate of my future career in his hands, stands in front of me.

"Ms. King, I checked the prescribed dosage of dobutamine for patient Lilly Jones in room 428, which you entered on the patient's chart during rounds earlier. Upon verification, dobutamine was not the physician's desired course of treatment for patient Jones, it was dopamine. Errors like this are unacceptable, Ms. King. I suggest you double-, no, triple-check the prescription order before you update a patient's chart."

My heart climbs into my throat and the acid in my stomach threaten to burn a hole right through me. If my carelessness has hurt a patient, I will never forgive myself. How could I have been so negligent and misinterpret dobutamine and dopamine? When I lip-read Dr. Melton's prescription, I was positive she said dobutamine.

Without turning around, I reach my hand backward and grab the notebook off the counter. I don't even bother to sign, or make Mr. Ellis read my lips. Writing quickly, I hand Mr. Ellis the notebook. **Is Lilly okay? I am incredibly sorry, Mr. Ellis. I was certain that I understood Dr. Melton correctly. From here on out, I will triple-check the prescription order. Like you said, my mistake is unacceptable.**

Mr. Ellis hands the notebook back to me, a scowl still on his face. "Patient Jones is fine. Like I said, I reviewed your notes from rounds with the physician and caught the discrepancy before the wrong medication was administered. Ms. King, you're a good pharmacist. You've done well, despite this mistake, be sure it doesn't happen again."

Watching Mr. Ellis walk away, tears sting my eyes. How could I have been so, so stupid? Glancing at my watch, I still have twenty minutes of my shift. Twenty minutes to hold in all the emotions that are threatening to burst out of me. My error could have seriously harmed that infant. What other mistakes have I made that haven't been caught?

I turn back to the computer and stare at the blinking cursor, second-guessing myself. Did I record Xavier Bexworth's prescription correctly? I took his information on rounds, too.

Time to triple-check.

I fire off an email to two other pharmacy technicians who were on rounds with me, and one to Xavier's nurse, checking the physician's order against the information I recorded.

Staring at the screen, I wait, unwilling to put another scrap of information onto the Bexworth chart until I'm certain I didn't make another mistake.

Goddammit, Harper. Children's lives are at stake; there is no room for error.

I can't get Mr. Ellis's words out of my head.

Waiting for the responses to my email, I open Lilly Jones's drug chart. Mr. Ellis noted the change of dobutamine to dopamine and signed off on it.

Bile rises in my throat. Me, of all people, I cannot make mistakes like this. There are a dozen people, if not more, looking for any reason to say I'm unfit to be a pharmacist, that being deaf is too big a hurdle to overcome in the field of medicine. I got lazy, complacent, and I could have seriously harmed a human being—an infant no less.

Even though the words are so similar and the two drugs are both inotropes, I shouldn't have confused the two—they don't even have the same number of syllables.

I choke down my tears. I don't have time to wallow right now. *Do your damn job, Harper, and do it right.*

My inbox confirms a new message. I click on the screen and read the email from the charge nurse overseeing the Bexworth case. The medications prescribed on rounds were exactly as I had listed. Thank God. Now to wait on the technicians' responses.

Staring at the computer, I flip back to Xavier's chart, feeling another tap on my shoulder. What now? How many screwups can I make in one day? Turning around, another pharmacy student, Trisha Miles, stands in front of me. Standing, I take my phone from my lab coat pocket. I unlock the screen and type. Hi, Trisha. What can I do for you?

Trisha and I have been in school together for several years. She's always helpful and a great pharmacist. She keeps me on my toes.

"I overheard what happened. For what it's worth, I messed up last week. We all make mistakes, Harper. Don't beat yourself up." She gives me a halfhearted smile, squeezes my shoulder, and turns to leave.

I appreciate Trisha's comforting words, but they don't help. I've worked too hard to let a misinterpretation derail my whole future.

Glancing at my watch, I flop back into the chair and swivel around to check my email. Sure enough, I have responses from the two techs. And my lipreading was accurate on the Bexworth round.

I put the finishing touch on Xavier's drug chart and sign off, ready to put this day behind me. And cry myself to sleep.

Shrugging my jacket on and fishing the keys out of my purse, I wave goodbye to Trisha and head down the hall, a terrible clawing in my chest. The second the hospital doors open to the outside, I can't hold the tears in anymore. I choke down sobs and let them stream down my cheeks.

Throughout my undergrad, and the last three years of grad school, I have never felt this awful. I'm just glad my mistake was caught before any serious damage was done. I don't even want to think about what could have happened had Mr. Ellis not went over my prescription orders.

Climbing behind the wheel of my VW Bug, I push the engine start button and rest my head on the steering wheel, letting the enormity of what I did drown me. I've always said that I can do anything a hearing person can do (and I can) but today proved just how hard my chosen profession really is for a deaf person. I have to up my game. Enlist Chloe's help; make her say drug names over and over again, until I can lip-read their subtle nuances without making mistakes.

See, I already have a plan. Today will be a small blip against the backdrop of my long, illustrious career.

Looking up, I swipe the tears off my cheeks, check my mirrors, and put the car in drive. All I want to do is go home, slip into some comfy clothes, snuggle with my dog, and hide under the covers.

* * *

Thor: You okay, Red? Thought I'd hear from you when you got off.

Me: Bad day. Sorry.

The second I lay my phone down on the bed, it flashes. Want to talk about it?

Me: No.

I slide my phone under my pillow and pat the mattress, calling Bobby closer. Such a good dog, he curls up right next to my face, leaving a sloppy, wet lick right on the tip of my nose. I rub his ears and let my eyes fall shut. If I close out the world, I won't have to relive my screwup.

I concentrate on the rise and fall of Bobby's little body, hoping the soothing rhythm will lull me into a deep sleep and erase this god-awful day.

Counting Bobby's breaths, I get to eighty and still can't get the image of Mr. Ellis standing over me, delivering my failure on a silver platter. The outside world is effing noisy.

Ninety…

Triple-check your work, Harper.

One hundred…

There's no room for error, Harper.

One hundred twenty-two…

You're a terrible pharmacist, Harper.

One hundred fifty-five…

You'll never make it in the hearing world, Harper.

Two hun—

Bright light burns my closed eyes and then it's gone. When the light flashes a second time, I jump out of bed, startled. Bobby's on his feet, looking just as confused. My door signaler glares again.

Shit. Who's here?

Wiping the drool from the corner of my mouth and patting my curls down, I yank open the door. Thor has a ginormous bag of Reese's Peanut Butter Cups in his hands.

Without so much as a hello, I grab his arm and pull him into my bedroom. I need those peanut butter cups, stat!

Grabbing the bag from his hand, I rip it open, and dig inside. Thor taps my shoulder, handing me his phone. That bad, huh?

I nod, and hand his phone back as I fall onto the bed.

I make quick work of the chocolate's wrapper and pop the mini piece of heaven in my mouth. Bobby completely snubs Thor and goes straight to sniffing the bag of candy likes it's cocaine—to him, it might as well be.

I push him back and shake my head. *No chocolate for dogs, little man.*

Thor lies down next to me and grabs a peanut butter cup from the bag. Unwrapping it, he takes a bite, nibbling the chocolate off, until it's a naked peanut butter cup. I roll my head to the right and stare at him. I've never seen anyone eat a Reese's like that. *"That was weird."*

He shrugs and bites into another, doing the same thing. "Makes it last longer. And you get to savor both parts. You should try it." He hands me a third chocolate.

Together, we peel the foil off, then the brown paper. Thor sets the candy against his front teeth and bites gently, pulling the chocolate shell off the peanut butter. I copy his actions, careful to only sink my teeth into the chocolate.

I make it all the way around the circle, ready to pull the top off. In the time that it has taken me to get this far, Thor's working on his fifth or sixth.

Screw it. I pop the semi-naked peanut butter cup in my mouth and grab another, feeling better already.

A mountain of gold foil and brown paper lies between us. Thor types something on his phone and passes it to me. Are you chatty when you're chocolate drunk?

I glare at him, but can't hide the smile on my lips. Maybe.

Thor: Good. What happened today?

He doesn't mince words. Right to the point. I take the

phone from his hands. I really messed up today. Lipreading error. Prescribed the wrong meds for an infant.

Thor: I'm sorry, Red. Is the baby okay?

Me: Yeah. Pharm manager caught the mistake before anything was administered. I feel wretched though.

Thor: Glad everyone's all right. Don't beat yourself up. I fuck up a hundred times a day. You're only human.

Turning onto his side, he scoots closer to me, and drapes his arm around my stomach. His chocolaty breath is warm against my cheek when he puts a kiss there.

I roll to my side, too, our faces centimeters apart. *"Thank you for knowing I needed you here, even when I didn't say so."*

"I hear you, babe." Pressing in, Thor's lips close around mine. This kiss is soft…quiet, meant to heal the soul, not set it on fire. Even when he kisses me, he knows exactly what I need.

I let me tongue linger on his mouth, tasting the sweetness of his lips before I pull away. Sitting up, I draw my legs in, and cross them. I motion for Thor to do the same thing. Grabbing the phone off the bed, I type, an idea striking my brain. I've got a surprise for you.

Thor: Oh, really?

I nod enthusiastically. For weeks now, I've been thinking about a name sign for Thor. I think I've finally nailed one down. It's perfect.

Me: I've got a sign for you. Copy me.

Dropping the phone between us, I raise my left hand to mirror Thor, knowing he's left-handed. I put my thumb between my index and middle fingers and motion like I'm hammering.

Thor replicates the motion. "What's it mean?" he asks.

I make the sign again and mouth his name. *"Thor."*

His eyes dance when his smile touches them.

Picking up the phone, I send him a message. Do you like it?

Thor: Let me show you just how much I love it.

He pinches my chin between his forefinger and thumb, drawing my mouth to his. This time, his kiss does set a fire as we fall, tangled together, onto the bed.

CHAPTER TWENTY

Harper

The door to the hospital closes with a whoosh behind me and I wave to Trisha who follows me out of the hospital.

"See you tomorrow. Bright and early," she says, her face widening into a yawn. "Sorry." She covers her mouth and shakes her head. Luckily, the light from inside the hospital is bright enough that I can see Trisha's face.

"I'll be here," I sign, mouthing the words, hoping she can see me well enough in the dim light to read my lips. I yawn, too, knowing exactly how she feels. I'm exhausted. I can't wait to get home, shower, and plop on the couch with Chloe. I've been looking forward to our date night with Ryan Gosling all week. *"Have a great night."* I sign.

"You too, Harper." Trisha crosses to the parking lot and heads to the side of the building, and I walk to my car in the front lot.

Unlocking my car, I climb inside, my stomach grumbling. I bet Chloe is already in the kitchen, whipping up her fabulous shrimp fajitas. I've had those suckers dancing in my head all week, like sugarplums dance at Christmastime.

I push the button on the dash to start the engine, my car rumbling to life. Even though it's the middle of October, the weather is unseasonably warm, which means I can still enjoy the luxury of driving with the top down. I press the button and the top disappears to the back. Pulling out of the parking lot, I head toward home, hungry for shrimp fajitas, Ryan Gosling, and the ginormous bag of peanut butter cups I've stashed in the pantry.

* * *

"What about Blue Valentine?*"* I ask, knowing I'll never change her mind on what she thinks is the best Ryan Gosling movie. *The Notebook* is Chloe's all-time favorite, the pinnacle of Ryan Gosling hotness and acting ability. *"Blue Valentine is a heart-breaking love story. And well acted by both G-O-S-L-I-N-G and W-I-L-L-I-A-M-S."*

"I agree, but it's not the best. R-Y-A-N and R-A-C-H-E-L even got swept up in the romance of The Notebook. *That's when you know it's good. When the lead actors even blur the lines between fiction and real life."*

Can't fault her logic. They were a hot couple. On and off the screen.

I take a bite of my fajita, marinade dribbling down my chin. Oh my goodness. Full-on food orgasm. *"Chloe, these are out-standing. Can you just skip* Cupcake Wars *and go on some other cooking show? You'd win with this recipe."*

"Thanks. They're so easy to make." She passes me a napkin, winking.

Diving back in for another bite, my phone flashes and a text message pops up on the screen. Thor: Home from the studio. So fucking tired. This two-job gig is going to be the death of me. How's movie night? Can't believe you're cheating on me with Ryan Gosling.

I put down my fajita, wiping my fingers on a napkin. Smiling, I pick up my phone, and type a response. How's the album coming? When do I get to hear it? Sorry, babe. *Crazy Stupid Love*'s up next. The RG lovefest continues.

Setting my phone on the cushion, I'm just about to pick up my fajita when a wadded-up napkin hits me in the head. My eyes flick to Chloe, who's giving me the "I just ate nails for breakfast, don't mess with me" look. Lips pursed and everything.

"What?"

"No cell phones on movie night. You know the rules." Finishing with a point in my direction, she eyes me.

"Sorry." I cringe. If he keeps texting, I'll need to be stealthy. *"Ready for the next movie?"* I ask as a peace offering, ignoring the flash of another incoming text message.

She nods and pops the last bite of her fajita into her mouth. Getting up from her end of the couch, she changes out the DVDs.

With her back to me, I take a sneak peek at my phone. Thor: I guess I can share you for tonight. But tomorrow, you're all mine. The record studio is throwing a party in our honor. Be my date?

Whoa! This is huge. He wants to take me somewhere his friends will be?

For so long, he's been careful not to let his personal life interfere when I'm around. Why has he been so leery of sharing all the parts of his life with me? He doesn't seem put off by my deafness, but maybe that's why he's kept me at arm's length all this time. Maybe he doesn't want everyone to know he's dating a deaf girl.

Worry takes up residence low in my gut, feeding on my most negative thoughts. He can't be ashamed of me, can he? When we're together, he's nothing but wonderful.

You thought the same thing about your parents all these years, too.

The heart-to-heart with my dad helped me understand where he was coming from, and our relationship is healing. But, it's going to take baby steps. The same thing can't be happening with Thor, not with this party invitation, right?

On her way back to the couch, Chloe hits the lights and the room is plunged into darkness as the title sequence begins. She and I are like a well-oiled marathon-movie-watching machine. She takes the DVDs in and out of the player, and I navigate the settings, turning on the subtitles. With a quick stash of my phone, I pick up the remote and get to work.

Finishing my dinner, I'm still reeling about Thor asking me to the recording studio's party. I pat my lap, and Bobby jumps up, walking in a few circles until he finds a comfortable place to curl up and snuggle. Petting his head with my right hand, I slide my left under my classic car fleece blanket, along with my phone, trying to bite back the giddy smile on my face. If I don't play it cool, Chloe will know exactly what I'm up to and banish me from future movie nights. *Gilmore Girls* is up next. Can't miss the season three rewatch.

Although, at this point, watching Ryan Gosling coach Steve Carell in the fine art of picking up women at a bar is barely holding my interest. I want to sneak upstairs, lock my bedroom door, and text Thor. With our busy schedules, we haven't gotten to see each other in the last four days. By our standards, that's a long friggin' time. With my phone hidden under the blanket, I type out another message.

I am so excited to go to that party with you!!! Yes! I'll be your date! Ever seen *Crazy Stupid Love*? It reminds me of you. You picked me up in a bar. You could totes school both of these guys on how to pick up a girl at a bar. ;-)

Two seconds later, I have a response. And the bottom drops out of my stomach. Acid spilling everywhere, burning up every cell and molecule in my body. Mom: Excuse me? I'm not sure I understand your text, Harper. What's going on? Are you out drinking? Someone picked you up in a bar? What party are you going to?

Shit! I sent Thor's text to my mother? I am such an idiot!

The temperature in the room skyrockets. I'm roasting under this damn blanket, but if I ditch it, Chloe will see that I'm texting, breaking movie-night law. And Bobby will hate me; he's snoring away.

Time for some damage control.

Me: Sorry, Mom. No, not drinking. At home watching a movie with Chloe. Didn't mean to send you that text.

Cringing, I wait for her reply. Keeping my eyes dead ahead,

I pretend to watch the movie, but inside, I'm freaking out. There is no way Mom is going to let this go.

Mom: I'm glad you're not out drinking. But what is this about being picked up at a bar? Are you seeing someone that met you at a bar?

While I read Mom's text, another one from Thor comes in. Now I know why Chloe banned texting from movie night. I've gotten myself into a crazy, stupid mess.

Thor: Unless you don't want to go? Not forcing you, or anything.

Before my attention dives back under the covers, I glance at Chloe. She's completely engrossed, curled up in her snoogie (Yes, she has a pet name for her blanket, don't judge), eating popcorn. I'm still good.

Me: Sorry. Yes! I'd love to go to the party with you! I hit send and pull up Mom's message, so I can reply. Me: Mom. Yes, I'm seeing someone I met at a bar. He's a nice guy.

I keep it simple. I'm quite sure that Thor's nice-guy status would be lost on my mother if she saw him. Let's just say, Mom's not the tattoos-and-grease, I'm-in-a-band kind of woman. And the even bigger obstacle will be convincing my mother that I can juggle a career and a love life.

Ryan Gosling's bare torso draws my attention back to the television. Damn, he looked hot in this movie.

Chloe turns her head in my direction, eyes wide. *"That is one beautiful man."* She signs. This is why she's my best friend. I think we share a brain.

"Speaking of beautiful men, whatever happened with Trey after you and Megan ran into him at The Cave the night you two

went out?" I ask. Yes, her ex-boyfriend is a colossal douche bag, but there's no denying that he is a gorgeous man. The last Chloe and I really talked, she mentioned that she'd seen him, but didn't go into details. So help me God, she better not be hooking up with him after what he did to her.

"Ancient history." She shoos away his name like a pesky fly. *"And good riddance."*

"You're okay?" I watch her face for any tells, the smile extinguishing the light from her eyes, a subtle downward turn of her mouth, anything that will lead me to believe that she isn't fine, but hiding behind her words.

"Perfect. Really. I've got a good thing going right now. I don't need Trey or his bullshit drama. I'm married to Cupcake Wars. *And R-Y-A-N G-O-S-L-I-N-G."* She points to the TV.

"Don't take this the wrong way, but I'm so happy that Trey is out of your life, for good. You're better off without him."

"None taken. And don't I know it." Pulling on the front of her hot pink snoogie, she readjusts her arms in the sleeves.

"I do have some bad news, though. You can't have R-Y-A-N, because I'm already married to him."

"Ha! I'm sure Thor might have a problem with that." She sticks her tongue out. *"What's up with you two, anyway?"*

"What do you mean?"

"From my perspective, it looks like you two are kinda perfect together." She winks.

Warmth spreads from the center of my chest. When it's just us, we are perfect. When the world pushes in and crowds us, that's when Thor backs away. But, this party invitation is a step in the right direction. *"We're good. He's a great guy. I just wish*"—I hesitate, dropping my hand on Bobby's head—*"he'd let me in. The second personal stuff comes up, he closes himself off."*

"Well, give him time. You know those hot, broody types, they have to keep an air of mystery about them, or their reputation is shot."

"Yeah. I guess you're right." I agree with her, but inside, I don't feel at ease. In my gut, I know Thor's dealing with something big…heavy. The other night, when he came over after my horrible day at the hospital, something was up with him, but I couldn't pry anything lose. Whatever it is, it's weighing him down.

"How's the Cupcake Wars *prep coming?"* I ask, noticing a flash on the other side of Bobby's head. If he hadn't been curled up on my lap, Chloe would have seen it go off.

"Megan and I have our game plan all laid out. I'm still watching reruns and taking notes on what the losing teams did wrong. If I know how they lost, I can do my best to not repeat their mistakes, and hopefully pull out the win."

"Good strategy." Leaning over Bobby, I grab my family-sized bag of Reese's Peanut Butter Cups off the coffee table. Tearing the bag apart at the seam, a peanut butter–chocolate cloud kisses my nose. I breathe in and hold it. When I die and go to heaven, this is what heaven will smell like.

Bobby perks up, too. *No chocolate for you, pooch.* I pat his head and give him a sad, frowny-faced headshake.

"Oh, I love this part, when H-A-N-N-A-H comes in from the rain, soaking wet and just lays one on J-A-C-O-B. So hot." Chloe points to the TV and whips her head to the front so she can see the action.

I lift the covers and peek at my phone. Two texts and one missed FaceTime?

Mom: First a nose ring and now a boyfriend you met in a bar? I hope you're not throwing this last year of grad school down the drain, Harper Alexis King.

She's pissed. Twenty-six years old and she's still busting out my middle name like I'm two. Some things never change. And when I didn't respond to her text right away, she FaceTimed me. *Nice one, Mom.* Heaven forbid I ever tell her about my mistake at the hospital.

Thor: Good. You had me worried for a sec. Been a damn tough week. I miss the fuck out of you, Red.

Keeping my head down, I shift my eyes in Chloe's direction before starting my message. Her eyes are front and center, all systems go, full throttle ahead. My thumbs move over the keys as fast as they can. Tough how? Everything okay? Miss you, too.

Chloe turns her head, and I drop the blanket like it's a hot potato, shoving my hand in the Reese's bag as a cover.

Her eyebrows pinch together as she signs. *"What's up? You're really jumpy."*

Tilting my head, I chew on my lip, playing dumb, plucking a peanut butter cup from the bag. *"No, not jumpy. Too much candy."* I hold out a foil-wrapped chocolate in offering.

Chloe nods and scoots closer to me on the couch. Taking the chocolate from my hand, Bobby sniffs the exchange. *"I'm glad we did this. A night vegging on the couch with my roomie was exactly what I needed."* Throwing her arm over my shoulder, she pulls me in for a hug, kissing my cheek.

"God, I've missed you. I don't know how much longer we're going to be able to do nights like this."

I nod, a twinge of sadness tugging at my heart. *"We're almost halfway through our rotations. Graduation is right around the corner."*

"Who knows where our jobs will take us." She shrugs. *"And I'm going to California this summer."* Chloe signs, then swipes at her eyes.

If she starts crying, so will I. *"And I'll be in the audience cheering you on."*

She stops, a huge grin blossoming on her face. *"You're coming to the taping?"*

"Hell yes. I wouldn't miss it."

"You, me, and Megan, loose in California? This summer is going to be epic!"

"Cupcakes and C-A-L-I!" I nod, smiling, the weight of an unknown future seeming a little lighter.

Chloe yawns. *"I can't think of a more perfect vacation."*

"Same." I pet Bobby and drop my head on Chloe's shoulder. *"I think after this one, I'm off to bed. I'm getting sleepy."* This time, it's my turn to yawn.

Watching the rest of the movie, all I can think about is Thor's worrisome text message, and a summer vacation in California with my best friend.

* * *

Tucked away in my bedroom, Bobby, curled at the foot of my bed, I unlock my phone. The last forty minutes of that movie were so long. Siting that close to Chloe, I couldn't keep up my surreptitious texting.

Tapping the messages app, three new texts await me. I touch Thor's name, first. I'll deal with Mom later. Right now, I'm more worried about why Thor's had a rough week.

Thor: More family shit. It'd just be nice to hold you right now.

Uh-oh. It seems he's always got a lot of bad stuff happening with his family. I wish he'd tell me what's going on. I click on the next message. You're what's good in my life. How did I end up with you?

That message was sent twenty-six minutes ago. A nagging, unsettled ache hits me low in the gut. Something awful has happened, I can feel it. Me: What's going on? This sounds serious. I'm worried. Do you want me to come over?

While I wait for his reply—God, I hope he replies—against my better judgment, I take a look at Mom's text: We are not through speaking about this, Harper. I refuse to let you throw away everything you've worked so hard to achieve.

Oh, Mom. When we had our heart-to-heart after Dad's party, I told her she had to step back and let me live my life. She wasn't too happy about that. I know she means well and has my best interest at heart, but she's going to have to let go and trust that I can make my own decisions. And my own mistakes.

Mom, I appreciate your concern. Rest assured, I am not throwing anything away. Grad school is fine. I'm studying and getting my projects finished when they need to be. Clinicals are going well. I'm enjoying my current rotation. My job at the YMCA is still wonderful. And yes, I'm making time to get to know a really kind, great man. I care about him. His name is Thor, and I would love for you to meet him, soon. This is my life, Mom. I love my life. I hit send and hope that does the trick.

Sitting up, I pull the blanket toward me, bringing Bobby closer. He gives me an annoyed side-glance, the whites of his eyes showing. Laying my head beside his, I run my hand between his ears, and he scoots closer, curling into a smaller ball of fur.

In the four years we've been together, Bobby and I have always understood each other. No words ever need to be exchanged, we just know. He knows when I need a lick on the nose, and I get when he wants to tack on five extra minutes to our walk. There's no pretense with Bobby. He accepts me for who I am, and I return the favor.

Why are people so difficult then? *Why can't they be like you, Bobby? I care about you, you care about me.* Simple.

Nope. People have to go and muck it up. Think they know what's best for someone else, or keep secrets.

A burst of light fills my dark room.

Keeping my head on the mattress next to Bobby, I reach behind me and grab my phone. Mom: Thor? Is that his real name? Is he the reason you got that thing in your nose?

I drop the phone on top the blankets and bury my head in Bobby's fur, a scream ripping through my insides. There's no getting through to her.

Me: Had the piercing before I met Thor. It's cute. Going to bed now.

Thor's message comes the second I send off my final note to Mom. Not home. I'd be crashing your Ryan Gosling date, if I were. My mind's going to dirty places, babe. Out drinking with the guys. Wasted.

Me: Do you have a DD? Be careful.

Warm, curled up next to Bobby, I wait for his text, my eyes getting heavier by the second. I refuse to fall asleep until I know he's got a safe way home. My nerves are giving me a second wind.

Sitting up, I give Bobby a scratch, and prop my back against the headboard, my phone flashing brightly.

Thor: After Dad's shit. Nice to be wassssted. Got DD babe.

Dad's shit? What the hell does that mean? So, drunk Thor gets horny and truthful. Good to know. Me: What's going on with your dad? Glad you have a DD.

Phone in my lap, I wait for him to explain. Minutes tick by and…nothing.

Me: Thor, are you okay? Did something happen with your dad? I'm worried.

Leaning my head back, I let my eyelids fall closed. *What are you keeping from me, Thorin Kline?*

CHAPTER TWENTY-ONE

HARPER

I knock on Thor's townhouse door. Waiting a minute or two, I knock again—or more like pound, using the side of my fist instead of my knuckles. I have no friggin' clue how loud I'm actually knocking. I could be signaling my arrival to his neighbors five units down, at the end of the cul-de-sac, for all I know. I should text him when I get here, instead.

Thor tears the door open, wearing nothing but gray jogging pants. He's always in a perpetual state of undress (not that I'm complaining). Why isn't he ready for the party? I glance down at my black skater dress, the one with the see-through neckline. Maybe I'm too overdressed for the party?

Cocking my head, I eye him, and gesture with an open palm, his choice of party attire. Grabbing my hand, he hauls me inside, not wasting a minute before kissing me.

Dear Lord, can this man kiss…among other things. Locking my arms around him, I melt into his warmth.

His hands slide down the backs of my arms, and he pulls

away. *"Bedroom. Now."* He signs.

My heart still pinches when he signs, giving an extra thump in appreciation. *"Bedroom? What about the party?"* I ask.

"Later." He signs. The fact that we can converse in short, signed sentences makes me incredibly giddy. *"I want to keep you mine for just a little bit longer."*

What does he mean? *"I am yours."*

Kissing the top of my hand, he fits his fingers between mine, and leads me through the living, into the kitchen, and up the stairs. Making an immediate right on the landing, he pulls me into his room, shuts the door, and kisses me again, harder this time.

His tongue slips between my lips, brushing against my mine. Heat blooms between my legs. With Thor, I'm always ready. Can't get enough of him.

Trailing his hand down my back, I feel the teeth of the zipper on my dress giving way. At the small of my back, he stops, my dress sliding off my body in a puddle of material at my feet. I should pick it up, but Thor's already moved onto my bra, flipping the hooks apart—*one, two, three.*

His eyes roam over every one of my curves, like a man locked in a Corvette dealership. Bringing his left hand up, he grazes the side of my breast and my legs threaten to give out from under me.

Moving his fingers inches lower, they travel to the underside, cupping me. I keep my eyes on his face, but he isn't looking at me, my tits have his undivided attention at the moment. It's like he's memorizing the way they lay, round and heavy against my chest.

His thumbs circle around my nipple, but don't make contact. Teasing. Sweet, sweet torment.

I suck in a breath, my head lolling back, absorbing every sensation. I want to remember all the places he touches me.

This is excruciating, welcomed torture. With Thor and me it's always full throttle, one of us demanding, spurring the other to go faster, but this...the way his fingers only make contact with the smallest amount of my skin, it's driving me mad.

He continues his slow, languid journey over my chest, exploring every inch of me, with only his fingertips. Eyes closed, open mouthed, I breathe faster and fuller, deliberately lifting my chest with each inhalation, begging him to touch more...take more. My legs shake, muscles burning...can't stand much...longer. I need to touch him, for him to hold me. Have his body on mine...*in mine.*

I flick my eyes open, reaching for his chest. I want him close. I'm dying to run my hands over his piercing. It's so hot. I love the way his breath hitches and how his moans vibrate in his chest when I touch it. But he steps away, shaking his head. *"My turn. Just enjoy."* Again, he signs this response, flawlessly.

Now I'm turned on as hell. I lean in to kiss him, show him how much it means to me that he wants to communicate the way I do. His left hand disappears from my chest, and comes between us. With an infinitesimal shake of his head, he signs, *"No."* against my lips, a shameless smirk tugging at the corners of his mouth.

No, huh? Not going to let me touch you yet? Pushing my boundaries, I open my mouth and drag my tongue along the side of his index finger. Defiance and longing burning up my insides. I can taste the lingering scent of his last cigarette.

His eyes go wide. I know he hates his hands, how beat up and rough they are. He's said before that his hands don't look right on my body, that I'm too soft…that his hands only sully my perfection. I disagree.

I circle my tongue around the tip of his index finger, sliding it between the pinched "No" sign. I feel his breath hitch, see his shoulders rise.

I love his hands. Talented, skilled, beautiful. Able to coax music from a silent instrument. They can make a car purr with life. Gentle. Protective. Strong. Loud when they speak.

Holding his gaze, I continue my little rebellion, pulling more of his finger into my mouth. Like the base of a flame, blue fire burns in his eyes. He shakes his head. "You are so naughty." I read on his lips, feeling the vibration of the words rumbling against his mouth.

Stealing his hand away, he places both of them on each side of my waist, dropping to his knees. The tip of his nose brushes side-to-side against my stomach and his shoulders rise.

Circling my arms around the back of his head, my fingers brush over his close-cropped scalp, each scratch igniting more longing inside me. Thor presses his cheek to the softness of my belly, and I hold him tighter.

How can I long for him to be closer than he already is?

I've fallen for him, that's why. He consumes me, heart and soul.

Thor trails his hands downward, over the curve of my ass, the backs of my thighs, until they rest on my lower hips. I keep working my fingers over his hair as he plants tiny kisses across my stomach. I gasp when his tongue dips into my belly button, and I press him closer.

Moving his palms up the front of my thighs, his fingers continue their northward pursuit, hooking inside the waistband of my black lace thong. Slowly, he peels his body away from mine as he drags my panties down.

I watch him and our eyes meet. His are dark and hooded, dangerous and sexy. Desire crashes into me, sending my insides flipping and rolling in the onslaught. My legs quiver, bending at the knees. I have to use Thor's head for support, catching myself before I fall.

Thor's quick, wrapping his arms around my legs to keep me from crashing. Once my balance is restored, he winks—knowing good and well the effect he's having on me and loving every minute of it—bringing his left hand down my calf…my ankle, he takes my panties along for the ride.

Stepping out of the pile of my discarded clothes, Thor puts his hands at my waist and gently pushes me backward, while he shuffles along on his knees. When the backs of my legs hit the edge of the bed, I fall, my breath catching in my throat.

Thor licks his lips, his hands resting on my knees. Slowly, he pushes my legs apart, never taking his eyes away from mine. He comes closer, fitting between me. Fitting his hands under my legs, he grips my ass, and yanks me toward him.

I surrender. Leaning back, but keeping my torso off the bed, I rest my upper body weight on my arms.

Pulling his hands free, he signs, *"Don't lie back. I want you to watch."*

Oh. Dear. Lord.

I nod, excitement and a hunger growing inside me.

Pressing my knees wider, he exhales. His warm breath hits me between the legs, fanning out over my center and inner thighs. It takes all my strength not to collapse on the bed. The second he touches me, all bets are off. I may not be able to hold out. But, dammit, I want to watch.

No more than an inch separates me from his mouth. I shift, lifting my ass off the bed, desperate to close the gap between us, but his hands clamp down on my legs, biceps bulging, and he halts my advance.

Thor shakes his head, his eyes flicking to mine. My legs hold him captive, and I can feel the vibrations of his low chuckle. With a wicked gleam in his eye, and a grin to match, he speaks. His lips move. Vocal cords vibrate. Sound waves travel from his body and into mine. "My fifty, need girl. So impatient."

Fifty, need girl? What the hell kind of dirty talk is that? Lust has fried my brain. I can't anymore. Lipreading capabilities have ceased. I may not know what he actually said, but I understand the last sentence clear as day.

I nod, lifting my right hand. *"Yes. For you."* So goddamn impatient.

His smirk grows wider, a hint of teeth peeking out from behind his lips. Leaning in, he exhales again. Along with his teasing breath comes another round of pummeling desire, swallowing me whole, like a wave in the ocean.

I drop my head back, dying…wanting and waiting for that blissful second when our bodies connect.

Thor's fingertips press into the tops of my thighs, and I lift my head.

"Watch me, Red."

I lip-read every word this time. I watch him.

He moves closer, his nose making contact first, brushing lightly, teasing the sensitive bundle of nerves at my center, sending a cascade of longing down my spine and into my toes.

Then it's his tongue, moving upward, over my folds with firm pressure, ending with a swirling motion around my clit. Arms shaking, I try to hold myself up. This is the hottest thing I've ever seen, and I can't tear my eyes away. But I can't take anymore. I want to lie back, let my legs fall open, and give myself to him, body and soul.

I sit up a little more and hold my weight on my right arm, wrapping my left around his head, pressing him further against me.

His tongue is magic. There are no other words for it. I lift my hips to his mouth, grinding against him. Panting, my breath coming faster. I hold him tighter, refusing to let go.

The ache at my core is ready to burst.

Thor drives his hand under my ass and yanks me against his mouth, fucking me with his tongue. The rhythms of our bodies are the perfect choreography to push me over the edge.

And I lose it.

My body quakes, white light shoots through the darkness of my closed lids, and a long breathy sigh escapes my mouth.

Pulling away, Thor smiles at me with a devilish grin, pride beaming from his eyes. I came hard, he should be proud of himself. There's no denying the man's skills.

Fumbling to sit up, my body weak and boneless, Thor slaps his palm against mine, helping me up. *"We're just getting started, sweetheart."* He signs, dropping his pants to the floor, his erection springing free.

I can't help it; my eyes shine bright and wide. It's like getting to eat chocolate and peanut butter every day for the rest of my life. Only it's Thor and infinitely better.

His body on full display, I rake my eyes over each hard, inked, muscled line. His taut abs twitch. Will he let me touch yet? Is it my turn to reduce him to a quivering mass of satiated bliss?

Planting my feet on the floor, I stand. At my full height, the top of my head barely comes to the center of his chest. But I like it this way. When I rest my head on him, my cheek is directly over his heart.

I crane my neck to look at him, placing my hands at his waist, fingers brushing over his rigid V-cut. On my tiptoes, I reach up, begging him to meet me halfway, needing to feel his mouth on mine.

He understands. Folding his arms around me, he bends, pressing a soft kiss to my lips. He tastes like me. My heart thumps heavy in my chest, a heady desire spreads through me, and I'm ready for more.

Our kiss is slow and consuming. I don't know when his breath becomes mine, but I take it willingly. Needing it. I want him inside me in every way he can be.

Thor, without loosening his grip, or breaking our kiss, walks us to the bed. Gently, he lays me down, his body covering mine. Spreading my legs, he fits between them. His dick presses so close to where I want it. Naughty girl that I am, I lift my hips, making the tip of his cock slide over my clit.

God, yes!

I do it again. And again.

Yessss!

And again.

Lifting and sliding. A glorious rhythm, giving way to so much need. Each time I push the limit, guiding him to my opening, hoping he slips inside.

Thor pushes my shoulders, and I fall back onto the mattress. He covers me, his entire body pressed to mine. Kissing down my cheek, to my neck, his strong arms holding me to him. I sign against his back. *"God, you feel amazing. Take me, T-H-O-R."*

He lifts slightly, and already, I'm missing his weight. Opening my eyes, I stare up at him. The dark stubble on his jaw is a little more rugged, like he hasn't trimmed it up in a day or two, giving him an edgier look.

"You are so hot."

"Are you signing against my back?" he asks, smiling.

Grinning, I do it again. *"Yes."*

"Don't stop. I love it." He kisses me again. Deeper this time. How is that even possible?

And then he stops.

"What's going on?"

Looking over his shoulder, toward the door, he climbs off me, and holds up his index finger, as he walks to the door. Holy shit. Someone's here!

Scrambling, I claw at the blanket on the bed, and pull it over my legs and chest, covering myself. Thor's got the door cracked, hiding his body behind it, talking to someone. Craning my neck, I try to peek around the door, to see who it is.

Thor shuts the door and turns around, shrugging. *"Sorry. Roommate."* Walking back to the bed, he cuts to the side, making his way to the nightstand. Pulling open a drawer, he rummages around, and holds up a small foil wrapper between his fingers. "Where were we?"

I don't need to read his lips this time, his actions are screaming. Ripping open the packet, Thor rolls the condom over his dick. Even with the interruption, he's still rock-hard.

Tossing back the blanket, he jumps into bed. *Oh!*

Grabbing my hips, he jerks me down on the mattress, and kicks his leg over my waist, pinning me beneath him.

He pierces me with his sky-blue eyes and my breath evens out, in awe of the beautiful man on top of me. How far we've come in such a short time together.

I've picked up and committed to memory so many of his subtle traits, little pieces of him that speak louder than any words can. *I know you, Thorin Kline.*

I touch the pulse at the side of his neck, feeling his life beneath my fingertips, thumping a hurried beat as his emotions run high. I know the horizontal creases on his forehead, markers of how much he carries, but doesn't share. Swiping my fingers above his brow, I smooth the lines, wanting to lighten his load. *Let me in, baby.*

Thor searches my face, giving a small shake of his head.

I know this look, too. It's a question. *How are you here with me?*

It's the same question I ask myself. Thor and I are so different. Tattoos and freckled porcelain. Hearing and deaf. But, when we're together, the lines blur. Ink gets smeared all over the glass, and the contrast fades. We're one. Without even a word, we know what the other needs. We reside in the other's universe and understand.

His eyes speak of passion and longing, the way a flame whispers over paper, consuming it. Boring into his gaze, I lift my hands between us. *"Consume me, Thor."* I sign against his lips. *"Set me on fire. Burn me up."*

Brushing the hair off my cheek, he hovers at my center. He kisses my fingers, and he pushes inside so slowly, inch by inch, filling and stretching me. Stealing my breath away.

My lids flutter closed. Can't…concentrate. Feels…so…good.

I tighten around him, throwing my arms around his neck, lifting my pelvis. *Take me, Thor.* I need him to quiet the ache between my legs.

Languidly, he pulls out, teasing. My breath hitches, and he slides back in, burying himself deeper. Rolling his hips with each deliberate, calculated thrust.

"More," I sign on his back, mouthing the words so he can see. *"Please."*

Harder. Faster.

"More of what, baby?" He pushes into me, thrusting just a little harder than before. "This?" Quicken his pace by a half-beat he pulls back out, and slams into me again.

"Again." I buck my hips, spurring him on.

Obliging my request, he pumps into me, faster and faster, building tension inside me like an architect. His dick hits so deep. *Oh, yes!*

I climb higher and higher until there's nowhere for me to go…until I want to fall.

To let go.

To scream.

It's right there, a ball of suppressed emotion, charged sexual energy, sitting in the back of my throat, ready to be unleashed.

Our bodies rocking together, he brings me to the edge.

Covering me, he sucks my bottom lip into his mouth and I…

I almost…

Now's your chance, Harper. Let him hear you.

Seventeen years of silence and Thor makes me want to speak. To shout his name.

He slams into me at the same time his tongue pushes past my lips. Kissing me deep, our tongues thrusting to the same rhythm as our bodies.

Thor's groan rumbles against my mouth, and my chest, he moves into me one last time, and I'm gone. My body hums…so fucking alive. I clamp down around him, my hands on his ass, begging him to stay, to drive into me farther…to fuck me with every inch of his dick.

He pushes. And I force him closer.

Oh, God! Thor!

The words are on my tongue. I want him to have them. To hear what he does to me.

What if he hates it? What if it turns him off?

He pulls out, slamming into me again. And again. Chasing his own release.

And I swallow the words lodged in my throat.

I won't ruin this for him.

Two more thrusts and he's gone. The *"Fuuuuuck,"* that roars from his mouth, resonates through my body. He shutters, collapsing on top of me.

We lie still for a while, catching our breath. Thor's head, pressed against my chest, rises and falls whenever I inhale and exhale. Along with the scratch of his hair under my palm, he's pulled me into a hypnotic, post-O trance.

Lifting his head, he puts his chin between my boobs, and smiles at me. He brings his hand up, and traces an outline around my lips. "Since the first day I saw you..." He pauses, touching the left side of my mouth. "I've loved your smile. Right here"—he taps—"it's just a little higher than the other side."

My smile's crooked? Self-consciously, I smile through a frown, touching the left side of my mouth, pulling and tugging at the corners, measuring.

"*Stop.*" Thor sets a vertical hand on top of his open palm. "*It's beautiful.*" With his hands on the mattress—one on each side of me—he does a push-up, crashes his mouth against the left side of my "crooked" smile, and hauls himself out of bed. "*Party time.*" He grins and turns around, giving me a lovely view of his perfect ass.

Thor disappears out of the bedroom, and into the hallway, heading in the direction of the bathroom. After that workout, I'd much rather just stay cuddled in bed all night. But, tonight's important to Thor. And I finally get to meet his friends. That's huge.

Flinging the blanket off, I dangle my feet over the side of the bed, while I glance around the room. My clothes remain in a crumpled heap in the center of his floor. Great. I have sex hair and my dress is a wrinkled mess. It won't take a bunch of rock musicians long to figure out why Thor's late for the party.

Taking inventory of my sex-crazed hair, I pat and shove the defiant curls back into submission.

Feet hitting the ground, I stalk over to the pile of black fabric, picking up my panties, bra, and then my dress. Wrinkled as fuck. *Damn.*

Thor returns, standing in the doorway, pulling on a pair of boxer briefs, eyebrows wagging. *"I can get used to coming in my room and seeing this view."* He moves his hand up and down gesturing at my nakedness.

Shaking out my dress, I give him a pointed glare. I can't really be mad at him, I was a very willing participant, but if I need to blame someone for my less than stellar appearance when meeting his friends for the first time, I'm bestowing him the honor.

Laying my clothes out on the bed, hoping some time away from the heap will help the wrinkle situation, I head toward the bathroom, myself. Putting a hand on Thor's stomach I slip between him and doorway. Before I'm in the hallway, I feel Thor's hand on my arm.

Turning around, I look up at him.

"Can I ask you something?"

He really has gotten good at signing. My heart pinches in my chest, impressed and so touched. *"Anything."* I nod.

"When we"—he points to the bed—*"when you came. I thought for a minute…It seemed like…"* He stops.

I wait a few beats, giving him time to recall his words and signs.

"*That you wanted to say something. That you were going to talk. Am I right?*"

How did he now? Moving my head up and down, I sign, "*Yes. I almost did.*"

"*Why did you hold back?*"

It hits me. How much he's put into this relationship. How hard he's trying. We're speaking the same language. He's signing, and I understand him. He understands me. Tears burn my eyes. Besides Chloe, no other person in my life has ever made an effort to communicate with me. "*I wanted to. I got scared.*"

"*Why?*" His brows pinch together. "*Harper, you don't E-V-E-R have to be scared with me.*"

Thor stares at me for a minute, his blue eyes darkening. Shoulders slumped, he walks over to the bed, resting his elbows on his knees. I don't think I could have hurt him any worse than if I had taken a baseball bat to Lizzy.

Padding across the room, I pull the sheet off the bed and wrap it around my shoulders, taking a seat beside him. I know how much he wants to hear my voice. He's asked me before. But, tonight proved that I can't. Even with the intimacy of being as close as two people can possibly be, I still couldn't. I wanted to…I just couldn't.

I bump my shoulder into his, getting his attention. "*Why is it so important to you?*" Asking the question, a little flare of anger ignites in my belly. Yes, I know what he wants. But what about what I want? It's my choice. If I don't want to speak, I don't have to. Why does he keep pressing the issue?

"*I want to hear your voice so fucking bad.*"

So, having me the way I am isn't enough? The anger inside

me isn't a flare, but a grenade and his words just pulled the pin. Grabbing my panties off the mattress, I shove one leg in at a time, then go to work on my bra. Getting dressed the first time was a hell of a lot easier.

Thor watches as I yank and tug my dress into place. Scanning the room for my shoes, I don't see them. Come to think of it, I don't remember taking them off. They've got to be downstairs.

Without a word, I walk to the doorway. His hand lands on my arm. Glancing over my shoulder, I see his lips move. "Where are you going?"

I whirl on him. *I'm leaving.* I clip my signs, anger coursing through my body. *I'm tired of you asking me to do something I'm not willing to give you. Seventeen years. I haven't spoken a goddamn word in seventeen fucking years. Respect my choices and leave it alone.* I drop my hands, shoulder's heaving. I'd be surprised if he got all of that, but right now, I'm so pissed, I could give zero fucks.

"You know what?" he yells. I know he's yelling because his mouth opens wider than it does when he speaks. And I can see the anger exploding in his eyes. "I've busted my ass learning ASL for *you.*" He points to me, poking a finger in my chest. "I want to communicate with you. I wish you cared to do the same for me."

Oh, so we're going to play the Who Cares More game, huh? Fuck you, Thorin Kline. "I was stupid to ever think a relationship with a hearing person could ever work. You don't understand. And let's not forget about all the secrets you keep from me. If you cared, you'd tell me what's going on with your mom. What shit *your dad has done. I'm so tired of you pushing me away. Not trusting ME!"*

Turing my back to him, I leave his room, and run down the stairs. In the living room, I grab my discarded shoes lying in front of the door, turn the knob and get the fuck out of his place before he comes after me.

Unlocking the Bug, I climb inside and push the engine start button. Bolting out of the parking lot, I head toward home, tears blurring my vision.

* * *

Fitting the key in the door, I push it open, already hating myself. What have I done? Bobby wags his tail at my feet, jumping up on his back legs, dancing around. Not even his Instagram-worthy mugging can pull me out of this slump. I want to sit on the couch, hide under my car blanket, eat a bowl of chocolate ice cream as big as my head, and dump peanut butter cups on top until I puke.

Chloe, sitting on the couch, looks up from the laptop perched on crisscrossed legs. Her large, black framed glasses sitting on the tip of her nose, she cocks her head and pushes them up. *"What happened to you? You look like Bobby when he gets kicked out of your bedroom on nights Thor sleeps over."* She pats the couch.

Falling onto the cushion beside her, Bobby jumps on my lap, licking my face. I pat his head, scooping him into my arms, hugging him.

"I won't have to kick him out anymore."

"*What happened?*"

Shaking my head, I let all the sadness, anger, and confusion come pouring out. I lay my head on Chloe's shoulder, tears slipping from my eyes. "*He wants to hear my voice.*"

"*Oh.*" More than anyone, Chloe knows how much I hate speaking. She accepts that about me and doesn't push.

"*If the two people in my life, who are supposed to love me no matter what, preferred it better when I didn't speak, why in the hell would Thor want to hear me?*"

Chloe shrugs, remaining quiet for a beat, then raises her hands. "*That's where trust comes in.*"

I lift my head to look at her. "*Trust? That's a two-way street. How can I trust someone who doesn't trust me? I've begged him to let me in. To trust me with the secret he keeps bottled up inside. And he stays quiet.*" Standing, I tuck Bobby under my arm and wipe my eyes on my shirtsleeve. "*That first date was a mistake. How many hearing boys do I have to go out with before I learn my lesson? I will never be enough the way I am.*"

Before Chloe can convince me I'm wrong, I turn on my heel, and hit the stairs. Bobby licks my face, knowing just want I need…without me saying a word.

CHAPTER TWENTY-TWO

THOR

"How many times do I have to tell you that you're not like him?" Mom scolds.

Yep. She's feeling better.

"You think your father would have ever learned another language for me? Hell, in the early days, I thought it was a sign of true love when he put his dirty underwear in the hamper. Guess how often that happened?"

I switch ears, pressing the phone between my face and shoulder as I unlock my back door. "Never."

"Twice. It happened twice in twenty years we were married. On our wedding night, and next day, during our honeymoon. You, son, are not your father. Who takes care of me? Sure as hell ain't your old man."

Dropping the keys on the counter, I book it up the stairs, taking them two at a time. "Think it's finally sinking in." I get it loud and clear. Even when Harper and I argued last week, the fiery rage that usually burns through me—especially when

I'm face to face with my dad—it didn't rear its ugly head. "You taking it easy, Ma?" I ask, pulling Lizzy's case from behind the nightstand. Flipping the latches, I grab Lizzy from the bed and tuck her away. We've got a date…hopefully.

"Yeah. Start my self-defense class tomorrow."

"No shit! That's great. I'm proud of you."

When Dad came sniffing around Mom's apartment complex a week or so after the attack, hoping to get his truck back, the cops nailed him. And since I convinced Mom to press charges, Raymond Kline won't be getting out of prison anytime soon. He can rot in there for all I care.

Mom's safe. She's taking steps to protect herself. The band is off to a fucking great start. For once, I don't feel like I have to look over my shoulder, or wait for the other shoe to drop. Can't remember a time in my life when I've felt so free.

Now I just have to get my girl back.

"Listen, Ma. I've got an appointment I'm running late for. Call you tomorrow? I want to hear all about your class." Jogging down the stairs, Lizzy in tow, I grab my keys, and head out the back door.

"Sure thing. And you let me know when I get to meet Harper? You can't keep her all to yourself, forever."

I can sure as hell try. Because I do…I want to keep her. Not share her with anyone. Forever. "I'll keep you posted." Unlocking the trunk on the Charger, I stow my guitar case.

"'Bye, baby. Love you."

"Love you, too. See you soon." I click the end button and fire up the engine. Before I back out, I send Harper another text. I know she's getting them, the read receipts confirm it.

Red, text me. Not giving up.

Tossing my phone on passenger seat and throwing the car into reverse, I back out, and head for the one place I know Harper won't be. I've got to enlist a little help if my plan is going to work.

Driving toward Harper and Chloe's house, another difference between me and my dad slams into me, separating us farther: I'm looking forward to showing Harper King how much I fucking adore her. No, scratch that. I don't just adore her, I love her. She's my last thought when I fall asleep at night, and the first when I wake up in the morning. I don't ever want that to chance. And even if she doesn't take me back, that won't change.

Before Harper, I was a selfish prick. An asshole. More like my dad than I wanted to admit. And to win Harper back, I need to prove to her that I'm not the old Thor. That I do trust her. I know she thinks I'm the most selfish person in the world right now. Wanting to hear her voice, for her to tell me how she feels, what *makes* her feel, was ever my only intent. For her to trust me.

I know her parents let her down when she was a kid. More than anyone, I know what that's like. And yes, our stories a different, but that doesn't mean either of us hurt any less because of what we lived through.

My broken bones healed, but Dad's words are like daily punches to the gut. I will carry his fucking voice with me for the rest of my life. And it's a struggle not to listen to his lies. That's why I need Harper. Her truths are louder than any of his bullshit.

I'm sure the same is true for Harper. At least, I hope so. Thank God she didn't have bruises to hide, or bones to set, but she has the open wounds of a relationship to stich back together. I'm glad her parents are trying to mend all those years of hurt and sadness, and are trying to do right by her. But the fact remains, their actions left lasting scar tissue around her heart.

It's no wonder my constant nagging sent her running. I kept ripping away at the scar tissue until it was sore and raw. I hurt her. And now it's time to repair the damage I caused. If it's not too late.

I fucking need her. I can't live without her. I refuse to allow some unspoken words and my fear of becoming something I'm not, get in our way.

Swinging the Charger into their driveway, I kill the engine, and climb out. Blood pounds loud in my ears, I thought the concert for the kindergarteners was going to be the hardest gig of my life. I was wrong by a long shot. If this goes down the way I want it to, my solo concert in two weeks will be the most difficult and most important gig of my fucking life.

I lift the guitar case from the trunk and slam the lid. Staring up at the house, all looks quiet. I hope she didn't forget I was coming over.

My boots fall heavy on the concrete walkway. I press the doorbell. And I wait. And hope.

Inside, Bobby barks. I can hear his little feet scratching against the door. Thirty seconds later, Chloe pulls it open, arms crossed over her chest, glaring at me.

"Hi?" I offer, giving her a sheepish grin. She looks pissed.

The refrain of Hall and Oates's "Maneater" plays on a loop in my brain.

She cocks an eyebrow, but still doesn't say anything.

Time to make nice with the best friend and gravel at her feet. "I know. I screwed up. That's why I need to see you. I need your help to fix it."

"Damn right, you screwed up. But"—a conspiratorial smile creeps to her lips—"it takes a good man to want to fix it. I'm glad you called." She pushes the door open wider and lets me inside.

Bobby demands my attention first, doing his little hindquarters dance, standing and spinning on his back legs. Crouching down, I scratch him behind his ears, and get an unsolicited face wash at the same time. "Hey there, buddy. Long time no see. I've missed you, too." Bobby yips his agreement, giving me a piece of his mind.

With one last pat on his head, I stand, Lizzy in hand, ready to get my plan started and my girl back. "Here's the deal. My ASL is getting better each day. But, I need some help working out the signs for a song I wrote. I was hoping you'd be the chick to help me out?"

"First of all, I'm not a chick. I don't cluck, and there's not a feather on me." She points.

This chi— Er, lady, has spunk. I like it.

"Second," she continues, "don't hurt Harper again. She's been miserable this whole week."

Her words hit me in the chest like an ax sticking right in my heart. Not that I'm glad Harper's been miserable, but, it's nice to hear that she's missing me. Why else would she be miserable? That glimmer of hope is all I need. This plan is going to fucking work.

"I didn't mean to hurt her. That was never my intention. I love her, Chloe. And I need to prove it to her. I need her to hear it."

The hard, protective, badass-friend armor falls away. "You love her?" She folds her hands over chest and her voice gets all squeaky and high pitched. When I told Griffin, he patted me on the back and told me to go get her.

Women are the weirdest fucking creatures.

I nod. "Will you help me, please?"

She shakes her head up and down, excitedly, a huge-ass grin on her face. "Let me hear the song."

"Thank you." A little anxiety burns away. One small piece of the puzzle coming together. Now, I just have to trust that the largest piece still fits next to me.

Unlatching the guitar case, I pull Lizzy onto my lap. Tuning her up, I give Chloe a small concert, singing the song over and over, while she translates my voice and words into motion.

* * *

Three weeks, one day, twenty-one hours, forty-two minutes, and twelve seconds. Thirteen seconds.

Fourteen seconds.

It's been too fucking long since I've seen or heard from Harper. I honestly thought she'd text me back once the anger and fire burned away. My girl is stubborn, I'll give her that. But, so am I. If Chloe comes through for me, I'll see Harper tonight.

Eighteen seconds.

I click my phone off and stuff it in my back pocket. Watching the clock isn't going to make Harper appear. If she does at all. Hell, she's gone three weeks without me, maybe I just need to face facts and find some way to move on. Maybe Harper's done and she's already moved on.

But, I've got to try. I want her to know that I haven't given up on us. And, if tonight doesn't work, then at least I'll know I gave it my all. Put my heart on the line. Gave it to her, no fucking strings attached. If she doesn't want it, it's going to hurt like a son of a bitch. It always will. But, at least I can say that I know what it's like to have had something real. Never thought I'd be that guy, but the second I saw her in the audience that night, my perspective shifted, the volume was turned up, and all I could hear was Harper King.

That's been the only thing keeping me going these last few weeks. Knowing *whom* I'm fighting for.

Come on, Chloe.

Under the diving board, I pace to the opposite end of the pool, my third complete lap.

Commence lap four. I kick the same baseball-sized rock that's kept me company, sending it down to the other end of the pool. On my return lap, I kick the mini boulder again. Rinse. Repeat.

Lap six. Kick. Turn back.

My phone vibrates against my ass cheek. Mid-kick, ready for lap seven, I pull my phone out faster than Harper can down a bag of mini Reese's. Glancing at the screen, I see Chloe's name, bright and promising. Umm…we're here. I think? This place is a dump. Are you sure this is the right address? I'm supposed to leave her here? Yeah, I'm not quite comfortable with that. This place looks like the hangout of a serial killer. You're not a serial killer, are you?

I roll my eyes as my thumbs scramble to hit the right keys. Goddammit! She better not leave. Yes. This is the right place. No, I am not a serial killer. Harper's been here before, she knows this place. Convince her to come in. Please.

This is going to be the hard part. If Harper is finished with me...with us, she won't come in and my plan is fucked. This is where Chloe has to sell it.

Chloe: Okaaaaay? (That was said with large amounts of skepticism.) She wants to know why you want to see her.

Fuck. Really? Like she doesn't know? Just tell her to come in and hear me out. After that, if she still wants to leave, I'll let her go.

My lungs burn in my chest. Goddamn. Hardest fucking text message I've ever had to type.

I check the clock, the app with the analogue version—I need the second hand. It's not a grandfather clock, but it will do. Phase two of my plan, if things go my way. A new clock on my body, only this one won't be a reminder of when I was broken; but a keepsake of when I was put back together...made whole.

Minutes tick by. No Harper. No messages.

When the five-minute mark passes with no communication, bile rise in my throat. The silence of this place is deafening.

She's not coming.

Kicking the rock on last time, I send it flying against the side of the pool. Walking back to my spot, I roll up the blanket and blow out the candles. Fucking candles. So much for doing the romantic thing.

Sitting on the cold concrete, I lean back against the side of the pool, and pull my knees up and rest my elbows on top. Turning my silent phone around in my hands, I'm tempted to text Chloe. To find out what happened. What good would that do me, though? At least this way, I can sugarcoat the truth. Lie to myself.

Rubbing a hand over my face, I check the time again. She was supposed to be here fourteen minutes ago.

I'm fucking cold. Time to pack it in.

Picking up my shit, I stow the blanket under my arm and gather the three lavender candles I brought at that girlie bed-and-bath place. A chuckle catches in my throat. I'd spent an ungodly amount of time in that store, smelling every fucking candle until I found the one that smelled like Harper.

Lavender candles. Not even a worthwhile consolation prize. More like a cruel joke. *Thanks for playing the game of love, Thorin. You lose, but take these scented candles to keep you warm and pining at night.*

Everything in one hand, I go to the rickety ladder, and pull myself onto the bottom rung. Halfway up, I peel my eyes away from my feet, and look to the pool deck. Harper's standing above me.

"Holy shit!" I yell, feet slipping on the rung. The ladder wobbles, but I manage to keep a strong grip. Not going to let an old rusted ladder throw me off its back like some fucking bull. Biting my bottom lip, my heart jumps in throat. Damn. If

I'm going to die of a fucking heart attack, at least Harper was the last person I saw. I can die a happy man.

Harper bends over and holds out her hand. Passing her the blanket and the candles, I climb the rest of the way up.

I don't know how it's possible, but in the three weeks we've been apart, she's gotten more beautiful. Her wild, red curls—the defiant ones—spring out from the rest of her hair like flames dancing in the moonlight.

She bites her left, lower lip, the crooked side, if she were smiling. Instead, she looks sad…withdrawn. I've never seen her like this. My Harper wears her crooked smile like a badge of honor, flashing it whenever she's given the opportunity. Her eyes always sparkle like sea glass. But not now, there's no light in her eyes.

I may not have taken my fist to her, but I did this. I broke all the things that lit her up inside. And now I need to put her back together and never break her again.

"Thanks for coming," I sign. I've been practicing my ass off. Even enrolled in a basic ASL course at the community college starting next semester. Not sure how I'm going to squeeze that into record studio life, but I will make it work. It's important to her, it's important to me. Plus, I fucking love that sparkle in her eyes when she watches me sign. Who would have ever thought Thorin Kline would be a college man with a girl on his arm.

She nods, handing my things back. Still no light in her eyes. *Work harder, Thor. Bring it back.*

Taking the blanket and candles, I set them on the ground. *"Not really how I picture this going down. But I'll take it. I'm glad you're here."*

"Chloe said I needed to hear you out." She shoves her hands in her pockets, curling her shoulders inward, bracing herself against the cold November air.

I reach for the blanket, unfurl it, and drape it over her shoulders. She doesn't protest or take it off, that's a small victory in the Thor column, right? At this point, I'm counting every little win in my favor.

"I'd like that."

The left side of her mouth twitches upward, the hint of a smile just below the surface. And I'll take that one, too.

Pulling in a lungful of cold, night air, I crack my knuckles, straighten my back, and tilt my head side-to-side, making my neck pop. My onstage ritual before any performance. Except this isn't a performance, it's the real damn thing. I may pour my heart and soul into every single song I play on stage, but tonight, I'm giving my heart away. I just hope she wants it.

"I've been practicing this a lot, but I'm still not very good." I know the signs, it's just getting my hands to make them, that's when I struggle. Harper and Chloe are so good. Their fingers and hands move over each word like poetry. My signing looks more like death metal.

"Just do your best." And she smiles. A small one, but it's real. And it's mine. For me. I'll fucking take it.

"I wrote you a song."

She cocks her head, leveling me with a pointed stare. I can see the skepticism in her eyes.

"Here goes."

Taking my phone from my back pocket, I unlock the screen and find the rough cut I recorded a few weeks ago. All the time

I would have spent with her, I spent in the studio, working out this song. Kept my mind off the fact that I wasn't with her.

"Will you hold this?" I ask, pushing my phone toward her. I'm going to need my hands free.

Harper takes it, our fingers brushing in the exchange. Okay, I may have set that up, I'm fucking dying to touch her.

"Press play whenever." I instruct, heart thumping in my ears. Signing a song is nothing like playing it on the guitar, and I'm nervous as hell. I don't want to fuck this up.

Harper's finger hovers over the play button, dropping on it with a quick tap. The sound is turned to full volume, so she can feel the tinny vibrations filtering through the small speakers.

The recording crackles with rawness, none of the studio magic to clean it up. Just me, Lizzy, and a microphone.

> *Saw you in the noisy crowd.*
> *A firelight in the dark.*
> *A blazing siren, bold and loud*
> *You claimed my beaten heart.*
>
> *Lost. Uncharted. But wanting it now.*
> *Can't ignore the sea glass siren.*
> *Hear me. Take me. This is my vow.*
> *The clouds begin to brighten.*
>
> *And I*
> *Live out loud.*
>
> *Live out loud through the fire.*

Live out loud through the pain.
Live out loud in the silence.
You're my everything.

With every breath, each strum of the guitar filtering out of my phone's speakers, I keep my eyes glued on Harper. Just like the night I first saw her at Mississippi Lights, I couldn't look away then…I can't look away now.

Live out loud through the pain.
Live out loud in the silence.
You're my everything.

The music ends with a loud *click* where I turned off recording equipment. Silence buzzes in my ears, the remnants of the lingering music waves in the night air.

Harper's breaths come fast. Still wrapped in my blanket, she bites her lower lip.

"*I'm sorry, R-E-D. I'm sorry for everything. For keeping secrets. Not letting you in. And for hurting you, making you feel less than, because that's not it. You mean more to me than Lizzy, and air, and all the stars in the fucking sky. And if I get the chance, I'll do better.*"

She sucks in a gulp of air.

"*I need you. The way you are. No changes.*" I step closer, hoping she'll welcome my advance. "*I want you. The way you are. No changes.*" Lifting the blanket from her shoulders, I let it fall to the ground. Unshed tears glisten in her eyes, looking more like sea glass than ever. "*I trust you. With my life. My heart.*

Everything that's me. I love you. The way you are, for who you are. Every part of you. And I guarantee my love will change. It will grow with each tick of the clock. I'm tired of keeping it quiet. I love you, Harper King."

She lets the tears fall. With my thumb, I brush one away as I circle my arms around her back, drawing her to my chest. When she doesn't pull away, I know everything's going to be okay.

I place a kiss on her forehead and close my eyes. Breathing her in, I memorize the way her body fits to mine, never wanting to forget what this feels like—to have her back in my arms after being gone for so long.

She reaches for me, putting her tiny hand against my cheek. Lowering my head, my lips find hers. A sweet kiss, unhurried, but heavy with wanting, our mouths brush together. This is the kind of kiss that writes poetry and love songs. The kind of kiss that leaves a mark, just like when lightning kisses the sand. It fuses us together, into something unique and strong.

When we finally pull apart, I stare into her green eyes, searching. "I'm sorry, Harper." I say again. Gently laying my hand against her mouth, I lower my middle and ring fingers, signing, *"I love you."*

She kisses my fingers and folds them into her hands. Our entwined hands fall to our side and she opens her mouth like she's going to say something.

Shaking my head, I lean in and kiss her before she tries. I didn't put this whole make up scene together in order to get something out of her. If she ever decides to speak out loud, it will be on her time, not because I put together some grand gesture to win her heart.

"I want you the way you are, no changes. I hear you loud and clear, Harper King." I press a hand to her heart, feeling it beat a fast and steady.

She kisses the corner of my mouth, tasting her salty tears on my lips. Warm and wonderful.

"I love you, too. Thor." She presses her hand against my mouth, *"I love you."*

And time stands still.

EPILOGUE

HARPER

Five months later…

"I'm so glad to have you home." I sign, sitting between Thor's sprawled legs on the couch. He pulls me close, wrapping his arms around my waist until my back is pressed to his chest. *"That tour was long."* For over two weeks, I've had to share him with the world. Tonight, he's all mine.

Well, maybe not all mine.

Not wanting to miss any opportunity to snuggle, Bobby jumps onto my lap wagging his tail. Thor's chest rumbles and he brings his hand up to scratch Bobby's head. Bobby's tail beats faster and he uses me as a stepladder to get closer to Thor. *"I'm not the only one who missed you."*

Thor pushes my hair to the side and rests his chin on my shoulder, giving Bobby better access to lick to his heart's content. I close my eyes, reveling in the feel of Thor's laughter. I love it. My whole body shakes and the vibrations from his voice are the best kind of music.

With enough puppy love, Thor falls back against the arm of

the couch and Bobby steps off my chest, making circles on my lap until he finds the most comfortable spot to curl into a ball.

I glance down at Thor's tattooed arms wrapped around my midsection. I love the way he holds me, so protective. With my index finger, I trace one of the many clocks he has inked on his skin. After our short breakup last fall, he finally told me what each clock meant to him—a reminder of all the times his father hurt him. It broke my heart when he told me. He still carries the haunting look of that broken little boy, despite his rough exterior. But, then there's light in his eyes, too. Hope.

My finger travels to the underside of his left forearm, to his newest tattoo, and the largest clock he has inked on his skin. He calls it "Harper's clock", because it reminds him of the moment I became his. Little does he know, but I became his the night we first met. I knew even then that what we shared was special.

I love Thor's tattoos; they're the physical manifestation of his resilience, his strength. He took a horrible, dark time in his life and turned it into something beautiful.

Thor pushes my hair to the side again, this time so he can kiss my neck. A smile blooms across my face at the feel of his lips on my skin. I can't think of a better way to spend an evening. God, I missed him.

Closing my eyes, I give myself over to the sensation—the electric zing that pulses through my veins each time his mouth presses against me takes my breath away. I squeeze his arms, forcing him to hold me tighter. With the whirlwind life the two of us lead now, the need to anchor myself to him is even stronger.

Thor wiggles his hands free from under mine, and I open my eyes. *"Today was nice."*

I nod, smiling. *"I had fun at your mom's. Glad I could help her get those pictures on the wall. How long has she been asking you to do that?"* Craning my neck around, I give him a quick, playful glare.

"A long time." He laughs, his chest rumbling against my back. *"Hey, cut the rock star some slack."*

"Not to long ago you were an auto mechanic, Mr. Rock Star," I chide.

The whole "I'm dating a friggin' rock star" notion got real when he had to give up his job at the lube shop. There just wasn't enough time in the day for Thor to live in both worlds. And when the interviews, screaming fans, sold-out concerts, and the paychecks started rolling in, I could tell that being a career musician suited him.

Outwardly, Thor's very modest about the whole professional musician gig, but when he gets up on stage, he burns so bright. He truly loves what he does. And he's damn good at it.

Every time I see him perform, it's like Mississippi Lights all over again. The hum of the music combine with the fire in Thor's eyes when he finds me in the audience, it blows my everloving mind.

"I loved working on cars."

I run my fingers over his, the calluses still thick, but the dark stain of motor oil has long since disappeared. *"But you love what you do now, right?"* Maybe I've read him wrong this whole time. Maybe he doesn't like the spotlight as much as he lets on.

"I do. Making music is all I've ever wanted to do. Cars will just have to be my hobby."

"Our hobby," I correct, leaning close and planting a kiss on his fingertips.

"Damn right, Red." He tightens his arms around me.

We're quiet for a while when it hits me, how much I love this…how much I love *him*. It's the simple moments like this that are the loudest. Our heart beats…our breaths…our bodies aligned so perfectly that everything's in sync. Every sensation is magnified. In the chaos of our daily lives, we lose this simplicity. But, it's the promise that after a long day apart, we get to come back together. As long as we have each other, we live each day out loud and to the fullest. The outside world doesn't matter, only what we have right here in each other's arms. This is all I want to hear.

And for the first time in seventeen years, I'm not scared to tell him how I feel.

Thor's been asking me for weeks if I'll move in with him, and I've been putting him off. I've always been a planner. Thor wasn't in my plan, and moving in together was an idea floating around in a whole different galaxy. Hell, I can already see the text messages from my mother, and they aren't good. Mom's still coming to terms with the whole "In a band and has tattoos" idea. But, she's working on it, for me.

Sitting up, I shift my body around. Bobby gives me a dirty look and jumps on the floor. Staring into Thor's blue eyes, I muster all my strength. *"Do you still want to move in together?"*

His left eyebrow quirks up. *"Yes. Why?"*

"I'm ready."

"*Really?*" Thor sits up this time, his smile growing by the second. "*You're serious?*"

I suck in a deep breath and concentrate on pushing it out, coordinating the flow of air along with the movement of my tongue and lips. "Yes," I say, the word rising from my throat and coming out of my mouth on a puff of air.

Thor's eyes widen, shining a magnificent color blue, like two blazing stars. He doesn't move for almost three heartbeats. "*You.*" He points at me. "*You just spoke. You said, 'yes.'*"

I nod, a huge-ass grin on my face. "*Yes.*"

"You just said you'd move in with me!" he shouts. His heavy voice resonates inside his body, and I can feel the vibrations. "You *said* it!" Putting his hands against my cheeks, he shakes his head. "Harper!" Leaning in, he kisses me. Soft and sweet.

"*I love you,*" he signs. "*So goddamn much.*"

Not afraid anymore, I kiss him back, hard. "I love you, Thor." I let the words fall from my lips and onto his.

His arms come around me and he deepens our kiss, taking my words into him.

Our hearts beat together and it's the loudest thing I've ever heard.

Acknowledgments

I can't believe I'm writing the acknowledgments for my fifth novel. It's so surreal! Thank you to all my readers who have gotten me to this point. If you weren't reading, then I wouldn't have five books on the shelves. Thank you.

To my agent, Louise Fury, your love, kindness, and guidance are invaluable to me. Thank you for believing in me, even when things aren't going so well. I love having you in my corner! And thank you, Kristin, for your amazing edits. You and Louise always steer my work in the right direction.

Thank you, Megha Parekh, for believing in my work. I couldn't have had a better editor to work on five books with! Thank you for everything! And to Lexi Smail, for all your guidance, and making the transition of editors seamless; I'm happy to have gotten to work with you!

To the Forever Yours team, thank you for the beautiful cover art, publicity, and getting my books into the hands of readers. I appreciate all you do for me!

A special thank-you to Meredith Tate, my friend and fount of New England knowledge! If I portrayed New Hampshire incorrectly, I take full responsibility. Meredith shared with me her love of her home state with me and I hope I did it justice. Thanks for your help, Mer, can't wait to try a cider doughnut one day!

My family. With this book especially, thank you. I know I put a lot on hold to get this book finished. Thank you for supporting me and understanding when Mom had to write. I love you endlessly.

And a final thank-you to my Lord and Savior, Jesus Christ. I'm blessed that you have given me the gift of storytelling. Thank you for giving me the opportunity to share my stories!

Author's Note

I loved writing Harper's story. From the first time I envisioned Harper, she was a strong-willed, intelligent, deaf woman. I loved getting to know her. She was a challenging and wonderful character to write. I owe and extra measure of thanks to Kristin Smith for directing me to so many wonderful Deaf resources, so I could bring Harper to life. I studied a lot of American Sign Language (ASL) for this book, read many books with deaf characters, and sought the advice of deaf and hard-of-hearing friends and acquaintances in order to make sure I portrayed Harper accurately and with sensitivity. Any unintentional errors fall solely on my shoulders and are not the fault of those I received information from.

In this story, Harper and other characters use American Sign Language. I love learning new languages, so taking a course in ASL at my local library was right up my ally. I understand that ASL does not translate well to the written word, and for storytelling purposes, the signed dialogue was written as if it were spoken. But, I tried hard to preserve some of the sign language when describing the characters hand movements and facial expressions.

I'm proud of Harper and I hope that you, the reader, are too! I'm glad she and Thor got to tell their unique love story!

PLEASE SEE THE NEXT PAGE FOR AN
EXCERPT FROM

MARIE MEYER'S *LONG ROAD HOME*

AVAILABLE NOW!

CHAPTER ONE

Ren

I swing my hip into the door, my hands overtaken by the giant garment bag containing the maid-of-honor dress my best friend chose for me. A bell sounds as I exit the bridal shop. Stepping onto the sidewalk, the warm breeze of an early June morning ruffles the plastic slung over my forearm. I speed-walk to my car, having exactly twenty-eight minutes to get to work. I am so late. There's no way in hell a final fitting should have taken forty minutes. I love Dylen, but being her maid of honor is beginning to fuck with my life.

Digging my keys from my purse, I slide my thumb over the unlock button, and my car's headlights wink in response. I yank the door open and snap the seat forward. Groping the interior wall of the car, my fingers brush over the plastic hook, and I tug it down, simultaneously losing the grip on my keys. They fall with a *thunk* onto the sidewalk.

"Shit! I don't have time for this!" I cram the dress into the car, prop the hanger on the hook, and take a step backward.

Bending over, I scoop the keys off the concrete just in time to hear a catcall. *Really?*

Standing, I whirl around. Two men in well-tailored suits, a few paces up the sidewalk, look over their shoulders and grin at me.

"Looking good, nursey. Loving the SpongeBob scrubs," the shorter one says—probably the same one that let out the disgusting whistle. "I'd like to visit your Bikini Bottom." The taller guy laughs and congratulates his buddy with a jab to the shoulder.

What morons.

Shaking my head, I give them the one-finger salute and round the car. "Oh, that's original," I shout, climbing into my car. If I wasn't already so late, I would have thought of a better comeback, but then again, they aren't worth my time. "Dicks," I growl under my breath. With my mood in the toilet, I start the car and ease out of the parking space.

Traffic is light through town, and thankfully, the interstate isn't backed up—an advantage to being late, I guess.

With the road wide open, I press my foot onto the accelerator and don't let up. The speedometer inches its way toward seventy and doesn't stop.

Cranking the volume on the radio, I let the sweet, sad lyrics of Tim McGraw and Taylor Swift's newest collaboration rid me of my lingering irritation at the male gender, and I fly down the freeway.

I tap out the beat of the song on the steering wheel, and with the next line on the tip of my tongue, I swallow the words as my eyes are drawn to the rearview mirror.

Red and blue flashing lights.

I glance at my speedometer and back off the gas pedal. I'm not going *that* fast. My heart drops into the acidic pit of my stomach. "You've got to be fucking kidding me," I groan, guiding my car to the shoulder. *Maybe if I just get out of the way, he'll go around me?*

No such luck.

The cruiser slows to a halt several feet behind my car. *Could this day get any worse?* I did not have time for this. I close my eyes, take a few deep breaths, and try to slow my racing pulse. Eight years of being a licensed driver with a spotless record are about to go down the drain.

With a sigh, I turn off the radio, and reach for my glove box. I withdraw my registration, and then go for my purse, tugging my license from my wallet, anything to speed along the process. However, glancing in my rearview, I can tell the police officer has designs to make this take as long as possible. What the hell is he doing? Why is he just sitting in his cruiser?

For three long minutes, I sit and stare at the road, watching car after car happily speed toward their destination, before I hear a tap on my passenger-side window.

Startled by his sudden appearance, my heart jumps into my throat. "Oh, goodness!" I choke, my hands flying to my chest.

Shaking, I press the button and the window lowers.

"Good day, ma'am." He nods, removing his sunglasses.

Hello, Green Eyes.

He's young. My age at least. And hot. Doughnuts aren't one of his staple foods. *Maybe being pulled over isn't so bad after all.* "Hi," I stutter. How I stumble on a one-syllable word, I don't know, but I did nonetheless.

"In a hurry?" he asks in a deep, authoritative voice.

"I'm sorry, Officer, I didn't think I was—"

"I clocked you at seventy-six," he says, cutting me off. He stares unblinkingly, like he's daring me to argue with his assessment.

"That's only eleven miles over," I say, pleading my case.

"Exactly, 'over' being the applicative word. The speed limit isn't a suggestion, miss." He cocks his head and brings his hand up, fingers wagging impatiently. "License and registration."

I pass the items over, and he clutches them between his giant thumb and forefinger.

He stands up to his full height, and I have to slouch in my seat to see him out the window. He squints his eyes in the sunlight, reading the information on my vehicle registration card. While he looks over my identification, my eyes fall to his nametag: C. Sinclair. I wonder what the "C" stands for. Am I allowed to ask? I try different names…*Chris Sinclair? Cameron? Calvin?*

My lips pull up at the corners. The only Calvin I know of is the one in the *Calvin and Hobbes* comics I read as a kid. This guy doesn't look like a Calvin to me.

Officer Sinclair taps my license on the window frame and bends low to peer into my car. I shoot up in my seat, trying to conceal the smile on my face. I wouldn't want him to think I thought this situation was funny. That might get me into more trouble. And there was no way I can tell him I was checking him out. Judging by his no-nonsense attitude, he would have no tolerance for that. "I'll be right back, Ms. Daniels," he grumbles, sounding irritated.

I watch him walk back to his car, his ass looking fine in my rearview. He may be Officer No Nonsense, but he is fun to look at.

Damn, look at his arms! I'd like to pin him to my Pinterest "arm porn" board. I can't help it, I gawk, unapologetically. Jesus, their circumference is larger than my head's. He's so freaking hot.

I pull my eyes from the rearview and scoop my phone off the passenger seat and type out a text to the charge nurse, letting her know why I'm so late.

My eyes flick from the rearview mirror to my dashboard clock. *What is he doing?* It's not like I have any outstanding warrants, or anything. I've never had so much as a parking ticket. Yet, he sits in his cruiser, typing away on his dashboard computer.

Five minutes later, he reappears at my window. "Okay, Ms. Daniels, we're about finished." With a flick of his wrist, he tosses back the cover of a small, thick book and begins scratching his pen across the paper. "I need a signature right here." He taps the paper with the pen, where he wants me to sign. Flipping the pad around, he holds it through the window.

Leaning over the passenger seat, I take the pen and scribble my name next to the "X" he's drawn. "There," I say, handing his pen back.

Without a word, he snatches it and rips the yellow paper off the top of the pad. "Slow down, Ms. Daniels." He holds the ticket between his big fingers, waiting for me to take it.

I mourn the death of my perfect driving record. Scowling, I

pluck the ticket from his hand and look up at him.

He pierces me with his green eyes, but still no congenial smile. No hint of humor in his demeanor. Zero bedside manner; it's a good thing he isn't a doctor. But, he's got the badass cop thing going for him.

"Thanks," I whisper, embarrassed that I got caught breaking the law.

Officer Sinclair steps away from my car but doesn't make a move to return to his cruiser. I put up the window, toss the ticket and my forms of identification onto the passenger seat, and then put the car in drive.

Remembering excerpts from *Rules of the Road*, I turn off my hazards and signal, waiting for the opportune moment to merge back onto the interstate. Each move I make, I feel Officer Sinclair's scrutinizing gaze, watching me…evaluating me. *Why is he just standing there? Back to your car, mister, nothing to see here. I'm a law-abiding citizen.*

Once I'm on the road, picking up speed—but careful not to exceed sixty-five—I sneak a peek in my rearview. He has his door open and is climbing inside.

I fumble with the settings on the cruise control and take my foot off the accelerator. At least this way, I won't run the risk of my heavy foot getting me into trouble again.

In my haste to get away from Officer Sinclair, I neglected to look at the ticket. How much do I owe the lovely state of Missouri for my disobedience?

Picking up the small, unassuming paper from the seat, I scan my eyes over the scribbled writing, looking for a dollar sign. Then I see it: $108.00.

One hundred and eight dollars? For eleven miles over? That's highway robbery. Literally! *Shit!* After shelling out a hundred and fifty bucks for my maid-of-honor dress, and footing the bill for Dylen's bachelorette party tonight, I'm flat broke. Looks like I'll be checking into a Starbucks rehabilitation program and breaking out the Folgers.

Great. The perfect beginning to a twelve-hour shift.

About the Author

Marie Meyer is a teacher who spends her days in the classroom and her nights writing heartfelt romances. She is a proud mommy and enjoys helping her oldest daughter train for the Special Olympics, making up silly stories with her youngest daughter, and bingeing on weeks of DVR'd television with her husband.

Learn more at:
MarieMeyer.com
Twitter, @MarieMWrites
Facebook.com/MarieMeyerBooks